ALTERUM

William F Cooper

Free short stories and articles are available at the author's website.

williamfcooper.com

Contents

PART ONE – VISITORS

Chapter 1

ALTERUM ... *Alterum was designed from the outset as a real world, not a simulation. While other companies focused on creating Massive Multi-Player Online Games, we worked with the world's best cognitive scientists to develop Lucid Synthetic Dreaming™.*

The Anglo-America Alterum Company (sometimes referred to as Jack Glory) is the unchallenged leader in providing alternate reality experiences.

When you are tired of playing games, come and experience the difference.

Alterum — Better than the real thing.

The Official Visitor's Guide to Alterum

Bella took his hand and inched closer to the edge of the roof. A crowd had gathered to watch them. It was only ten floors, but that was exactly what they had been looking for. Once they stepped off the ledge, there was no going back. No time to change their minds.

"You ready to do this?"

"Do you think it will work?"

"There's only one way to find out."

*

The agent pulled over when he reached the roadblock. As he walked towards the barricade, he hand-signed 'ID show'. The device around his neck burst to life and an image of his badge floated in the air between him and the officer manning the barrier. The image rotated. One side showed the legend AIP, Agente In Patria, across a flag made up of thirteen red and white stripes and a Union Jack in the top left-hand corner. The flip side showed his name and a 3D photograph. The officer inspected the badge for a few seconds, as if deciding whether to let him pass. The agent stood impassively, waiting for the display of impotent authority to conclude. Eventually, the officer nodded his approval and let him pass. He strolled towards the waiting detective.

"Cunard."

"Officer Fischer." Cunard squinted up at the building opposite. There were two figures standing on the rooftop. "Patrians, I assume?"

"You assume correctly. Two esteemed visitors from your wonderful world. Fucking up everyone else's night. Situation normal."

"They'll never come back to Alterum. I can assure you of that."

"Well, that's good to know. Glad to hear it will be a new group of assholes next week or next month. Different faces, same arrogant attitude. They treat this place like a playground."

"They're base jumpers. You've got them here too."

"Not like this." Fischer gestured and the two jumpers were displayed for Cunard. "We've got a drone up there. As you can see, no parachutes."

"Shit. Not again."

"Shit indeed. Who goes on vacation to another world just to kill themselves?"

"I ..."

"It's a rhetorical question, Cunard. The answer is fucked-up Patrians. So many people want to visit your world. They talk about how wonderful it must be. If these visitors are anything to judge by, count me out."

"Can I speak to them?"

"Go ahead." Fischer flicked his hand in Cunard's direction, giving him control of the floating image.

"This is AIP Cunard. Identify yourself."

"Are you here to talk us down?"

"Something like that."

"It's not going to happen."

"You won't be coming back anytime soon if you jump. Is that what you want?"

They looked at each other and the woman laughed. "Let's do this."

Cunard and Fischer watched as the figures plunged through the air. The man seemed to shout something as he fell. Their bodies hit the ground with a dull thud.

"Well, it could be worse I guess," said Fischer. "They could have been up there all night."

"You're all heart."

"So, if you can sign off that there is no crime scene here of interest to the AIP, I will scrape these idiots off the ground and return them to the port. The rest of us mere mortals can then get on with the remainder of our lives. How does that sound?"

"Sounds good." Cunard shook his head. "Just need to check something first." They walked across the road to where the bodies lay. Blood was seeping from the broken remains. Cunard took some shoe covers and gloves from his pocket. He offered a set to Fischer.

"I'm fine. I don't need to walk through blood to find out what happened here."

"Suit yourself."

Cunard put on the protective covers and stepped towards the first body. Kneeling, he turned the head towards him, and using a penlight, he inspected the eyes. They were misted over as if he had been dead for days. Cunard bowed his head and sighed. He stood and walked towards the second jumper, the woman. Leaning down he had no need to touch the body this time. The corpse was lying face-up. The skull was smashed, its contents sprayed in every direction. The eyes were intact—the eyes were always intact. However, in comparison to her friend, these were clear and shining.

"Shit."

"Have you finished your psychological profile?"

Cunard stood up. "Yes. All finished."

"And?"

"They wanted to experience the thrill of almost dying. Subject number two was willing to risk it all. She had a total commitment to risk-taking regardless of the cost. Number one, not so much."

"Excellent work, Sherlock. I'll make a note of that. No wait, I won't bother." Fischer spat on the ground. "'Cos I don't give a shit."

"Your humanity is an example to us all."

"*Gleichfalls.*"

Cunard grinned. "*Genau.*"

Fischer winced. "The pronunciation was good, but not quite the right context. Keep practicing though. One day you and I are going to have an actual conversation in German."

"I look forward to it."

"Okay." Fischer then bellowed at the assembled crew, "Let's bag up these tourists, hose the street, and get downtown to watch drunk people fight each other. It's Saturday night, baby."

*

Two days later, traffic was light in the Battery Tunnel and Cunard reached the ship terminal in Red Hook sooner than he expected.

The vessel *Lucitania* loomed large over the small reception building with its solitary guard on show. It was a facade of normality. There were other guards monitoring every approach. Armed security cameras covered the perimeter and surrounding streets, ready to deal with any serious assaults on the dock. The ship that never sailed shone bright against the night sky. Every cabin lit up, giving the impression of a horizontal tower.

Cunard and the guard knew each other, but he threw his badge into the air between them regardless. Protocols had to be observed here at the crossing port. The guard gestured towards the badge and a solid line of red light scanned it before turning green.

"You're expected in the radio room."

"I'm early."

"It's Director Clive."

Cunard passed straight through the terminal building and walked across the gangway. A colleague met him as he boarded the ship. They were keen to hurry him along. It irritated him, and he let it show. "What is so urgent?"

"It's on a need-to-know basis and apparently I don't need to know. Why would I, as the Station Chief?"

Cunard said, "So, are you enjoying your promotion?"

The chief flipped his middle finger at Cunard.

The radio room was named after the traditional comms rooms of old ocean liners. It looked more like an air traffic control tower. Banks of screens covered the walls. In the center was a fishbowl of a room with a frozen image of Director Clive floating over a table. The entrance to the bowl was an air hatch.

Cunard poured himself a coffee, watching the frustration in the chief's eyes as he did so.

"Don't keep the director waiting."

"For fifty milliseconds?" Cunard opened the door and entered the air hatch. He placed his hand on a panel next to the interior door, and after a brief wait it slid open. Director Clive's image was no longer frozen. Cunard looked at the clock on the wall outside the bowl. The second-hand was moving so fast it was no longer possible to follow its position. The radio room staff moved back and forward in a blur.

The floating image spoke. "Agent Cunard. Good to see you."

"Likewise, Director Clive."

"Let me introduce you to Mary Landsberg." A spinning hologram appeared next to Clive. It showed the face of a woman in her mid-thirties, with shoulder-length blonde hair and piercing blue eyes. "She's in a pod as we speak and will be with you shortly."

"Have we had any results back on the jumpers yet?"

"Who?"

"We had two jumpers a couple of days ago. One of them was clear-eyed. I sent in a report."

"I see. One moment. Let me check."

"Thank you."

Director Clive leaned out of shot and spoke to someone off-screen. "Okay, they are looking into it. That was two hours ago?"

"It was about forty-eight hours ago local time, so yeah, roughly two hours."

Cunard looked outside of the glass bowl at the clock again. One hour had already passed since he entered the briefing room. Feeling dazed like he often did, he took a sip of his coffee and tried to focus on Director Clive.

"Mary is a forensic finance cryptologist. The best there is."

"Right." Cunard pursed his lips, making a show of looking impressed.

"You do know what that is, don't you?"

"Yes." Cunard knew what was coming next. The director had no doubt only recently had it explained and therefore wanted to explain it to someone else.

"It's a person who can track down transfers of cryptocurrency. It's a particularly important job."

"So, are we looking at money laundering?" asked Cunard.

"No. It is plain old-fashioned theft."

"Right. So, I assume someone extraordinarily rich has had a significant amount of Chain stolen. Do we suspect it was it an Alterran?"

"That's what I like about you, Cunard. No need to spell things out."

"Well, you wouldn't get involved for a low-level tourist mugging, would you?"

"All our visitors are important. Some, however, are more important than others. Chukaisha Tower opens tomorrow, next month your time. We cannot have the confidence of high-net-worth individuals being shaken."

"What about the station chief? He doesn't appear to be in the loop."

"He's not. The fewer people that know about this, the better. Our security is tight, but I suspect that some of our colleagues share more than they should. We need to close out the situation before it leaks."

"I am honored by your confidence in me."

Clive gave a wry smile. "And I am not taken in by your bullshit."

Theirs was an uneasy relationship, but they had the measure of each other, and they both took pleasure from that.

"I won't keep you any longer. The radio room is an uncomfortable experience. Mary can fill you in on the details."

"Any news on that other item?"

Clive looked down and concentrated, reading from a screen.

"Yes, one emerged from his pod unscathed. He used his safe word before he hit the ground. Refused to talk to us. Naturally, he is banned from returning. The other one, she was badly scrambled. Catatonic coma and profound bradycardia. We have had people recover, but it's unlikely in this case." Director Clive thought for a moment. "Why do they do it?"

"Who knows, but it's on the rise and the Alterrans don't like it."

"We don't care what they like or don't like, Cunard. Do not go native on us. They are not real."

"Real enough to steal someone's money."

"Real enough to worry about, not real enough for us to care about their feelings."

Chapter 2

SAFE WORD ... *Your safety is our paramount concern and Alterum has a lower risk profile than any real-world destination. As part of our focus on client well-being we provide every visitor to Alterum with their own unique safe word. This is something you can choose or have selected for you. Speak to your travel agent prior to your departure from one of our state-of-the-art crossing ports.*

If at any time you wish to make an unplanned exit from Alterum (sometimes referred to as "leaping"), simply state your safe word loudly and clearly three times. Please remember, however, that this is for emergency purposes only. If you use your safe word, the visit is considered complete, and you will not be able to re-enter Alterum without a new booking. Partial and full refunds will be void in the case of unscheduled exits.

Note: All visitors travel at their own risk and AAAC considers booking as a waiver of liability.

Alterum—See it, feel it, love it

The Official Visitor's Guide to Alterum

When Mary opened her eyes, she assumed something had gone wrong with the crossing. She was still in the flotation pod. Soft pink light illuminated the smooth white interior. The gentle hum of life-support and waste evacuation equipment preparing to disengage from her body was a welcome sound. She suffered from mild claustrophobia and the pod had not been a peaceful experience.

It was only when she pushed open the lid that Mary realized she had indeed crossed. The room was subtly different, and a voice recording confirmed it.

Welcome to Alterum. You have arrived at crossing port Lucitania. You will find a shower facility and a change of clothing here in your cabin. Take your time to adjust to your new surroundings and enjoy a complementary coffee. Once you are ready to leave, activate your Handi and you will be given further instructions.

Fighting back a sense of panic, Mary took a shower to wash off the residue of viscous floatation liquid. Where she was, it was not real. She was still in a pod. This was a lucid dream, but only a dream. She wanted to wake up and rip off the devices to which she was hooked up. Her safe word played over and over in her head. She now understood why it had to be spoken out loud. If it were merely a case of thinking it, she would be back in the London Isle of Dogs crossing port where she started her day. Out of curiosity she flicked the shower mixer tap all the way round and braced for the hot water. It burned as painfully as it would in real life. She gave out a yell and killed the water.

Stepping from the shower, Mary poured herself a coffee and looked out of the cabin window. It was night here. The sense of disconnection returned. She took a drink of her coffee and shuddered. It was strong and bitter. Deciding there was no point in delaying further, she got dressed and picked up the handset on the table. It responded to her touch.

To activate hand gesture mode, use your personal start signal.

It was the same voice as her Handi back home. That was good. Mary ran fingers through her hair behind her ears. She could feel the embedded neuro-processors that would allow her to see and hear what the Handi transmitted. Placing the lanyard around her neck, she positioned one hand in front of the device and gave the usual wake-up gesture.

Hand gesture activated.

She gestured a location query.

Cruise Terminal 5, Red Hook, Brooklyn.

"Real world or Alterum?"

I don't understand your question. Can you ask it another way?

"Am I in Alterum or the real world?"

You are in Cruise Terminal 5, Red Hook, Brooklyn.

Mary shook her head. She placed a hand on a touchpad on the wall and the door opened. She stepped out of the cabin. The corridor seemed to stretch forever, door after door on each side.

"What now?" She raised her palms and shrugged. A beam of light flashed from the Handi to the floor, forming a green arrow.

Please follow the—

"Yes," she interrupted. "I get the picture."

*

Cunard was in the meeting room when she arrived. He stood and introduced himself.

"I made you a coffee."

"No thanks. I've already had one."

"Wasn't too good though, was it? Try it." He pointed at the mug sitting on the table.

Mary sat down and took a drink. It was better. A lot better. "Why all of this? Waking up in a pod? The cruise ship?"

"First time in Alterum, I assume?"

"People pay a lot of money to come here. You would think their first experience would be better than a cheap IRL coffee. If it's fake, it should be a good fake."

Cunard sat back and waited for Mary to stop talking.

"I know I'm rambling. I'm not happy with all of this. Knowing I am still somewhere else. It's ..." She sighed and gave up trying to articulate how she felt.

"It can disorientate you the first time, so let me explain as best I can. You arrive in a pod because you left in a pod. The bitter coffee is deliberate. It's all about hitting your senses. Making you feel. Giving you time to adapt before you go out there and get yourself into trouble.

"On this ship everyone is from the real world but using expressions like IRL and fake world are strictly off limits as soon as we leave the port. We are not from the 'real world', we are from Patria. Patria is a parallel world that figured out how to break through to this dimension, this multiverse. As a result, we established relations with Alterum. We are Patrians. I am an agent of Patria. You are here on business, and I am your escort."

"Sure, whatever, but can't you zap NPC's memories if they learn too much?"

"This is not a game. Alterrans are not considered 'non-player characters', and believe it or not, we do not control the rules, so no, I can't zap their memories."

Mary drank her coffee as Cunard spoke. She felt her breath slowly returning to a normal rhythm and only then realized that she had been hyperventilating. "Okay."

"There are many misconceptions about this place. Treat it is as if it were real. It's the best way to avoid getting yourself into any trouble."

"Don't worry. Any problems and I will click my heels three times and I'm back in Kansas."

Cunard nodded without smiling. "If you ever feel threatened, use your safe word. Do not hesitate. Too many people think this is a game. Let me repeat myself, Alterum is not a game. Not by a long shot. You'll realize that soon enough, but please believe me."

"You make it sound like a dangerous place for a holiday."

"You're not on vacation. Someone has stolen a lot of money and my guess is they will not give it back without a struggle. That means they are dangerous."

Pushing the now empty cup away from her, Mary paused for a second before answering. "You do know this is what I do in the real world, in Patria? It's always about money. It's always about a lot of money. Guess what? It's dangerous there too."

"I am sure it is, just don't get too relaxed."

"Not much chance of that with Dr Gloom as my guide?" The Handi flashed as she spoke. "Looks like he's ready to talk."

Cunard was about to ask who the client was, but let it go. He would find out as soon as Mary accepted the incoming call.

A floating head appeared above the table, then flickered and reappeared, complete with a body. The image floated back through the desk until it appeared to be sitting on a chair opposite them. Mary was puzzled when she saw the man opposite. He was in his late thirties or early forties. He had short dark hair and eyes that were probably brown but were so dark that they appeared to be black. His crisp white business shirt covered an obviously well-toned body.

Cunard grunted. "Morgan. Couldn't happen to a nicer guy."

"Still babysitting tourists?" The figure spoke in a deep, powerful voice.

15

"How much did they sting you for?"

"Wait ...You are Morgan?" Mary struggled to contain a puzzled expression.

"Andrew Morgan, yes."

"But ..."

"You were expecting someone older. It is a reasonable assumption."

Cunard explained to Mary, "If you pay a premium, you can enter Alterum in pretty much any form you like."

"I'm an old man, Miss Landsberg. I have a few years of life left and I will not waste them in a crippled state when I can live like this," he patted his chest. "You know, I have to admit, I never felt this good in Patria and I'm never going back."

Mary turned to Cunard. "What about you? Is that how you look in the real—in Patria, or am I the only one that is myself?" She turned back to Morgan. "Oh, and it's Mrs. Landsberg, not Miss."

"Of course. You married ten years ago but kept your birth name. Your husband is Mr. James Finnegan. I would have preferred to stick with Landsberg too. You have a daughter. She is what age? Six, I believe."

"Why do you know that?"

"I find it helps to understand the people who work for me."

"Frankly, I find that a little disturbing. What about Cunard here? What do you know about him?"

"Ah, the Agente In Patria. I know nothing about him outside of this place. Jack Glory keeps it that way. Nothing but a code name and yes, your instinct is correct, a false appearance."

"It works for me." Cunard put his hands behind his head and leaned back in the chair.

"They believe it prevents them being influenced here or threatened back home. Stupid, since there are no real crimes here in Alterum."

"And yet you've had a large amount of Chain stolen," said Cunard.

Morgan leaned in. "By Alterrans, not Patrians. That is the difference, Cunard. It has got nothing to do with the AIP. I simply need you to look after Mrs. Landsberg while she tracks down the missing money."

"You've sent me the details I've asked for?" Mary gestured, and a list of documents floated between them. "The Chain wallet ID, the old key, how much was left in the wallet at the time of the key change, the details of the last valid transaction?"

"It's all there."

"Do you have any idea of who did this?" She tapped on the documents to confirm they were all she needed.

"I know exactly who did it, but I'll deal with that side of things. Your job is to get my money back."

"Right, we can do it that way, but it's usually easier if I know who to focus on."

Morgan smiled but it never quite reached his eyes. "Let's go with what you've got, shall we? I'll meet you in person in a couple of hours for an update. I've been told that you're good. That's why I am paying a lot of money for you. I expect quick results, and you to track my money down using what information I have already given you. If, however, you do need more data, I will give it to you then."

"I think—"

"I've sent you the address for our meeting." Morgan cut the connection. His face disappeared leaving a headless body for a second before it too flickered and faded.

"Morgan? You're not picky about who you work for, are you?"

17

"You have a code name and this ..." she looked him up and down. "Your appearance is fake. At least I am transparent. Are you a man or a woman, black or white?"

"Yes." Cunard said. "Next question?"

*

"Where to?" asked Mary as they crossed the deserted parking lot and made their way to Cunard's car.

"We'll swing by your hotel before meeting up with Morgan. You got everything you need from him?"

Mary had been again checking the files as they had made their way off the *Lucitania* and through the terminal building. Documents floated in the air as she walked, only visible to her in private mode. "I think so. Eighty million Chain. I've never seen this much in a wallet before."

"He's a rich guy with expensive tastes."

"But eighty million? The whole point of wallets is that they are like cash, untraceable. If someone gets your wallet ID and key, it's theirs. That's why people keep Chain accounts and use wallets for smaller values."

"Tell me this. Who would have a use for a wallet of that value in Patria?"

Mary shrugged as if the answer was obvious. "Criminals. It's perfect for hiding and laundering money."

Cunard flicked the doors open with his Handi. "Exactly." He got into the driver's side leaving Mary staring into the darkness of the night.

She leaned into the car. "Morgan is one the richest men on earth. It's a huge amount of Chain, but only a drop in the ocean compared to his net worth. And anyway, why launder money in a theme park?"

"Get in. I want to show you something."

*

They drove in silence as Mary continued to inspect the files. Reaching the Battery Tunnel after about ten minutes, Cunard checked the message sign above the entrance.

Governors Island Exit. Zero-minute queue.

"Good."

Mary glanced up. "That's new."

"It is."

After taking the exit, they emerged onto the small island park. Cunard drove to the top of Outlook Hill and parked.

"It's the best time to come. The place is packed during the day."

They stepped out of the car and made their way to the vantage point. It gave spectacular views across to the Manhattan skyline. The smell of salt water hung in the air.

"Yes, it's a nice view."

Cunard breathed deep. "Ah, fresh air and condescension. Love it."

"I ..."

"Watch and learn." Cunard drew a large circle in front of him and the distant skyline was magnified by his Handi. "New York." He then placed the palm of one hand on the circle and pushed it sideways. "New Jersey. Oh wait. What's that?" He put both hands on the image and pushed them apart, magnifying the scene further.

"What the—"

"You've never even read up on Alterum, have you?"

Mary shook her head as she studied the view. It was Big Ben and the British Houses of Parliament. They were on the opposite sides of the Hudson River where New Jersey should have been. "What the hell?"

"This is not Patria. It is similar, but it is different."

19

"You don't say. Can I?" She pointed at the magnification lens.

Cunard gestured control over to her and Mary moved the view left and right, taking in the sight.

"New York London is the official name. Locals refer to it as Nylon City."

"Why did they make it like this? I thought Alterum was a duplicate of Earth?"

"Here's where it gets interesting. That is exactly what was intended when they designed and created this place. An accurate replica of Patria."

"So, how did it become this Frankenstein city?"

"That's a question I don't think there's a good answer to. We created it, but we gave it the ability to change. It was built on AI principals. Once started, it evolved according to its own logic and history. It still is evolving. It moves too fast for us to control what this reality is becoming. One hour passes in Patria, twenty-four hours pass here. We are the creators, but we think too slowly to influence it. Only by stepping into this world can we even try to affect it. That's why the AIP was formed."

"You make it sound as if we are gods and the AIP are angels."

"Perhaps we are. Perhaps the world you and I come from is the same. Moving too fast for a god of infinite time. Populated by angels that carry out God's work, but who are never truly in control."

"Messiah complex, much?"

"On the contrary, this place makes me doubt the power of any god, real or imagined."

"Okay, so this has been a lot of fun, but I think I need a drink and the company of someone not quite so gloomy."

Cunard looked at her. "Getting real enough for you?"

"More than I want. Let's go."

*

Driving back down the hill they re-entered the tunnel and headed towards the city. Cunard put on the radio.

"The night-time shows are always worth a listen."

...and I may sound mad, but we are ruled by an alien elite.

You mean Patrians?

That's all a cover. There's no such place as Patria, but the people who call themselves Patrian are part of the conspiracy. The elite and the Patrians. They are the same thing. There's no difference between them.

What conspiracy is that?

The conspiracy to fuck us over. To kill us, to rape us, to do whatever they want for their own pleasure. That's what the elite do. We are their playthings. They are pedophiles and killers and abusers.

And what proof do you have?

Wake up, man. Wake up.

Okay. So, are you Waking? Are you part of the Waking Army?

It doesn't matter if I am with the WA or not. Listen to what I'm saying. Look around you. Look at that new trading center in Canary Wharf. Who owns it? Ask and see what you find out. That's all I'm saying. Ask the question.

Some people say it's bringing a lot of jobs to Nylon City. They say it's helping to revive the area.

And you think the normal people will be allowed to stay once it's open? Who's the crazy one now?

The caller pronounced the Waking Army acronym, the WA, with the commonly used pronunciation 'Wah'.

"It's bizarre," said Mary.

"Except the crazies are mostly right."

21

"That's what I mean. What if our conspiracy theorists are right too?"

The car emerged from the tunnel and Cunard took the first exit. "Yeah, this place gets you that way. You hungry?"

Mary shook her head, then stopped. "Wait, is that a Seoul Fried Chicken? Pull over."

Chapter 3

CURRENCY ... *As part of your booking, you will need to purchase local currency for items not covered in your package. Currency can be provided for any of the local markets depending on where you are visiting in Alterum.*

Chain is the only real-world currency that is capable of being transferred to Alterum and has become the money of choice for many specialist experiences. Please check with your travel agent and ensure you have enough funds in both local currency and a Chain wallet for the experience you planned for.

If you wish to arrange additional funds once you have arrived, Chain can be transferred directly to a locally available wallet.

Note: As well as Chain cash wallets, Chain Exchange accounts are also available, but these are only suitable for long-term visitors. If any currency is unspent at the end of your trip, your wallet will be returned from Alterum, and all remaining funds will be available IRL (in real world).

Alterum—The only limit is your imagination

The Official Visitor's Guide to Alterum

So, I guess you were kind of hungry."

Mary took a break from devouring her food and breathed in the aroma of fast food. "I love SFC, especially the Golden Kari."

"I can see that."

"I can't believe you took the coriander and lime."

"Cilantro."

"Whatever. In London it's coriander, but no matter what you call it, it's still the herb of the devil."

Cunard grinned.

"Oh, so you do occasionally crack a smile."

"Yeah, sometimes. Towards the end of a tour of duty, the smiles get less frequent. The crackpot on the radio, he's not far from the truth. Patrians come here to blow off steam. The normal rules don't apply as far as most visitors are concerned."

"Sounds like Magaluf in the summer."

"Sorry?"

"A bad joke. A lot of English people go to Spain and behave appallingly for two weeks every summer and then wonder why the locals hate us. If you take anyone out of their normal environment, the social niceties drop away. So, how badly do they behave here?"

"It varies, but everyone lets their usual morals take a break to some extent during their stay."

"Like me." Mary picked up her last piece of chicken.

"You're going to let your morals take a break, are you?"

"I already have." She waved the chicken at Cunard. "In the—in Patria, I'm vegetarian. SFC is one of the few things I miss about meat." Mary popped the chicken into her mouth, twisted it and pulled out the bone. She spoke with a mouthful of food. "And I've got to say, this is quite possibly the best chicken I've ever had. Although to be fair, I've been only dreaming about it for five years."

"Looks like I better keep an eye on you then."

"Do people have affairs?"

"It's not uncommon but calling it an affair is probably giving more credit than it deserves in most cases."

"Do you?"

"I'd need to be in a relationship for that to be possible."

"Ah." Mary sucked on a straw and took a drink of bubble tea. "Would you have an affair with me? I'm not saying I would, but you know, theoretically. What about a Patrian who is married outside?"

Cunard asked carefully, "Is that what you want? Is it more than the chicken you've been missing?"

Mary burst out laughing. "I miss a lot of things, Mr. code-name Cunard, but I'm making conversation, not a proposal. I think it was nice of the company to give you such a pleasant appearance. It must make life that little easier if you did, you know …"

"I will take your word about my appearance."

"If only I'd known, I could have asked for a different body too."

Cunard wiped the remainder of the chili sauce from his lips. "It's not so bad."

"Well, thank you. What a charmer you are with all your head-turning compliments."

"So, how does someone become a forensic cryptologist?"

Mary shrugged. "I'm good at coding and problem-solving. Most of the time, I work from home. It's the perfect job for an introvert."

Cunard's eyes widened. "You, an introvert?"

"Yes. Is that so hard to be believe as a tall, dark, handsome man who quite possibly is all or none of those things?" Mary leaned to one side and pulled a face.

"Are you sure you're not asking me to have an affair?"

"I've already satisfied the bad girl in me."

"So, you prefer an illicit piece of chicken to sex?"

"If I'm going abandon my morals, it will be deep fried chicken every time."

"Right." Cunard gathered up the packaging onto the plastic tray. "We should go to the hotel so you can get started."

"I've might have been sinning, but I have also been working." Mary used her Handi to show Cunard a hub-and-spoke network diagram. Light pulsed between the various endpoints. "I'm a multi-tasker."

"So, what exactly am I looking at?"

Mary said, "You are looking at me passing one Chain back and forward from a Chain wallet to a Chain exchange. Ping-pong, back and forward. How does that help me, you ask?"

Cunard was silent.

"Ask me how that helps."

"Okay, how does that help?"

"I'm glad you asked. I like to verbalize my thoughts so that people can tell me how clever I am. Remember that when I've finished talking." She took another drink of the bubble tea before continuing. "People think of a Chain exchange as a bank account and a Chain wallet as cash. Correct for the exchange. Wrong for the wallet. They are both accounts. The Chain wallet is like an old-fashioned numbered account in a Swiss bank. If I've got the ID and password, I control it. No proof of identity is required, unlike a standard account.

"But here comes the interesting thing. There is no central host, no one bank or exchange that controls it. There is a distributed ledger with thousands of computers that check if they all agree on the amount and the transactions."

"This I knew." Cunard drummed his fingers on the table. "Should I tell you how clever you are yet?"

Mary went on, "But that means there is a lot of traffic between the ledgers."

"Okay, you are clever. You're finding the ledgers?"

Mary pointed at the spokes in the diagram. "Exactly. Sometimes I hit the same one more than once, but if I do it often enough …You are looking at a map that is building of Alterran ledgers. I then place a sniffer-bot on each one I find."

"Once you've found enough of them, how do you identify the wallet? The traffic will be encrypted."

"It is, and it isn't. The Chain wallet is traceable if you have certain information and the right tools. Do you remember the information I asked Morgan for? Anyway, I can't control the wallet with that information, but I can watch for any traffic related to it."

"And its location?"

"With the sniffer-bots, yes. It's impossible to completely turn off the location services of a Handi."

"How legal are your tools?"

In Patria? As legal as the thefts they are used to track down. Here? Well, apparently there are no laws for us to worry about."

"It would be faster if we knew who they were."

Mary closed the display. "Morgan has that covered, but yes it would."

"I don't trust him. If the Waking Army is involved, this could get messy. It's a strong possibility. I think we should cover off that angle while your bots do their work. How would you like to see some live music?"

"Sure, I guess. What did you have in mind?"

Chapter 4

LAW … *Like all tourist destinations, Alterum has its own customs and regulations. Although you are not subject to local laws, we ask that you respect these during your visit. This will make the experience more authentic and will also ensure that future visitors continue to be given a warm welcome.*

If you do find yourself in trouble with law enforcement, please identify yourself as a Patrian and contact our nearest office which will resolve any issues.

Note: If you have been accused of a serious crime, you may have to be moved to another destination within Alterum for the remainder of your trip. Repeated serious violation of local laws may result in a temporary ban or increased fees for future trips.

Alterum—Life is a rehearsal; this is the show.

The Official Visitor's Guide to Alterum

The ground had rushed up faster than Bella expected, and then there was darkness. Darkness, but she was still alive. She had done it. She had survived the jump. She needed to shake off the numbness and get up. Bella tried to move her arms, but it didn't feel as if there was anything there. She tried to move her legs. The same. That was when she began to panic. She told herself to take a deep breath, but knew there was no breath to take, no eyes to open. Bella could not feel anything. She was consciousness, nothing more.

She became aware of a quiet voice in a distant corner of her mind. It was an echo of her younger self, a schooldays poetry recital.

Alone, alone, all alone,

Alone on a wide sea

And never a saint took pity on

My soul in agony

Were these quiet voices always present? Were they normally drowned out by the distraction of sensations, by sight and sound and smell and touch? It seemed to Bella that there were other rooms in her mind that she was only now noticing. Part of her, but just out of reach.

Maybe it would pass, she thought. She would count to a hundred and then try to feel something. One … It seemed to pass so slowly, that first number. When she had finished thinking it, she would say the next number. That was the plan, but how would she be able to space them without the metronome of her physical existence and the world to which it was attached? The number one stretched out ahead of Bella, seemingly without end.

*

Cunard was about to cross the Manhattan-Westminster bridge when a call came in. It was Detective Fischer.

"Hey, Cunard. I need you. Same place as before."

"Another jumper?"

"No, the same one."

"You're joking, right?"

"*Doch*. She's on the roof. I took the call from a resident. I've kept it to myself, but if you could hurry up, that would be great."

"Shit. Okay, I'm on my way." Cunard disconnected. "Mary, I'll need to drop you off at the hotel. You'll be safe there. I've got my day job to do."

"What was that about, a suicide risk?"

"Not exactly. She jumped a few days ago. Back home she is in a coma in one of our pods. In this world, she is dead. Not quite as dead as I thought though. I'll pick you up in time for our meeting with Morgan, and you can call me if you need anything."

Mary laughed. "Wait, you can't say 'not quite as dead as I thought' without an explanation. What does that mean?"

"She's a ghost. At least here in Alterum she is one."

"You are going to see a ghost?"

"Talk to a ghost. Persuade her that she's dead and then ..."

"And you think for one minute that I am going to miss out on this? I'm coming with you."

Cunard frowned. "It's not as much fun as you might think."

"I don't care. I'm coming with you. How the hell did she become a ghost?"

"She didn't say her safe word and wasn't in a pod here in Alterum. That meant the pod on Patria wasn't ready and didn't fire up in time. When that happens, people usually get stuck in the void. Detached from both worlds. By the time the system realizes and tries to bring them out of their induced paralysis, they have dissociated permanently. They still exist somewhere deep inside, but they have separated from their body. Few recover from it. Occasionally they come back as a ghost."

"Are there Alterran ghosts too?"

"There's no evidence they exist. It's one of the many things that freak Alterrans out about us."

When they arrived, they made their way to the roof of the building. A shimmering figure of a woman was standing at the edge of the building. Fischer was talking to her. He waved them over.

"Cunard, this is Bella. And this is?" He looked towards Mary.

"I'm Mary, pleased to meet you both."

"I didn't know," said the ghost.

Cunard nodded sympathetically. "I know."

"Ged, what happened to Ged?"

Fischer shook his head.

"I thought I could beat the jump." The ghost sobbed. "But what do I do now? Am I stuck here? Stuck like this?"

"You can believe yourself back," said Mary.

"I'm afraid not, Tinkerbell. Exactly who is this?" Fischer hooked a thumb at Mary.

Cunard raised his hand. "Please let me handle this. I know your intentions are good, but it's a little more complicated than that."

The ghost stared at Cunard. "Tell me what to do."

Cunard rubbed the back of his neck. "You need to jump again. That's the only way out."

"I don't know if I can."

"You've done it once," said Fischer. "It should be easy the second time around."

"I can't."

"It is the only way out, Bella," Cunard said.

The ghost began to cry. "It was so lonely. I can't go back there. When I jumped, there was a darkness. Nothing there but me. I can't go back."

"You won't go there this time," said Cunard. "You'll push through to the other side."

"And then I saw a light. I approached it and I was back on the roof."

"The light will be there this time too. The light will guide you to the other side."

Mary noticed Fischer rolling his eyes. "How can you be sure?" she asked Cunard.

"It's happened before. I know."

31

"Cunard has a direct line to the afterlife. He's well connected," said Fischer.

The ghost cried, "What if you're wrong? I can't go back to that place. I can't go back."

"It will be fine. Trust me. You need to jump."

Mary watched Fischer's amused reaction. "How do you *know*, Cunard?" she repeated.

Cunard avoided her gaze. "Look, there's no other choice. It's either that or you exist here in a ghost form."

"That's a choice Bella should make."

"I can't go back."

"Well, I've got a job to do," said Fischer. "You can't leave her here, if she's not going to jump."

"I think it would be better for everybody if you did."

The ghost was still sobbing.

"Well, she won't, so what are we going to do with her?" said Mary.

Fischer shook his head. "You need to take her with you."

Cunard stared into space.

"You know it makes sense."

"I know, but …"

"What other choice do you have? Leave her here and wait for the WA to turn up? They would love her. More grist to the mill."

"Who is the WA?" asked the ghost.

"Crazies," said Fischer with a hint of sarcasm. "The Waking Army. They believe this is all a dream controlled by Patrians. The whole world. Everything." Fischer banged his chest. "This is imaginary." He stomped his foot. "So is this building. All of it. Who could believe such a thing?"

"But—" began the ghost.

Cunard quickly lifted a finger to his mouth. "Okay, I'll take you with us."

*

"We'd done it all," said the ghost. "The Troll Wall in Norway. Table Mountain in South Africa. Then we started doing the urban jumps. Burj Khalifa, Petronas Towers. It is the greatest rush in the world."

"I get that," said Mary. "But why come here? How can doing it in this place compare to real life?"

"Have you ever had a dream about falling and then waking up before you hit the ground?"

"Yes."

"It's one of the most common nightmares. It feels real at the time, doesn't it?"

"Yes, but it's a dream."

"It's not a lucid synthetic dream though," mumbled Cunard from the front of the car.

"Always the company man," replied Mary. "I'm surprised you didn't put in a trademark at the end of that. "Lucid Synthetic Dreaming, trademark Jack Glory."

"He's right though. Here it feels real, and we can go sub-thirty meters. No one jumps below thirty, it's too dangerous, but here you can. You might walk away with an injury, but you drag yourself back to the crossing, go home, and that's the end of your injury."

"Or you say your safe word before it's too late," said Cunard. "Like your friend."

"He wasn't meant to do that."

"You didn't have parachutes. How was that going to work? If you want to commit suicide, do it in Patria, not here."

"We weren't trying to kill ourselves. Have you ever stayed in the dream as you hit the ground when you fall?"

"Never," said Mary.

"No one does. But what if you could?"

"Go on."

"There's this rumor about Alterum. It's big in the adventure community. All these people who have done everything they can, trying to take it to the next level. We call it, jumping the tag."

"What?"

"The Alterum tag line. 'If Dreams were real'. Do a search on it. If dreams were real, how would you finish off that sentence? How would you finish the tag line? If dreams were real, I could fly. If dreams were real, I would be immortal. We believe it is possible to break the normal rules of nature here. That tag line is a hidden message for the rich who pay for the privilege."

"So, you thought you'd jump off a building to test it. How did that work out for you?"

Mary shook her head. "Cunard, really."

Bella said, "I still believe it."

"You just haven't found the key?"

"Or I didn't believe it strongly enough. I don't know."

"You two have a lot in common. Positive thinking does not change reality. Not in Patria, and not here in Alterum."

"Well, I think it does," replied the ghost.

"Me too," said Mary.

"I am an AIP agent. If it was possible to have special powers, don't you think I would know about it? Don't you think that I would have some?"

"Maybe you do," said Mary. "You're just such a pessimist you don't realize it."

The ghost laughed and started to fade.

"Oh Bella, you're becoming invisible."

The ghost held an arm up to her face. "What's happening?"

"If dreams were real," said Mary, "I would be invisible."

The ghost laughed again. "You're right."

"What about that, Cunard? How many ghosts do you know in the real world? How many people that can make themselves invisible?"

Cunard shrugged. "There are a few differences."

"Watch." The ghost faded completely from view.

"That's amazing, Bella."

"I've jumped the tag."

Cunard shook his head. "We're here."

Chapter 5

NIGHTLIFE … *Alterum has nightlife to rival anything available IRL.*

If you have previously visited Alterum, you may notice many changes since your last trip. This is especially true for destinations such as New York London.

Time moves faster in Alterum. Twenty-four times faster to be precise. When did you last visit? A year ago? Twenty-four years have passed. Restaurants will have come in and out of fashion, opened and closed since you were last here. Nightclubs have an even shorter lifespan, so you are best to check a local guidebook on your arrival. The Native Guide to Nylon City is the most comprehensive publication and is available for download on your Handi.

Running continuously for decades, MGSB nightclub is one of the few mainstays that never seems to lose its appeal. This icon of New York London is the place to go for live music seven days a week. Still operating at the time of writing, this is a must-visit venue for all music lovers. The Music Gormandiser's Sound Booth (to use its full name) has been voted a top-ten attraction of the year by travel writers on no less than twenty occasions. Here you will discover the sound of two worlds that have combined to create something unique, the Nylon Slur. So, grab a cocktail from the bar, sit back and enjoy the chilled-out atmosphere of this legendary nightclub.

Alterum—Reality amplified.

The Official Visitor's Guide to Alterum

E va checked her make-up in the mirror and adjusted the eyeliner to perfect the Cleopatra wings. "I've put the word out. We will find him."

The figure sitting in the corner of the dressing room spoke in a whisper. "If Morgan has him …"

"We can't afford for this to divert us. We are too close. We find him, we tidy this up and we move forward."

"Thank you, Eva."

She stood and smoothed down her dress. "Don't thank me. We are family. We celebrate together, we mourn together, we stay together."

The tightly packed tables of the club were fully occupied. Each one had a fixed phone and an illuminated number floating above it. Eva acknowledged the crowd as she strolled towards the center-stage microphone. The band, in sync with her timing, was note-perfect as she leaned into the mic and sang in a slow, slurred, almost speaking voice.

You like potato and I like potahto

You like Siddhartha and I like Sinatra

Siddhartha, Sinatra, Sinatra Siddhartha

Let's call the whole thing off

The trumpet climbed towards a high note as if announcing the arrival of a full-stop and the band swung into a new melody. Eva was no longer speaking the words, her powerful contralto voice reaching every corner of the room.

I'm gonna live till I die!

I'm gonna laugh 'stead of cry,

I'm gonna take the town and turn it upside down

The audience roared its approval. Someone stood on their seat and shouted, "Up the WA," as he waved three fingers in the shape of a W. Other hands raised into the air, repeating the sign.

Eva laughed and spoke into the mic. "You might think that. I couldn't possibly comment."

*

Eva joined them in a private booth after she finished her act. A waiter brought sparkling water and sat it on the table. She waited for him to leave before she spoke.

"What do you have for me this time, lover?"

"A ghost," said Mary, before Cunard could speak. "Believe it or not, a real-life ghost."

Eva glanced at Mary, then shifted her gaze to where the invisible Bella was sitting. "I believe it."

"You can see me?"

"I can sense you. It might help if you make yourself visible. No one in this club is going to mind."

As Bella re-appeared Mary shuffled in her seat to make more room. "You've seen ghosts before? We don't have them in Patria."

"They are ten-a-penny here. We get quite bored with them."

Cunard told Mary, "Eva is … different. We can talk freely."

"Oh right. Are you Patrian?"

Cunard spoke before Eva could reply. "It's complicated."

"It's not complicated. I am Alterran but originally from Patria. Now, shall we get down to business?" Eva took a drink of water.

"I need you to put your feelers out. Find out if there is any word on the theft of some Chain from a Patrian."

"Who is the Patrian and how much?"

"Andrew Morgan, and it is a substantial amount. I want to know if the Waking Army is involved."

"It doesn't sound like them, but yeah, I'll see what I can do."

"He is exactly the kind of person they would like to hit. He says he knows who stole it but won't give us any names. That makes me nervous. I don't want him going to war with the WA."

"There would only be one winner if he was stupid enough to do that."

Cunard frowned. "Exactly. We cannot afford to spook the new investors. I need you to work your connections. If they are involved, they need to step back and return the Chain."

Eva flashed a sarcastic smile "Yeah, like that will happen. It would be easier for you to take out Morgan."

"Now who's dreaming?"

Eva turned to the ghost. "How long has it been since you failed to cross?"

"I was stuck in limbo for a long time. I don't know, months."

Eva looked at Cunard for an answer.

"A couple of days, Alterum time. Two hours in Patria."

Surprised, Bella spoke. "Two hours? That's all? I cannot go back."

"You've not told her, have you?"

"Not yet."

"Told me what?"

Cunard muttered something under his breath. "When your vacation is due to end, you will be transferred to a medical facility. The connection to Alterum broken."

"I will go back to limbo, won't I?"

"And if she had jumped again?" asked Mary.

Cunard avoided eye contact. "Mmh. She would have possibly survived."

"Or?"

Eva answered for him. "Yeah, or she would have gone back to the void a little earlier than the disconnect. The company doesn't like ghosts. They talk too much and feed into the whole conspiracy theory. Except, of course, that it's not really a conspiracy, if it's all true. One day you Patrians will accept the Book of Shadows and we can end this whole charade."

Mary thought about what the ghost had said. "Think carefully, Bella. How much of your holiday did you have left when you jumped?"

"We wanted to have time to enjoy our powers. It was day one of a two-day break. Two days Patrian. We spent a week here beforehand."

Mary crunched the numbers. "You had a month and a half Alterran time booked." Mary paused to think. "You were in limbo two days Alterran. You must have … somewhere between twenty-four and forty Alterum days left."

"And then?"

"Some people do return. It's not impossible, but I won't lie to you." Eva shot a disapproving look at Cunard. "Few people make it back. Stay with me, and we will try to work it out."

"I don't know," said Cunard.

"No, you don't know, do you? Bella, you choose. You can go where you please in Alterum. No one can stop you. If you come with me, I may ask you to do things that will make you feel uncomfortable. It will be to help you get home. You have zero chance with him, or one percent with me."

Chapter 6

RELIGION ... *Worried about missing your church service?*

All major religions and denominations are catered for in Alterum's larger population centers and many are run by IRL religious leaders on a rotation basis.

Although mainstream religions are not widely accepted by Alterrans, many locals follow the teachings of the Book of Shadows. Sometimes described as more philosophy than religion, the Book of Shadows was founded by Alterrans and has developed a small, but growing, IRL following. The more curious and adventurous visitors may enjoy experiencing this unique belief system in its original setting.

Alterum—Seeing is believing.

The Official Visitor's Guide to Alterum

As they drove in silence, Mary checked the bots she had deployed. She let out an involuntary sound as she pieced together some of the alerts into a recognizable pattern.

"What have you spotted?"

Mary pivoted round towards Cunard. "You were going to send her back there?"

"She is going back to the void. It's a matter of time, no matter what Eva says."

"At least Eva has not lost her humanity."

Cunard grinned.

"What does that mean?"

"Nothing."

Mary thought for a second. "She's fully Alterran, isn't she?"

Cunard give an almost imperceptible nod.

"But she thinks she's Patrian?"

"She knows exactly what she is. When Alterum was being built, they seeded it with replicas of actual people and let the AI engine learn from their behavior. Her real self is from Patria, and she is a replica."

"That must be a terrible knowledge to have. It could drive you insane."

"It did with some of the other seeds apparently, but not Eva. She is a believer in the Book of Shadows. 'Everything is false, and everything is real'. It works for her. She knows what she is and considers herself real. Who are we to judge? Now, have you got any news for Morgan? We're almost there."

Mary turned her focus back to the air screen. "When a wallet transaction is made, it must hit a few ledgers directly from the source device to trigger a valid update request. When a key update is made, it's a much larger number. I have logged hundreds of ledgers being hit by Morgan's wallet with the same timestamp. Someone has changed the key."

"You can track it, right?"

"I'm on it. My sniffers will track the update back to a cell station and then we can monitor the surrounding cells for the device ID. We'll get the location within a few feet."

*

"Does everyone do business in nightclubs here?"

"Only at night. Stay close." Cunard walked towards the entrance, ignoring the queue that had formed along the sidewalk next to the converted theater building. The signage on the marquee declared 'Nylon Zoo', each letter formed by light bulbs.

Most of the people queuing wore long overcoats pulled tight against the cold. As they reached the entrance Mary understood why. As each guest approached the roped-off entrance, they opened their coat to display their club-wear for inspection. The door attendants would make their decision, letting them enter or sending them away with a variation of 'not tonight'. Those that were granted entry were given a wristband which, upon contact with their skin, projected a number directly above them. It reminded Mary of the table numbers in MGSB, except it was the guests that were numbered here.

Cunard flashed his badge. "We're here to see Morgan. He's expecting us." The security moved to the side and offered them a wristband. "We're not here to prom."

The larger of the two doormen shrugged. "You'll need it to enter his suite. If you walk through the promenade zone, someone will find you and take you to him."

Cunard reluctantly took the band and passed the other to Mary.

She slipped it on her wrist and glanced upwards. The number "262F" followed her. As they entered the venue, a bus boy passed them. Balancing a plastic container full of empty glasses on his head, he was dressed in sneakers, Lycra shorts and nothing else. She tracked him until she was distracted by a woman in a sheer black mesh zentai suit that covered her head and entire body. She was wearing nothing other than the suit except platform heels which were also encased by the transparent material. Mary felt Cunard's hand on her shoulder.

"Stay with me."

She followed him into the center of the venue, feeling distinctly overdressed. The music was loud but not overwhelming. "Why is no one dancing?"

It was an exaggeration, but he knew what she meant. Most of the clubbers were walking back and forward as if on a catwalk. "Look up." He pointed to what appeared to be the original theater mezzanine level. It was split into VIP suites separated from the venue by soundproofed windows. Each one had a glass elevator connecting it to the ground floor.

In one suite Mary could see a middle-aged couple sitting on a white leather sofa, drinking cocktails, and pointing down at the crowd. A laser beam projected from their suite and hit a floating number on the dance floor. It turned red and a security guard approached the woman below the number. Mary watched fascinated as the woman was escorted to the correct elevator. The couple in the VIP suite stood up and disappeared as their guest rose above the crowd.

"Seriously?"

"It's not called the Zoo for nothing. People prom back and forward until they are picked to spend time with the rich and the famous. Many of the people up there are visiting wealthy Patrians. So, would you call that an affair?"

A light shot out from another booth and illuminated Cunard and Mary's numbers. Mary shook her head. "Classy."

"You know, there is a VIP side door. Morgan made us come through the public entrance to demonstrate our place in his world."

*

Morgan met them as the elevator arrived at his private suite overlooking the club. Cunard, surprised by what he saw, observed him closely for a second before speaking. "Are you okay?"

His hair was damp as if he were just out of the shower. He was wearing jeans and was barefoot and bare-chested apart from a large crucifix that hung round his neck. His eyes were fully dilated. Cunard noticed a tremor in his hands.

Cunard asked, "Should we leave you to it and come back in the morning?"

"Come in. I don't have time to waste. How are you finding our new frontier, Miss Landsberg?"

"Sorry?"

"Alterum. Has it seeped into your soul yet?"

Cunard glanced at Mary and rolled his eyes. He stepped out of the elevator.

Mary followed and took in the layout. There were no sofas in this suite. Instead, there was a single armchair positioned to overlook the club. A table behind it was crowded with spirit bottles and glasses. There were two doors on the back wall, one with an exit sign above it.

"Well?" Morgan stared at Mary intently.

"It's not what I expected, but I don't know what I did expect. I thought you were an old man, and to be honest I did not see you as someone who was religious." Mary pointed at his crucifix.

Morgan made a gesture to bring up the lights. When it did not work, he clenched his hands together to steady the tremor before realizing he was not wearing his Handi. "Room," he raised his voice. "Lighter." He stared at the crucifix with a puzzled expression. "This?" He held it up in front of his face. "I wasn't. But here we need something more. We have to … otherwise …" Morgan noticed a spot of blood on his chest that had been hidden by the cross. He stopped talking and stared at it, transfixed. He rubbed the mark with the palm of his hand, spreading the stain until it was no longer visible.

Mary watched the cleaning motion and felt her heart rate rise. She changed the subject. "I have got some movement on the wallet. The key has been changed again. That gives me a device ID to track. I should have the location within an hour."

Morgan listened impassively, then checked his chest again, moving the crucifix left and right. Satisfied that the blood was gone he turned his attention back to his visitors. "Well done. Good work, Mrs. Finnegan."

Mary ignored the Finnegan remark. She recognized his attempts to create a reaction and this time she would not oblige.

"Drink?" Cunard and Mary shook their heads. Morgan sneered as he walked unsteadily to the table and poured himself a bourbon. "You have no idea, Cunard. No idea what's coming, do you?"

"Why don't you tell me?"

"War. War is coming and all Jack Glory sees is revenue and profits."

"I thought that was something you, of all people, would understand."

"Things are changing here. Over the last few years everything has become about Chain. It used to be it was only used by Patrian service companies. Now, Alterran street vendors want Chain to sell you a hotdog. You don't get it, do you?"

Cunard shook his head. "What is there to get?"

"People moving in and buying up real estate. You own a property for one year and it is twenty years here because of the time difference. Even with low inflation the returns are super-charged."

"And?"

"And the real world can't compete. It used to be only the smart money that came to Alterum. Now it's all the money. All of it."

"Well, I'm sorry we forced you to bring in eighty million Chain. I will pass on your concerns to Director Clive. In the meantime, we will have whoever stole it in the next hour or two. It would have been easier it you had given us their name in the first place."

"Names. There were two of them. They worked for me. I had the key, of course. They had half each in case one of them was ever compromised. Then *both* were compromised. What are the odds?"

Mary glanced nervously at Cunard. "They either talk, or I hack their device. Either way, we're going to get your money back."

"They won't talk. It's the WA. The WA don't talk." Morgan turned and walked away from his visitors to the back of the suite. He mumbled as he waved his glass. "Room. Open internal door." The door swung wide, and Morgan shuffled out of sight.

Mary mouthed silently, "What the hell?"

Cunard reached inside his jacket and took out his gun. He motioned for Mary to stay where she was.

Ignoring him, she followed him into the back room, becoming aware of a pungent metallic odor as she was confronted by the scene. She wanted to shout her safe word but was frozen to the spot.

A naked battered figure was chained to the wall. Head hanging forward, body covered in lacerations and dripping blood. An instrument trolley sat to one side. At the other end of the small room was a bed covered in a black satin sheet that was crumpled and unevenly spread, revealing a patch of blood-soaked white bed linen beneath.

Morgan spoke to the broken figure. "Roberts, we have visitors."

The head lifted as if to look at them, but the eyes were gone. The mouth was a distorted mess of flesh. The barely living corpse moaned and created a gargling sound as it did so.

"The WA don't talk." Morgan waved in the direction of his victim as if providing proof. "Bring the other one to me, but he won't talk either. I guarantee it."

Cunard walked forward, gun raised. "Then Mary will hack their device like she said." He pointed at the tortured victim's forehead and pulled the trigger.

Morgan watched Cunard return the gun to his jacket and spoke calmly as if he had been presented with no more than a minor inconvenience. "Was that necessary? I hadn't finished."

Mary was transfixed at what she had witnessed. She felt something tracking down her cheek. Lifting her hand to wipe away what she assumed to be blood, she studied her fingers and realized she was crying.

*

"He's an animal," said Mary. "I can't stay. Take me back to the port."

They were sitting in the car outside of Nylon Zoo.

"Let's take a breath. You're going to track the device ID, hack it, and then leave."

"He is a monster, Cunard. I'm not helping him get his money back. If you don't take me to the port, I will use my safe word."

Cunard spoke slowly in a quiet and gentle tone. "He is a monster. That's why you will finish the job."

She studied his expression carefully. "You're saying, let's get the job done, then I go back to my normal life? Is that the way you see this working?"

"Look, Patria is your real world. It's where everything you care about is. Do you think Morgan can be one thing here and something different there?"

"What are you suggesting? You think he would harm my family?"

Cunard shrugged. "I don't know. People like him, they make a point of letting you know they have something on you. They let your imagination do the rest."

"Is that why the AIP have assumed identities?"

"It's part of the reason. As soon as Chain flowed into Alterum, the edges between here and Patria became blurred. Everyone wants a piece of the action and there are no laws here that apply outside. The AIP creates what law there is between the two worlds. We can have people removed permanently. That is a painful thing, financially and personally. If they could influence or pressure an agent …"

"You need to report him."

"I will and he will not be removed."

"But he—"

"Butchered an Alterran. And he is bringing in massive amounts of Chain. Every transaction in and out of here goes through the Alterum Vault Exchange Service. They charge a transaction fee and AVES is owned by the company. All those transactions are where the real money for the company is these days. It's not the pod fees paid by tourists."

"So, he gets away with it? I've got to play nice and track down whoever stole his money, and the same thing happens to them?"

Cunard said nothing.

"Right. Let's get this over as quickly as we can."

*

"This is not what I was expecting." Mary inspected Cunard's apartment.

"It's got everything I need."

"And nothing else. Like literally nothing else."

"Would you like something to drink?"

"Tea, if you have it." Mary sat down at the table and gestured to bring her sniffer-bots to life.

Cunard put some tea bags into a French Press and poured in the boiling water as she worked. She observed him from the corner of her eye, wondering what he really thought of his job and the people he worked for. What he had done in the nightclub, it was horrific, but it was an act of mercy. Who was this man?

"What time is it?"

"Just past midnight."

"How long have I been here?"

"In Alterum? Six, seven hours. Seems longer, doesn't it?"

"No, I mean how long in Patria?"

Cunard did a quick calculation. "Fifteen, twenty minutes."

"My daughter will be on her morning break with her friends in the playground. The funny thing is, I didn't think I'd miss her because I knew I'd be back in time for the school pickup. But you know what?" Cunard opened his mouth to speak. Mary lifted a hand to stop him. "I miss her. I know I have not missed her dinnertime or bath time or bedtime or anything, but I feel as if I have, and it aches. Does that make me an obsessed mother?"

"Is there another kind?"

"Probably not." Her focus returned to the screen. "That's interesting. No transactions."

Cunard frowned. "What?"

"It's eighty million."

"And?"

"Don't you see? There have only been key changes, no transactions. The wallet must still have its original value. It should have been at least partially split up by now. Distributed in small values to a thousand untraceable wallets. It's been untouched since it was moved."

"Which means what exactly?"

"I don't know. It could mean it was an unplanned, opportunist theft. They hadn't planned ahead to have the forward wallets ready."

"So, it's possible to recover the whole amount?"

"Yes. By the time I am usually called in, I'm lucky to get back half. Usually, it's less. I get a bonus for a twenty-five percent recovery rate. We need to get the location of the device."

"How much longer?"

"Any time now." The string of scrolling cell IDs ground to a halt. "And now we convert to a physical location."

A geo-location address appeared. Mary gestured and the streets of New York London displayed in front of them. The view zoomed in and planted a map pin on the visualization.

"Looks like you're going back to where you started."

"Is that …"

Cunard nodded. "The Isle of Dogs. Chukaisha Tower, to be precise."

Chapter 7

RETIREMENT AND LONG-STAY PACKAGES ... *With a retirement or long-stay package provided by AAAC, it is now possible to move permanently to Alterum.*

Entering Alterum with an enhanced package makes you eligible for age and physical form choice. Select the age you wish to enter Alterum at, select the physical form you wish to enter Alterum with.

With this package you will be cared for in an ICU grade Lucid Synthetic Dreaming™ pod, ensuring that if you ever leave Alterum, you will return in the best physical shape possible.

Alterum—The life you never had.

The Official Visitor's Guide to Alterum

After crossing the Westminster-Manhattan bridge, Mary realized the exit ramp brought them onto the left-hand side of the road. "Seriously? They haven't standardized which side to drive on?"

Cunard said, "If they won't settle on one name for the Hudson Thames, what chance is there for anything else? It's one city, but it can sometimes be a little schizophrenic. How does it feel to be home?"

"We should exchange names and contact details and I will let you know when I get there."

As they continued the drive to the Isle of Dogs, Cunard contacted Eva.

She told him, "It's not the WA."

"You sure about that?"

"No, I'm not, but that's what I'm being told."

"Do they still trust you?"

"I've never asked them, lover. One thing though. They told me that an employee of Morgan has gone missing."

"You got a name for me?"

"Don Harper. Seemingly he was close to Morgan, and he vanished yesterday."

"Any reason the WA would be interested in him?"

"They are interested in a lot of people. They're probably interested in you."

"Okay. Thanks anyway. How's the ghost?"

Mary frowned. "How is Bella?" she corrected him.

"She's a fast learner. She can control her visibility already. Don't give up on her, Cunard."

"Sure. Anyway, talk later." He waited until the line closed and then turned to Mary. "Now we have a name."

*

The tower dominated the landscape. It was on the edge of the Docklands' existing business district and had views out across the river to Washington Heights. It was complete, but the surrounding parkland was still in the process of being landscaped. Temporary lights illuminated the area as the laborers worked through the night.

"Chukaisha Tower. The future of Alterum."

Mary looked up and followed the lights of the tower as they disappeared into the darkness above. "Impressive. The location has been stable for the last hour. According to my scan, it's on the forty-first floor."

Cunard flashed his ID at the security guards, and they were allowed into the building where another guard was patrolling the reception area.

"We need to get to level forty-one."

"The control floor, sure." The guard pointed to an elevator on the exterior wall.

Cunard explained as they began their ascent. "The tower is operating in test mode, but the official opening is next month. Director Clive will be here for that. First visit in years."

"It must be important." Mary studied the view. A run-down smaller tower was located at the boundary of the parkland. "I'm surprised the council estate hasn't been bulldozed. Not quite the right look."

Cunard followed her gaze. "Oh, the projects? Urban renewal at its best."

"Real estate at its cheapest."

The elevator came to a smooth stop, and the doors opened to reveal a control room not unlike the radio room on the *Lucitania*. They stepped out and Mary swept her arm across the room. Her Handi sprayed laser beams in every direction. The beams then moved in a rolling wave formation like the swelling water of an ocean wave.

"This isn't going to take long, is it?" Cunard pointed towards the elevators in the center of the floor. One had a flashing light above it, indicating it was due to stop. "I think we've been made. The external lift is slower. It was no coincidence we were directed to that one. Just enough time for us to appreciate the views and let someone catch up with us." Cunard pulled out his gun. "Be ready to use your safe word if necessary."

"The Handi responsible, it's over there." She moved in the direction of the signal.

Cunard stepped towards the elevator and crouched. The door opened to a burst of gunfire.

"Drop your weapons," Cunard shouted. "I've got you covered."

Three figures rushed from the open door, firing as they emerged.

"Mary, safe word." Cunard let off a rapid-fire round of shots. One of the three figures slumped to the floor. There was a pause in the gunfire and

Cunard scanned the room for Mary. She was nowhere to be seen. "No need for anyone else to get hurt."

Gunshot sprayed around him. Cunard kept low and moved rapidly between desks. A gunman suddenly stood up and scattered bullets randomly. Cunard aimed at an overhead light behind him and fired. The light exploded and he turned, presenting a clearer target. They were face to face. The gunman looked shocked and scared. Cunard took aim and shot twice in quick succession. One chest shot followed by a head shot. Both connected and he collapsed.

"Well done, agent. A great effort."

Cunard spun round to find the third man standing behind a chair, holding his gun to Mary's head. She was semi-conscious.

"Wait."

"As you say, no one needs to get hurt. Put your gun down and she will be unharmed."

He reluctantly dropped his weapon.

"Kick it towards me."

Cunard did as he was directed.

"That was a sensible choice." The gunman pointed his gun away from Mary's head and shot a Handi device sitting on the desk. The sound of breaking glass was repeated as he fired again. "She was a little reckless. Stayed to find the Handi. She is more determined than any of us thought. Still, problem solved and no need for her to die."

Mary began to regain consciousness. "Cunard," she mumbled, looking at the ruined device.

"Perfect." The gunman stepped away from Mary, keeping his gun pointed at Cunard. He raised three fingers with his free hand, creating a W sign. "The waking will no longer sleep, and the AIP are not welcome here."

Mary tried to shout but managed little more than a hoarse whisper. "No."

A shot rang out. The gunman crumpled to the floor. Cunard glanced over his shoulder and saw Fischer near the external elevator with his gun drawn.

"Could you have cut it any finer?"

"*Gern geschehen.* It was nothing."

Cunard moved towards Mary and whispered so that Fischer could not hear. "Why didn't you use your safe word?"

"My family ..."

"Don't mind me." Fischer strolled over, assessing the surrounding carnage. "They might have to redecorate for the grand opening." He picked up the destroyed Handi and turned it over, inspecting it from every angle before dropping it back on the desk.

Cunard took hold of Mary's hand and squeezed it tight. "You and I need to talk."

"What are you doing here?" Fischer asked.

"Some missing Chain."

Fischer glanced at the Handi. "And now it's gone? Was it worth dying for?" He glanced at Mary. "I take it you got him into this?"

"He made a 'W' sign. I think it was the WA." Mary's voice was slurred, and her eyes still glazed.

"This one," he hooked his thumb at Mary. "This one is smart, real *schlau*. The WA have been quiet lately. You, Cunard, were the victim and *jungfrau* Maria here was the witness until I showed up and saved your ass."

"Why are you here? How did you know where I was?"

Fischer smiled. "*Bruder. Kumpel.* I like you. You know that, but it's not all about you." He gestured and a missing person report flashed in the air between them. "Don Harper, New York resident, has been AWOL for over twenty-four hours. Reported by a friend. Normally we would not care until he had been gone for a few days, but he works as a building engineer here in Chukaisha Tower and it's about to open. So, it is kind of a big deal, *oder?*"

*

The body of a building guard lay sprawled on the ground floor as they exited the elevator.

"He was barely alive when I got here," Fischer walked towards the corpse. "He said he had to obey them because they had his family. I hoped to find Harper here, not you."

"If I come across him, I'll be sure to get in touch."

Fischer stood over the dead body and raised two fingers on each hand to make separate 'V' shapes. "The shadow may fade." He brought his hands together to form a 'W'. "But the source remains."

Chapter 8

NON-PLAYER CHARACTERS ... *Alterum is not a game, and the residents are not "Non-Player Characters". This is what makes our world unique.*

Each local you meet is an autonomous AI construct that evolved naturally. They are born, work, raise families and die within Alterum. They are self-aware and believe that they experience pain and emotion. No other online experience offers this level of reality.

For this reason, we do not refer to the locals as NPCs and we do not refer to our world as the Real World or IRL. Our world is referred to as Patria. They have been told that 'Patrians' created technology which allows us to cross over into other multiverses including Alterum.

We ask you to respect this mythology during your stay. This will help you and future visitors to fully experience a hyper-reality instead of a mere simulation.

Alterum—Perfect one day, better the next.

The Official Visitor's Guide to Alterum

I 'm sorry, Mary. I shouldn't have spooked you about your family, but you're no good to them in a coma. The next time I tell you to use your safe word, use it."

"I assume that was something to do with the Book of Shadows. That sign that Fischer made?"

"Don't change the subject."

"The thing is, the WA use a 'W' as their sign and so did Fischer. So, what's the difference between the Book of Shadows and the WA?"

"One finger."

"We need to find Harper. If Morgan gets to him first …"

"I know."

"And I will decide when I leave. Not you, not Morgan, but me."

"That's a nice luxury to have."

Mary turned to Cunard. "How do we find him?"

"I don't know. I guess now that we have his name, we could cross-check the ID of the Handi at the tower, see if it was his. Then we could perhaps request access to all cell records and look for hotspots of activity."

"Right."

"Which I have already done. Which is why we are heading towards the main location on his records."

"Oh, right."

*

The Empire Hotel had a crumbling and pock-marked facade. A man was slumped on the ground next to the small single door entrance. He held up a paper cup as they approached.

"Change."

Cunard stepped over the man's outstretched legs. "No cash on me, sorry."

The reception was a small square room with a hole in the wall and a security door to the left. The sign above the reception window was faded and yellow.

No ID required for cash rentals

Cunard waved in the direction of the sign. "Looks like he valued his privacy."

After they rang the bell, an old woman appeared. She was wearing a face mask attached to a small oxygen bottle that she carried in her arms like a baby. She dissected them with her stare and then held the mask away from her face to speak.

"We're full."

"Glad to hear it." Cunard flicked his badge into the air between them.

"You're not local," she grunted. "We want nothing to do with Jackboots here."

"Nonetheless, I have authority to enter and search without a warrant." Cunard threw up a picture of Don Harper. "Which floor?"

"I don't recognize him."

"Then I guess I'll have to search the place room by room."

"You won't find him. He's not been here today."

"The man you don't recognize. This man, Don Harper?"

The woman put on her mask and breathed deeply. She placed a hand on the counter as if to steady herself.

"Are you alright?" asked Mary.

"She's fine. She's stalling."

"AIP shit," the woman mumbled in a voice distorted by the mask.

"Sorry, I didn't quite catch that?"

A voice whispered from the backroom. The woman turned back and listened as something was said. She slowly took off her mask. "Five oh two. Fifth floor."

"And the key."

She gestured and the image of a key floated between them.

Cunard pointed at the key and then his Handi. The key shot towards him and evaporated. "Thank you." Cunard held up four fingers, creating the same "W" shape made by Fischer earlier. "May you find peace in the shadow."

"No peace without justice," she replied, flicking her middle finger at him.

Cunard turned towards the security door and gestured a key turning. The solid metal entrance swung open.

"Thank you," Mary said to the woman. "We mean no harm."

"But you do harm."

Mary followed Cunard through the door, waiting for it to close before speaking. "Jackboot doesn't sound as friendly as Jack Glory."

"What do you want me to say?"

"That we're the good guys."

"We're not. We are not the good guys. We do what we want here and the Alterrans must put up with it. She hates me because she has good reason to hate the AIP."

"So, why do you stay?"

Cunard shrugged. "The money is good. You know, the only people they hate more than the AIP are tourists."

Stepping out of the elevator on the fifth floor, they found themselves in a grand hallway with marble floors, deep rich oak doors, and prints of Pre-Raphaelite paintings on the wall. There were only two apartments, 501 and 502.

"This is not what I expected, but it's a good a hiding place."

Cunard faced 502 and repeated the key-turning gesture. The door swung open, and they entered the apartment. It had a long narrow hallway leading into a large open-plan living area. The lights switched on as they made their way through the space. The apartment was luxurious and spacious, and it was a mess. Bottles of wine and spirits lying around the floor, drug paraphernalia on a table next to the sofa.

"Mr. Harper has some unhealthy habits." Cunard rubbed a finger on the remainder of white dust scattered across the table surface and sniffed it. "Some expensive habits."

Mary took in the apartment and spotted a fixed terminal on a desk. She pressed the power button and the logo of the hotel appeared as it came to life and spoke.

Please use your key to access all services

Cunard flicked the key to Mary. "See what you can find, and I will check out the rest of the place."

Mary sat down and began to type at the keyboard, making gesture and vocal commands between keystrokes.

Cunard opened the fridge and pulled out a bottle of cold press coffee. He unscrewed the top and took a small drink. Mary raised an eyebrow. Cunard took another one out and sat it in front of her as she worked.

"I didn't realize it was the food you were checking out."

"No point in them going to waste. You have access to the best of everything here if you have the money." Cunard pointed back at the table. "Those drugs, they are beyond anything you will find back home."

"The best cocaine money can buy?"

"Not cocaine. Not anything you would have come across before. Every drug here is tailored for an exact experience. The white stuff is Sild Nitrate. Combines the effects of amyl nitrite and sildenafil without crashing your blood pressure."

Mary said, "I'm a boring mother who stays in most weekends. I don't know what that means."

"The best sex you will ever have."

"Okay, well now you really are trying to make me feel boring."

"After the tower, I wouldn't accuse you of that."

"He last used this terminal two days ago." Mary tilted her head. "These drugs, are they addictive?"

"Depends on what you mean by addictive. Physically no, but psychologically? Too much of a good thing can make normal life unbearable."

"So, maybe you would visit a rehab if you were going to give them up?"

"What have you found?"

Mary gestured at the screen and displayed a video into the space between them. A woman in a cable knit cardigan walked in the grounds of a beautiful garden with a sandstone building behind her. The woman announced, "We are here when you are ready, because you do not have to do this on your own. The Hermitage Retreat will guide you back to your best self."

Mary waved the image back into the terminal. "He searched for this five times in the last month."

"Good work." Cunard put down his bottled coffee. "Worth a visit."

"One minute," Mary tapped quickly on the keyboard and then spoke to the computer. "Download." A stream of light pulsed from the screen to Mary's Handi. "In case there is anything else of interest."

"Finished?" asked Cunard.

"Yes."

Cunard took out his gun, pointed it at the screen and fired. "If we can access this, so can someone else. Let's go."

An elegantly dressed woman in the elevator smiled at them as they entered, then bowed her head to avoid eye contact. Cunard and Mary paid little attention to her until the lift stopped on the ground floor and she made no move to exit with them. The doors began to close, and she spoke. "His real name is James Packard, not Harper."

Cunard gestured towards the elevator, but this time it did not obey his command to open. The woman's face was obscured as she leaned forward. "James Packard."

*

"Anything of interest?" Mary was driving as Cunard investigated the name.

"That would be an understatement. He's not Alterran. James Packard is Patrian. He arrived here on a two-month package. That's four years local time. No sign of him spending any of the money he brought with him and he's halfway through his visit. He is still here somewhere."

Mary spoke quietly, as much to herself as to Cunard. "It's a good plan. Come here and impersonate an Alterran. Make it look like the WA."

"Perhaps." Cunard pointed ahead. "It's the next turn on the left."

They drove across the gravel driveway into the grounds of the building from the video. Most of the house was in darkness, a set of carriage lights illuminating the entrance.

The door opened as they climbed the steps. A male nurse in a crisp white uniform greeted them. "I'm sorry but visits and admissions are not available overnight."

Cunard flashed his badge then showed the nurse the picture of Packard. "We need to find this man urgently. His safety depends on it. He could be registered as Don Harper, James Packard, or some other name. He's Patrian, so don't give me any run-around about maintaining client confidentiality."

"I am aware of the rights of the AIP. Please follow me."

"So, he is a patient?" Mary asked.

"Client. We don't have patients. We have a dedicated facility for Patrians, staffed by Patrian nurses. Yes, he's here." The nurse showed them the stairway behind reception. "Top of the stairs and turn right. It has its own security."

The entrance to the Patrian wing had a secure glass door. They were expected and the nurse on duty buzzed them through. "My colleague said you're looking for John Emerson."

"James Packard, Don Harper, John Emerson … I don't care what he's called, but I need to see this person now." Cunard displayed Packard's picture.

"People often use an alias," the nurse explained. "Keeps the whole thing confidential. John's room is the third one down."

"How is he?" asked Mary.

The nurse frowned. "Typical tourist addict. They think they are invincible when they arrive, so they take it to the limit. He came in a couple of days ago looking like he was going to die. Five blood transfusions cycled with Fentanyl Redux have fixed him up. He's due to leave tomorrow. He'll most likely cycle through here a few times during his stay."

Cunard frowned, recognizing the type. "Okay. We need to speak to him urgently. It is an AIP matter. Do not let anyone else in."

Cunard knocked gently on the door. "Mr. Emerson?"

"Yes."

Cunard entered the room slowly and deliberately. A balding middle-aged man was sitting on an armchair. He studied Cunard's badge with alarm. Cunard said quickly, "Please don't leap. We have to talk."

"I've got nothing to say."

"We know you took the Chain from Morgan," said Mary. "We want to help you fix it."

"There's nothing to fix. I've done nothing wrong."

"He seems to think you have," said Mary. "He thinks you and one of your colleagues stole it. We saw your colleague tonight."

"Roberts wouldn't talk to you."

"Roberts won't talk to anyone ever again. Morgan made sure of that."

Packard was suddenly lost in thought. "No …"

"Morgan is dangerous," said Mary. "You need to return it. You won't be safe unless you do."

Packard shook his head. "Why would he do that to Roberts? It makes no sense."

"That kind of money will make people do terrible things."

"But …" Packard again drifted off for a second before coming back to focus. "Roberts was Alterran. He wouldn't touch me."

"I wouldn't be so sure."

"It doesn't make sense," Packard repeated.

Packard's confusion hit Mary like a revelation. "He has the new key, doesn't he?"

Packard nodded. "We went to the tower together. I changed the key on my Handi and left it there. I put a repeater on my device. It will look like it's updating the key without changing it. It's timed to repeat every twenty-four hours."

Mary smiled having worked out the puzzle. "He wants it to look as if it's stolen. As a Chain wallet he can still access it. All of this, me coming here to find it, it was all just to corroborate the theft."

Cunard said, "I've been an idiot. He needed to tidy up the loose ends. You find the Handi in Chukaisha Tower, I get burned, but only after you've been convinced it's the work of the WA. Fischer was right. I was the victim, and you were the witness."

"He wouldn't touch me. I'm Patrian." Packard stared at Cunard, looking for confirmation.

"You got the job in the tower to create a local identity?"

"I was meant to go straight home afterwards, but I met someone through work. We became close, I decided to stay if I could. She was going to help me disappear. I needed to get clean first."

"This person you became close to, she knows about this?"

"We love each other. Do you think he'll come after me?"

Cunard stared at Packard. "Listen to me carefully. When you deviated from the plan, you became one of the loose ends."

"What do I do?"

"Give me the key," said Mary. "It's the only way to stop you being a target. If I control the wallet, he has nothing to gain from harming you. It's over."

Packard pleaded, "You've got to protect me."

As Cunard was about to reply, a series of red dots began floating around the room. They were coming from outside the window. "Shit." He pulled Mary to the floor as the dots began to center rapidly on Packard.

Packard, confused at Cunard's movements, saw several lights racing across the floor towards him. He followed the moving dots as they began zeroing in on his heart. He stood up from his armchair. The targets followed him, remaining centered on his chest.

"Leap, Packard, *leap*," shouted Cunard.

Packard slumped back down on the seat. "I can't."

The glass from the window shattered and bullets sprayed the frozen Packard. He was pushed further into the chair and slumped as the bullets kept coming, now ripping his face apart. Then, as quickly as it had started, it went quiet. The target lasers disappeared.

Cunard crawled over to the window and using his Handi displayed an image of drones disappearing into the night sky beyond the driveway. Taking no chances, he stayed low and crawled back towards Mary. "We need to go." He opened the door and, still crawling, pulled her out into the hallway. The duty nurse ran towards them as they got up from the floor.

"Stay back," said Cunard. "There's nothing you can do for him."

The nurse came to a sudden halt.

"Are you okay?" Cunard held onto Mary. She was sprayed with Packard's blood. He probably was too, but he would deal with that later.

"Define *okay*. How did he know where Packard was? Did someone follow us?"

"Perhaps he always knew."

The nurse, shocked by the sound of gunfire and the sight of Cunard and Mary, faced them like a statue.

Cunard asked her, "Did you let anyone know we were here?"

She turned grey. "It's protocol."

Stabbing at the nurse with a finger Mary shouted, "Who owns the Hermitage?"

"I only work here. I don't know."

"You're Patrian. You wouldn't come here without knowing who you work for." Mary moved towards her, and the nurse took a step back.

Cunard pulled out his gun and aimed at the nurse. "How about I count to five and then I blow your brains out, just like Packard?"

"You wouldn't."

"It doesn't matter if I do. I'm giving you five seconds to leap. Five seconds to say your safe word." Cunard made a show of straightening his arm and improving his aim. "Five … four … three … two …"

"No, please."

"Packard didn't want to leap either. Why would that be, I wonder?"

"Please." The nurse was now shaking.

"Could it be that you can't? That a condition of your employment was to come here without a safe word? That would be an effective way of controlling employees, wouldn't it?"

The nurse said nothing, her silence an admission.

"So, let's try again. I'm going to count down from five and blow your brains out. Who do you work for? Five …four …"

"Youzoo. I work for Youzoo."

"That's here. What about back home?"

The nurse shook her head.

"And here we go again. Five … four … three …two …" Cunard fired his gun past the nurse's head, lodging a bullet in the wall behind her. "One and a half … one …"

"Sea Defender."

"Thank you." Cunard let off another round at the entrance, shattering the glass doors. "Mary, stay behind me."

As they reached the top of the staircase, he surveyed the ground floor. No sign of life. They began to move slowly down towards the reception area. When they reached the bottom of the stairs, red and blue lights silently flashed across the windows. Cunard reached back and held Mary by one shoulder, pushing her down as he crouched. "Let's make sure they are friendlies."

The door burst open and uniformed officers rushed the building, guns pointed. They spotted Cunard and screamed at him, "Gun down, hands where we can see them."

Cunard dropped his weapon and put his hands up. Mary followed his lead.

"Stand up slowly."

Again, they followed the barked instructions. Two members of the SWAT team moved in sync as they approached them. A plain-clothed figure appeared in the entrance. It was Fischer.

"Stand down, men. This is Agent Cunard of the AIP." The officers stopped but did not lower their guns. "I said stand down."

The officers checked with each other and slowly lowered their weapons. Cunard bent down and retrieved his gun.

"Patrian scum," one of the officers mumbled as Cunard and Mary went to Fischer.

"Sorry?"

"Patrian scum," the officer repeated, this time loud enough for everyone to hear. A few of his colleagues grunted in agreement.

Fischer stood between them and spoke to the officer. "He speaks very highly of you too. Now let them pass."

"Thanks." Mary touched Fischer's arm as she spoke.

"You two should get out of here. The AIP are not popular with the uniforms."

"You seem to be showing up everywhere tonight."

"And that is a good thing. I thought you might lead me to Harper. Was I correct?"

Cunard nodded. "He's dead. He was Patrian, so nothing for you to worry about."

"*Aber andererseits*, that does worry me. I worry about all Alterrans being blamed and collectively punished."

"Not this time. It's a disagreement between Patrians."

*

Mary leaned back into the car seat and shut her eyes. She then turned towards Cunard. "One and a half?"

"You never used fractions when you were counting down?"

"When I was five, maybe. One and a quarter, one and a fifth, one and a sixth," she spoke in a childlike voice, shaking her head and laughing.

"So, what is the name of the company that hired you?"

"I think you can guess. Sea Defender is the holding company for most of Morgan's business interests. And Youzoo?"

"Privately held with a deliberately obscured ownership trail."

"But you've heard of it?" said Mary.

"You visited one of its establishments tonight, Nylon Zoo. It also owns a large chunk of the rec drugs market." Mary seemed puzzled. "Recreational drugs. None of it is illegal here, and it's becoming another reason why Patrians visit. Makes sense that they would also own the rehab clinic people use to get clean before heading home."

"So, Morgan knew where Packard was?"

"Looks like it. Harming a Patrian would be a last resort, even for him. But as soon he knew we had found him, Packard was finished. One thing, Mary. Do you have a safe word? Was coming here without one a precondition of your contract?"

"No, I do have one."

"Things are getting messy."

Mary leaned over and whispered in Cunard's ear. He laughed then frowned, an unspoken question.

She said, "Yes, seriously. That's it."

"Good. So, you're just reckless then?"

"Like you ..." Mary realized something. "You don't have one, do you?"

Cunard said, "Keeps me motivated."

"What the hell?"

"No AIP agents have them. We are here for a tour of duty. You don't get to opt out when things get tough."

"That's crazy. Why can't you leap and then re-spawn?"

Cunard looked at her. "Re-spawn?"

"Or whatever it is you do when you die in a game."

"This is not a game. By the time you got back in the 'game' as you call it, it would be at least a day later."

"And?"

"And whatever situation you were in would be long gone. The rise of the WA meant it that wasn't an option."

"Are they that strong?"

"Against people that won't stand their ground, yes."

"And now Morgan's doing the same."

"It makes sense. They have skin in the game this way, and he has more control over them."

"Why would the company let his people come without a safe word? I thought that was against the rules."

"It is. Only agents are permitted entry without one."

"So ..."

"So, he has people in the company. It's the only way he could pull it off."

"You've got him then. They won't let him away with that. You've got him."

"I guess it depends on *who* he owns in Jack Glory."

Mary glared at Cunard then gestured to make a connection with her Handi. "Stay quiet."

The line connected and Morgan answered.

"Ms Landsberg. How are we progressing? Where are you?"

"On my way to see you. I have taken this as far as I can. The trail is now completely dead."

"I see."

"I'm going home as soon as I've updated you in person." There was silence at the other end of the connection. "Morgan?"

"Okay. Come to my apartment and come alone."

"Cunard comes with me. For protection."

"Protection from whom?"

"That's the question, isn't it?"

"If you are that nervous, please go straight to the port. I will not allow the AIP into my home. Thank you for your work. I'm sorry you weren't able to earn your bonus."

"I *am* going to meet with you before I go. You will want to hear what I have to say. Oh, and I will get my bonus. Cunard will wait outside."

Again, there was silence. Mary splayed her fingers. She mouthed silently as she counted down dropping a finger on each number. *Five, four, three, two.* She then bent her index finger without bringing it down completely and mouthed, *A half.*

"Okay. I don't know what we must discuss, but I'll see you. Only you."

"I'll be there in thirty minutes."

"Ms Landsberg, I—" Mary cut the connection before Morgan could finish.

"So, the plan is?"

"You think I have a plan? I'm flattered."

"You *do* have a plan? Tell me you have a plan."

"Kind of. He's not sure how much we know."

"So, the safe thing is to void us."

"You, not me." She smiled.

"Right. And your logic behind this is …"

"Because he didn't try to kill me when he had the chance."

"And you believe that he will hesitate to attack you or your family once you're back in Patria?"

Chapter 9

CROSSING … *Crossing back at the end of your trip can sometimes be bittersweet.*

Video and photographs of your vacation cannot be transferred, ensuring that what happens in Alterum, stays in Alterum. Once you have emerged from your pod, however, you will be given the option of recording an interview.

The interview is yours to keep and will be the perfect memory prompt. Our interviewers are all experienced travelers and will tease out the experiences and sensations that brought your trip to life.

For those willing to share, the interviews will also be used for training purposes to improve the experience of future and returning travelers.

Alterum—A world of memories.

The Official Visitor's Guide to Alterum

The entrance to Morgan's apartment block overlooking Central Park was guarded by two large men in expensive suits, not the uniformed doorman of the other nearby buildings. They studied Cunard and Mary.

"We're here to—" Mary was cut off before she could continue.

"We know who you are," one of the guards said, as he scanned them both.

Cunard gestured and scanned the guards in return. "Patrians." It was a statement rather than a question.

"They're clean." The guards stood aside, and one opened the door. "The lady only. And please remove your Handi."

"Hope you've got your safe word memorized." Cunard stared at the larger of the two men as Mary gave him the Handi for safe keeping.

"Always," replied the guard, holding the door open as she passed through.

The inside of the building resembled a small hotel. There was a reception desk with an attendant talking on the phone. "Yes sir, she has arrived ... Of course, sir, I'll send her straight up." He put down the phone.

"Which floor?"

"I will take care of that, madame."

The elevator opened into a wide spacious room with floor to ceiling windows. Morgan was standing outside on the balcony, smoking a cigar. Every bit the successful businessperson again, his manner and appearance at the club a distant memory. He motioned for her to join him.

"Quite the view, wouldn't you agree?"

"It is."

"This apartment block was built to give views over both New York and London. Below us, Central Park. In one direction, Big Ben, and in the other direction, Chukaisha Tower. It was one of the first uniquely Alterran buildings of majestic scale. It belongs to Nylon City rather than being a shadow of another world."

"Impressive."

"It's more than that. You miss the point. Alterum is real. Some people get it, but not many. Not even the esteemed Jack Glory."

"But you do?"

"I do. Most people still think of this place as entertainment, a holiday destination and nothing more. When Chukaisha Tower goes online, everything will change. I mean everything." Morgan put down his cigar and closed his hands together in an embrace. "The two worlds will become inextricably linked.

"Electronic trades can take place faster than mere humans can keep up. Automated trading needs to be choked because without human oversight it leads to artificial spikes and crashes. Chukaisha Tower solves that problem once and for all. The time differential here means traders can monitor and correct automated trading in real-time."

Mary tilted her head as she listened to Morgan. "And here, manual trades can be carried out at the same speed as the IRL automated trading systems?"

"Exactly. Patrian traders are moving here in their thousands, buying up real estate, preparing to join the gold rush. And soon Alterum will be a large part of the real-world economy. No one will be able to shut it down. If they did, the economy would collapse as access to any money locked in here was lost. It would effectively disappear overnight. You might as well make a bonfire of paper currency and watch it burn."

Mary's eyes narrowed as the magnitude of the change sunk in. "Power in Alterum will become power in the real world."

Morgan smiled. "You get it."

"Why did you steal your own money? And why go to the pretense of trying to recover it?"

"Is that what I did?"

"Packard confirmed it. He told us everything before you had him killed. The visit to the tower to change the key. All of it."

Morgan was quiet and contemplative as he retrieved a fresh cigar. She let the silence sit between them. After Morgan lit up, he blew smoke up into the night and sighed. "If someone stole your money, surely you would try to recover it? If I hadn't tried to recover it, who would believe it was ever stolen?"

"And if the WA had it, who would doubt that?"

"And if they were seen to have attacked an Agente In Patria and infiltrated the tower, even better. Because they have, you know. The company needs to root it out or we are all going to suffer." Morgan frowned, looking genuinely worried. "The WA may be treated as delusional by everyone here, but they're not idiots. They are organized, they know the truth even if few of their compatriots believe them. They are not going to let this world be taken over by outsiders without a fight. The company has to be mobilized against them and sooner rather than later."

"You could have warned the company if you know so much about the WA. But then, there is more to it, isn't there?"

"No laws have been broken."

"No Patrian laws."

Morgan laughed deeply. "Oh, my dear. Patrian laws? It didn't take long for you to feel at home here, did it?"

Mary bristled at the condescending tone. "I'm not sure Packard would agree either."

"I'm sure he wouldn't, but then again, he signed a disclaimer when he came here. We all did. The company is not responsible for any short-term or long-term psychological or neurological damage incurred while visiting Alterum. It would be hard to hold a visitor liable when the company has no liability, wouldn't you agree?

"Look, I didn't want to harm him, but he was a mess. He came for a job but got hooked on the local vices and people. He turned out to be quite unreliable."

Mary said, "I've had enough of this. Pay my fee including the bonus and I will report whatever you want, but I need to know you will leave me and my family alone."

Morgan stared at her blank-faced. "Report what you know. Two employees stole the money for the WA. One was Alterran, the other a drug addled Patrian. The wallet is gone and unrecoverable."

"And that's it? We are safe?"

"Of course, you are. I wouldn't want to commit a real crime, would I?"

"And Cunard?"

"He can take care of himself. You and your family are safe. The company will finally wake up to the threat of the WA. Everyone wins."

Mary's eyes filled with tears. "Okay, I'm leaving."

"One more thing. Did Packard share anything else I should be aware of?"

Mary appeared puzzled, wiped a tear from her cheek and shook her head.

*

Cunard and Mary were sitting in the car, looking across to Morgan's building. She had given him a full account of the meeting.

"Do you believe him?" asked Mary.

"Which part?"

"The part about not harming me?"

"Not for a second."

Mary nodded. "Do you think he believed me?"

"Hopefully not. We'll soon find out." They sat in silence, staring ahead for a few moments before Cunard turned towards Mary. "What are you thinking?"

"I'm thinking I didn't get to eat as much chicken as I expected."

"Right." He grinned.

"Also, there's something more to the theft. Something doesn't add up."

"You've worked in this field a long time, haven't you?"

"Yes."

"Then you already have the answer."

She asked, "What do you mean?"

"Once you have done one deployment here, there's nothing completely new. It all starts becoming variations of the same things. I'm sure it's the same in your line of work. So, ask yourself, why does anyone ever want a Chain wallet with such a large value and why do they want it to disappear?"

Mary thought for a few seconds. "Like I said before, it's usually about hiding a crime."

"Morgan wants the cash to disappear?"

"He wants the Chain to disappear."

"What's the difference?"

"It is money, but it is also a ledger. Do you see?"

Cunard shook his head.

"Unlike physical bank notes, Chain wallets record all transactions. Where the money came from, where it went to."

"He's hiding transactions. That's what you're saying?"

"Maybe he's cleaning up. He has no intention of ever returning to the real world. He told us that. He doesn't want to go back to an old dying body. The only thing that could pull him back is the taxman or the law."

"And?"

"And he wouldn't be the first businessman to have a secret ledger. Chain wallets have been used to bribe, to buy into black markets, to pay for killings. And it's not just transactions that are usually in the ledger. People store documents, notes, video, photographs, in Chain. And because it's a ledger, nothing ever gets deleted."

"But if it's cash, why would ..." Cunard paused.

"What?"

"Chain wallets can be transferred back and forward between Patria and Alterum, but it has to go through the Company's AVES Interchange. You cannot carry out an AVES transfer without a record of the sender, recipient, and amount. That's information that the authorities cannot usually get about wallets. They never know who owns a Chain wallet. It all makes sense. AVES has been exempted from regulatory disclosure because Alterum was not recognized as a tier-one financial system."

"Was? You used the past tense."

"The tower has changed all that. Alterum will be part of the world finance markets and only got its license based on an agreement that AVES would also come under the same regulations as Patria. There has been a concern that Alterum has become a destination for dirty money. So, the deal was, you give us AVES disclosure, we give you a license."

"Let me guess, they backdated the disclosure requirement?"

"They did. Very controversial and there was pushback, but it was a showstopper for the authorities. Jack Glory didn't care. It wanted the license approved. As soon as the tower officially opens, regulators get access. A large value amount like that will flash red on their monitoring systems."

"So, the Chain wallet will be linked to him, and they can demand access. It wouldn't matter if he distributed the money, the ledger would still be there. He probably thought he'd beaten the system until the backdated disclosure was agreed."

Cunard nodded. "By setting up the WA he hoped to derail the opening, but if that didn't work, the wallet was gone anyway."

"The tower was a ticking bomb." Mary gestured and the time displayed. "We've been here fifteen minutes. How long do we give it?"

81

"As long as it takes."

"Oh, sorry. Were you waiting for me?" a disembodied voice whispered.

Mary turned around and spoke to the back seat. "Did you get it?"

"Yes. Now, if we could get going, I'd like to appear. All this being invisible takes a lot of effort, you know."

Cunard started the car and drove away from the building. As he did so Bella appeared with a wide grin.

"That was the best. I went straight off the balcony and base-jumped without a parachute. Without ending up back in the void. I actually did it."

"And you got the key?"

"You were right. As soon as you left, he logged into the wallet to check it."

"I think I told the truth with the right amount of uncertainty. Don't you agree, Cunard?"

"He was agitated until he logged in," said the ghost. "And the first thing he did was change the key. But I got it for you."

"You are a guardian angel," said Mary.

"I'm a ghost, but you're welcome."

"And we will look after you, won't we, Cunard?"

"I'll keep my side of the bargain. If I live long enough."

*

Back in Cunard's apartment Mary brought up a Chain screen. Two options floated in front of her, Wallet and Exchange. Mary selected Wallet and was prompted for an account number and password.

"Let's see how good Bella was at memorizing this," she said.

Cunard watched anxiously as Mary typed in the key. They were in. She turned and smiled at Cunard.

He asked, "What has he been up to?"

"I have no idea and it would take weeks of digging to find out. I can guarantee there is enough in here to hang him though."

"Can you take a copy of the transactions?"

"I can do better than that." Mary tapped away at the floating keyboard and selected the key update function. "He seemed keen to have his money stolen, so let's steal it."

Cunard said, "We need to get you protection back home. He will come for you and your family. You know that don't you?"

"And the wallet is now mine." Mary continued to tap away. "I will just leave a note for whoever reviews this." Once she had finished typing, she selected AVES, then entered an account number and pointed to a privacy drop-down box. 'Open Transactions'. She hit enter and watched the logo spin with the words 'Transfer Processing' displayed.

"Where are you sending it?"

"To a drop box used by the IRS. When they open a formal investigation into someone, they demand read access to all accounts. I've sent them the wallet ID and granted them full access."

Cunard placed his hand on Mary's shoulder. "You are very clever."

"I'm good at what I do. Now promise me you will look after Bella."

"I will do what I can. Once this transfer is finished, do you want to grab a last taste of Seoul Fried Chicken before you leave?"

Mary shook her head. "They still slaughter the animals, don't they?"

Cunard blinked.

"You see, that was kind of why I gave it up back home. I have no idea of who or what you are, but give me hug agent, Cunard." Mary pulled him towards her.

"It's not over yet. Not for either of us."

"You think? You can be a little stupid for someone so clever. That's why I'm hugging you."

Cunard said, "Right." A connecting tone sounded, and he pulled away to accept the call. It was Fischer. "*Wie geht's?*"

"I got word that some of Morgan's men are on their way to your apartment. I don't think they're dropping by for coffee."

"Shit." Cunard checked Mary's screen. It was still transferring. "Can you get your men to hold them off? Pull them in for a vehicle check? Anything?"

"It's not my men that gave me the word, Cunard. Some civilian friends who are unlikely to put themselves on the line for a Patrian."

"No peace without justice?"

"Something like that. I'm on the London side of the river. I won't get there in time. You're on your own this time. Sorry, *kumpel.*"

"*Kein* problem, Fischer. Thanks for the warning."

"You're getting better, you know. We'll have that conversation sometime soon. *Tschuss.*"

"It must be serious," said Cunard, as he went to the window. "Fischer doesn't complement my German very often." Checking the street below, he saw four men enter the building. "Why is the transfer taking so long?"

He came away from the window, pulled open a drawer of his desk and removed a semi-automatic and flicked the safety lock. "Time for you to go, Mary. Don't argue. I'll hold them off until the transfer is complete."

Mary's eyes bulged, tears forming. "I've got a child to think about."

"You don't need to explain. Please go before it's too late."

"Who are you, Cunard? Who are you out there?"

"I'll look you up when my tour of duty finishes."

"Do that."

Cunard raised his voice. "Leap."

Mary stepped back and clicked her heels three times, laughing and crying as she did so. "There's no place like home, home, HOME." And with that she fell to the floor.

Cunard examined the screen floating in the air. The transfer was almost complete but there was no way out of the apartment. There was a knock at the door as someone spoke.

"Mr. Cunard, I have an urgent message for you."

As Cunard stepped forward the door knocked again. Standing square in front of it he held his weapon at waist height and opened fire. The wood splintered as he sprayed side to side. He heard a muffled groan on the other side. Cunard kept firing as he walked backwards. He did not have much ammunition left. He looked at the screen. 'Transfer Complete' flashed in green as he finished his last round. He threw his weapon to the floor and pulled out his handgun. He kicked over the desk to use as a shield. Crouching, he pointed his revolver at the entrance and waited.

The door was strafed from the other side. Cunard wondered how many he had hit and how many were left but made his peace with the outcome he expected. The entrance buckled and collapsed inward. Laser guides scanned the room. From his vantage point he could see a drone float in the doorway. He took a deep breath and decided he was not going to go out hiding behind furniture. He leapt forward firing off rounds at the drone, hitting it and watching it fall, but not before he too was hit in the shoulder, sending what felt like an electric shock through his chest and arm. His gun arm fell to his side, and Cunard collapsed as his legs gave way. There was no pain in them, but they felt numb. Realizing he had dropped his weapon, he crawled towards it as he heard the pop of a low impact explosion and felt tear gas sting his eyes and catch in his throat. More rounds were fired as he inched towards his gun. Mary lay within his line of sight, a crumpled corpse with dead eyes. Safe. As he reached out to grasp his weapon, he became aware of a man standing over him.

"No need for that." The man stepped closer and kicked the weapon out of reach.

Cunard knew he was finished. He prepared himself for the void and the unending loneliness of that empty place. A surprising thought spoke to him from somewhere deep inside, *the shadow fades but the source remains.*

"Now that we've dealt with your visitors, why don't we see about getting an ambulance for you?"

Cunard looked up. The figure standing over him was blurred through his streaming eyes. "Who are you?"

The man raised three fingers to make a W sign. "We wouldn't normally help. But hey, there are exceptions to every rule. Be sure to let your people know that the WA had nothing to do with tonight's events. We wouldn't want to delay the opening of the tower, would we?"

Cunard slipped out of consciousness as he heard the man call emergency services.

*

Cunard hobbled uncomfortably to the chair in the middle of the radio room. The air hatch closed behind him, and the floating head began to move at normal speed as those outside sped up.

"How are you, Cunard?" asked Director Clive.

"I'm getting there. Still a little difficult walking."

"Five bullets. Two in the upper body and three in the legs. You will be on desk duty for a few more weeks. Unless you want to come home early?"

"Thank you, Director, but I will see out my deployment."

"Good man. We need people like you on the ground now that the tower is open. It won't be long before Nylon City rivals its real-world namesakes for market share."

"How is Landsberg?"

"Well, as you know, it's only been a few days out here, but she's fine. We have organized for protection in case Morgan has any notions of revenge. He has been extracted and the IRS is keeping him busy. We have also identified everyone involved in bypassing the safe word protocol and have relieved them of their employment."

"He is capable of anything. He's a sociopath."

Director Clive said, "Perhaps, but his sociopathy is practical in its nature. There is nothing to be gained in harming her. Rest assured though; she will be protected."

"And the other matter I requested?"

The director gazed off-screen. "Your ghost would, under normal circumstances, have been moved to a medical facility by now."

"She was extremely helpful."

"We can't afford to have ghosts haunting the city. If she shared her experience with other visitors ... well, it wouldn't be good for business."

"Controlled properly she would be an invaluable asset. She can go where no one else can."

"True, but still ..."

"Don't you think it's strange that the WA wanted the tower opened?"

"The WA? You mean the Waking Army. I do wonder if we've left you in there for too long."

"They saved my life. That doesn't make sense. We need to find out what they are up to. I believe the ghost can help with that. I don't know how else we would infiltrate them quickly."

Director Clive paused before speaking. "You clearly harbor doubts about your other asset."

"I still trust Eva. I'm just not sure they do."

"Alright. I take your point. You think the ghost has some loyalty to you?"

"If she knows I've kept her in Alterum, yes."

"Mmh. Look, she can stay until the end of your tour of duty. If she is loyal, it is to you, not Jack Glory. Keep her on a tight leash and report back immediately if you have any concerns."

"Thank you, Director."

"Cunard, you have done the company a great service. You deserve our trust. The tower will take us to the next level and your stock options will make you wealthy."

"You won't regret it, Director."

"One more thing, Cunard. When we have rooted out the Waking Army, we will destroy them without mercy. There will be no exceptions."

"Understood."

"These people are not real, but I know how it can stop feeling like that once you've been in there a while. Two weeks after you are back home, you will stop thinking about them. I am speaking from experience. Do you know how much Alterran time I spent there early in my career?"

"Yes." Cunard replied.

Director Clive burst into laughter. "You are extremely polite, Cunard. So, I've bored you with my tales one too many times?"

"More than one too many." Cunard afforded himself a smile.

After leaving the radio room, he made his way back to the parking lot and slid painfully into his car. Selecting autopilot, he directed it to take him to his new apartment. He preferred to drive, but that was not practical for the time being. The vehicle moved slowly and stopped at the gate. The guard leaned in and then waved him through. As the car picked up speed, Cunard spoke to the empty passenger seat.

"That should buy you some time."

Bella materialized and replied. "You didn't need to take me with you. I trust you."

"I said I would be honest with you, and I keep my word."

"How long have I got?"

"Longer than you had a few minutes ago."

PART TWO – AGENTS

Chapter 10

THE GOLDEN RULES ... There are three rules that guide everything you do as an agent:

> *1.   You must never allow a visitor to come to harm by the actions of others or by your own inaction.*
>
> *2.   You must obey all directives of a company superior unless this violates the first rule.*
>
> *3.   You must avoid situations that could lead to your own harm unless this violates the first or second rule.*

There are few jobs that carry the level of responsibility expected of a company agent. These rules are simple to understand but only a select few can follow them. We believe that you are a member of this elite group.

Agente In Patria Handbook

Cunard entered the elevator and waited for the door to close. "You're here, aren't you?"

Bella materialized, back to him, looking out at the city as they climbed the exterior of Chukaisha Tower.

"How long now?" she asked.

"One week less than the last time you asked."

"And how long is that?"

"Two months. Satisfied?"

Bella turned and faced him. "You're good. I wonder when you will start avoiding the question."

Cunard was tempted to admit that he had requested an extension. He resisted. The best way to keep her trust was to make sure Bella thought he did not care. She would see that as the sign of weakness. As soon as that happened, they would enter a spiral of suspicion and distrust. She would watch him night and day. He would have to watch everything he said and did, knowing that she was watching.

He said, "We've both known how this works. I can't stay in Alterum forever. The company doesn't trust you to work with another handler. It is what it is."

Bella turned away and looked out at the city again. "I'll miss it. It feels like home now."

The elevator came to a stop. "I don't need to say this, but—"

"No, you don't." She vanished as the door opened. "Happy now?"

Cunard approached the function suite and threw his ID into the air. Two guards, one Patrian, one Alterran, nodded and let him pass. The great and the good were all in attendance. Both worlds mixing in easy company. The mayors were there, the heads of the trading companies operating out of the tower, local celebrities, and the stars of the trading floors.

A voice whispered in his ear "Isn't this pleasant? Two worlds in harmony."

Cunard muttered, as if to himself, "You know I hate it when you do that."

"It is what it is."

Fischer approached him. "I didn't think this was your kind of thing."

"*Gleichfalls.*"

"It isn't. I am with the mayor's security detail."

"What's she worried about, Patrians or Londoners?"

Fischer laughed. "Oh, I'm sure both are a cause for concern, but the truth is, she has more to fear from her own party colleagues than anyone else."

The two mayors were talking to each other, surrounded by a coterie of hangers-on. She wore a red dress that was elegant without being too formal. Draped round her neck was a sapphire and diamond necklace. The London mayor wore a dark blue suit, white shirt, and a red bow tie.

"The red, white and blue versus the red, white and blue," said Bella.

Fischer pretended to look for her. "Bella, there you are. As always, you are positively translucent."

Cunard surveyed the scene. Although there were no physical differences between Patrians and Alterrans, he could tell them apart with ease. It was something subtle in the movement, the way they held themselves, the mannerisms. Looking at the elite of two worlds, the difference was still there. He was struck how the mayors were surrounded by Alterrans. Not a Patrian amongst the group working hard to impress them with their nodding and feigned attention. The managers of the trading companies, similarly, were mixing with each other and attended to by Patrians.

And then there was the rest. The floor traders, not wearing tuxedos and formal gowns, but dressed like, and talking with, the local celebrities. This group marked and displayed their wealth as ostentatiously as they could. They were lighthouses transmitting their status as brightly as they could. Bold colors and plunging necklines, gold watches hanging loosely off wrists, their movement catching and throwing light, the timepieces looking as if they could slip off and fall to the floor at any moment. A tease that said to the world, 'I wear my wealth casually and losing this would be of little concern.' The watches never did fall. The links were added and removed until just the right level of affectation was achieved. This group mingled together, happy to bask in each other's glow.

Separate to the subtle signs, there was another much more obvious way to tell Patrians and Alterrans apart.

Bella shared her opinion. "Show business for the ugly."

Cunard asked, "The traders?"

"Duh."

"Cruel, but true," said Fischer. "I'm sure there must be some good-looking Patrians, but *Mein Gott*, do you guys send the rejects?"

Cunard said, "Bella, I'm going to miss you when …" He was conscious of Fischer's presence. "When we move on to other things."

"That thought will give me much joy in the eternity that awaits."

"*Neidlich.* I better get back to the boss. Enjoy your evening."

After he was out of earshot Cunard said, "You see that group there? The tall Alterran, he's a member of the Manor gang. They seem to be mixing a lot with the traders. We need to find out what's going on. It could be nothing or it could be something. Stick close to him and see what you can find out. His name is Slender."

"Okay. One more thing before I go."

"What?" There was silence. "What?" he repeated. Again silence. *Shit,* she had done it again.

"Have you found something to your amusement, lover?"

Cunard turned to find Eva approaching him. "All my favorite people in one place."

Eva leaned in and kissed him on the cheek. "Is Bella here? Where is she?"

"Either standing next to us laughing at me, or over there with that group," he pointed.

"What's your interest in the Manor? Are they leading nice respectable Patrians astray?"

*

Hesh turned the tap and waited. After a few seconds, a trickle appeared. He cupped his hands to catch it and rubbed his face. It was just enough to wake himself, but not enough to get clean. He didn't see the point in using a towel. Sliding open the window in the small bathroom, he looked across to Chukaisha Tower. Spotlights swung back and forth in the night air as cars deposited guests near the entrance.

The visibility was not as good as they had promised. When the new cladding had been proposed, they were told it would be as if there was nothing there between them and the rest of the world. A glass covering that would provide privacy looking in and clarity looking out. It was a lie. The world outside now seemed dull, as if he had sunglasses on. Not too bad during the day, but dark and depressing at night.

He placed a plug in the sink and left the tap running. After he left his apartment, he found Maria waiting by the elevator, the button illuminated. "I don't think it's coming," she said. "We should take the stairs."

"How long have you been waiting?"

"Too long. Have you got water today?"

"Can't you see I washed myself? Spick and span, Maria. Spick and span."

She frowned. "Come on. Let's go." She took hold of his arm and pulled him towards the stairwell.

"Hey, you're not my Ma."

"Closest thing you've got."

He followed her. Maria had been his neighbor for as long as he had lived there. He'd moved into the tower block when he was twelve. Maria had always been kind to them. She gave them food parcels in the early days before his real Ma got a job. That went on for six months. Two months in, Hesh asked why she never bought him ice cream. She laughed and called him a few names in Spanish, but she brought some the next day. It became a game between them.

"Hey Maria, how come you never bring me bacon?" he once asked.

"So, now you're a real Londoner, you eat bacon?"

"There're no rules to life, Maria. I think I'd like it."

"Yes, and your Ma wouldn't."

That was a long time ago. Now it was just Hesh and Maria, and truth be told, he would leave if he could. Despite all the promises, this place was getting worse instead of better. They snaked their way down the stairs with its narrow turns, designed as an emergency escape route and taking up as little space as possible. Maria held on to the rail.

"I'll walk in front in case you fall."

"I guess it keeps me fit, if nothing else."

"Walking downstairs doesn't get you fit, old woman. That's just controlled falling. Let's see you walk up them."

"No, I will be waiting for the lift on the way back."

"Oath."

They met a neighbor on the way down. Alexandra was wearing a short blue dress with matching shoes. Hesh stole a long gaze as she walked in front of them, beautiful but clumsy in her heels.

"Are you going clubbing, Alex?" asked Maria.

"We're heading up west after the ceremony."

"You should take Hesham with you."

He shook his head but waited to hear her response.

"I've got a date, Maria."

"You should date, Hesham."

"Maria, please" he said.

Alexandra laughed. "It's okay, Hesh. She's allowed to say whatever she wants at that age. I can't wait to be old."

"Sixty-eight. I'm only sixty-eight."

"Like I said."

"Oath. Listen, old woman, keep your nose attached to your face. Got me?"

This time Maria laughed.

Alexandra moved faster than them and was soon out of sight.

"Hey, Maria," Hesh said in a young voice. "How come you never bring me women?"

"Well, it's not for a want of trying. You should ask her out."

"You heard her. She's got a date."

"So, ask her out when she's not got a date."

"If she's hooked, she's hooked. I don't walk on other people's territory."

Maria gripped his arm and paused. "No woman is anyone's territory. Your Ma was no one's territory and that's why she walked away. Never forget that."

He saw the steel in her eye and a hint of a tear forming. "It's banter. I don't mean it." A whole conversation, a complete history of their relationship, passed between them in a look. He took a deep breath and gave her a hug.

She said, "But it's how people behave. They treat each other like territory. No man, no woman, is anyone's territory."

He nodded. "Come on, old woman. We don't want to miss the free booze. Just as well Ma isn't here to see how you've corrupted me with the demon drink."

"Alex?" Maria shouted, her voice echoing down the stairwell.

"Yes, Maria?" A voice came back.

"This date tonight … Are you his territory?"

"No, Maria."

"What are you doing at the weekend?"

"Depends. Who's asking?"

Maria raised her eyebrows and nodded at Hesh.

"I'm asking," he yelled.

"Well, okay … But you're not bringing Maria."

"Oath."

By the time they reached the bottom, Hesh was sweating. The stairwell was airless and after twenty floors he felt it. It was a relief to push open the fire door and feel the breeze that constantly swirled around the base of the building. Most of the residents were already there. A decorator's table had been set up next to the entrance. It was covered with large ice buckets holding a mix of alcoholic and soft drinks.

"Help yourself," said Denis, who was adding more bottles to be chilled.

"What are you doing tomorrow night?" Hesh asked.

Denis paused and looked at them before frowning and continuing with his work without replying.

Maria gave a Hesh a dig in the ribs with her elbow as she pulled out two beers. They walked away from the tower and looked back. What had once been a dull concrete building was now covered in the gleaming façade of glass, each pane so perfectly joined that it appeared to be a single continuous sheet covering the whole structure.

Maria clinked her bottle off Hesh's. "Who wouldn't want to live in something as beautiful as that?"

*

The function room consisted of a large bar area next to the entrance, with an auditorium-style seating which terraced down a full floor level. Eva and her band were set up on the stage and playing a set of mostly easy-listening swing music. Behind them was a two-story window with the city in the distance. Cunard sat back in his seat and closed his eyes. He loved her voice. It transported him to somewhere peaceful in his mind. It was a place that was hard to find in normal circumstances. It had been two years since the Tower had opened and his time in Alterum was coming to an end.

He could ask to do another tour of duty instead of the extension he had asked for. It would probably be rejected, and he was not sure he had the heart for it. He would not be allowed back for three years. Unlike the short gap he had between his first two visits, which was the rule for a third tour. Seventy-two years would have passed here. Every acquaintance would be gone or so old they might as well be. That was the way Jack Glory liked it. No possibility of being tainted by previous relationships. Fischer would be dead, new mayors, new gangs even. The Manor did not exist during his first visit. The only constant had been Eva. She was a seed personality. She had been in Alterum from near the beginning. Never aging, always with her tentacles across the very soul of the city. The Alterrans accepted her as one of their own, but assumed she was Patrian. That helped explained her ageless existence.

The song finished and the band took a break. Eva came and sat next to him. "I guess I must be losing it." She looked around.

There was only a light smattering of people sitting down to watch the band. The rest of the guests were still in the bar area, the noise of their chatter a background drone.

"You're not losing it," said Cunard. "Never have, never will. Why did you agree to the gig in the first place? It's not your crowd."

"This new breed of Patrians, they don't come to my club. If I am going to understand them, I need to come to them."

"Why bother?"

Eva silently looked at the ceiling for few seconds before answering. "Do you know what happened to the other seeds?"

"I've read the handbook."

"Well, I'm sure that makes you an expert on what the company wants you to think."

Cunard looked wry. The propaganda was as strong and inaccurate when it was aimed at employees as it was for visitors. "I hear they died in their sleep after long and satisfying lives."

Eva took a drink of water. "I could believe they would tell you that. Or nothing at all."

"It was the latter. I've read the handbook and there is nothing but a cursory mention of seeds. Myth, rumor. Each one less reliable than the last."

"Their influence … our influence … was too strong for the intersubjective. It was designed that way. We built this world and when it was finished, we were disposable. So, we were mostly disposed of unless we were useful."

"And this means you have to play gigs for this lot?" Cunard waved dismissively.

"It means I need to understand new elements. These last few years have been the most significant in our history since the rift. We only had an occasional Patrian living here long-term. Mostly agents like you. That didn't impact our world. But this, this tower with its long-term visitors? This will shift it in ways none of us truly understand. When you have lived for as long as I have, you either understand the intersubjective or it sweeps you aside."

Cunard looked down at his feet tapping involuntarily on the floor. "I don't know how you do it, Eva. I'm weary after two visits."

She placed a hand on his arm. "Remember when we first met?"

He nodded. "That was a lifetime ago. I wanted to experience everything this world had to offer."

"Just like our trader friends in the bar. And now? Am I too old for you?"

"You always have been." He smiled with his eyes.

"There is a reason why you are weary, Cunard. It's because you don't commit to anything. I know who I am. I belong to something that is bigger than me, and if it swallows me up? So be it."

"Why would it swallow you up?"

"Because it has to at some point."

"Only if you are with the WA. Working against the company."

There. He had said it. Did he swing the conversation in this direction or did she? He was always going to ask her tonight, but had she just manipulated him into asking? It had been hanging in the air for months now. Perhaps they both needed it out in the open.

"It doesn't matter."

"It really does," he replied.

"At some point the company will have me disposed of. Why is Bella still here? Because you persuaded them that she is useful. Only the useful survive. I'm Alterran. That is the side I chose. There was a path that suited both of us for a while, but the day is coming when the path splits."

"It splits now if you are with the WA. If you are, walk away …"

"If I was with them, it would be a choice I made years ago. If I walked away now, I wouldn't be on any side. I would be weary like you. Do you recommend the place your mind inhabits?"

"You're good." He examined Eva for a hint of the truth.

Eva's hand slid down his arm and locked fingers with his. "No one lives forever, Cunard, and believe it or not, I don't want to either."

And with that he was certain. She wouldn't be here if he took a third tour of duty.

*

Hesh found Joe towards the edge of the gathering. He had taken one of the ice buckets and some beer.

"Alright, Hesh?"

"Excellent." He took the bottle offered to him. "So, this is what we got out of it?" He held up the beer and tilted it towards Chukaisha Tower. "Cheers."

"It's just the start."

"Sure, it is," Hesh shook his head. "How come there's no workers on-site since the cladding was finished? You really believe these guys?"

"I don't know, but it isn't any worse, is it?"

"Isn't it? The cladding isn't about making our lives better. It's about them not having to look at us."

"Bullshit."

"Then why are we down here with plastic buckets and discount booze, and they are all celebrating their generosity up there?" Hesh made a circling motion and zoomed in on the one patch of light in the tower opposite. He could only afford a cheap Handi, and the image was dull and pixelated. A band could be seen with its back to them, blurred figures moving around on what appeared to be the floor above.

"You are so sour, Hesh. It's not the best beer, but it's free." His friend took a drink and looked up at the tower block. "Our place looks slick, man. What's so bad about that?"

"It's not our place. That's just it. Nothing belongs to us. It's our people, but it's not our place."

Joe held up a 'W' sign. "What are you going to do, join the WA? Fight the good fight."

"Nah, why would I join them? You think Patrians are our only enemy? Did they let the tower block rot, did they cut back the maintenance crew? The WA ain't doing anything for us. They're too busy fighting a holy war. I've got no love for Patrians, but we do more harm to each other than they have ever done."

"Man, you are too serious for me. Drink some more beer before you make me top myself."

Hesh laughed. "Okay, friend. Okay, but I'm warning you, it gets worse when I'm drunk."

Joe pulled a roll-up from his jacket pocket. "What you have, Hesh, is a chemical imbalance. It leads to cellular stress." He tapped Hesh's forehead. "You need to fix that by counteracting it with something that triggers healthy neurotrophic function." He put the joint in his mouth, lit up, and inhaled deeply. "Exhibit A."

"Who told you that?"

"My psych. She was trying to get me on Trilithium, but what does she know?" He passed the joint to Hesh.

They were interrupted by the sound of someone tapping on a microphone. They looked round and saw the local councilor on a makeshift platform.

"Ladies and gentlemen. Thank you for coming out tonight to mark the start of the Wolseley Tower regeneration project. It has been a long time coming, but we did it. We got this thing started.

"If it weren't for the drive and determination of people like Denis Frere and the rest of the resident's committee, we would never have done it.

"This is the just the beginning. Once the cladding display is switched on, the council and the trust will receive half of the profit from all advertising. That money is going to provide a steady income stream that will be re-invested in Wolseley Tower.

"And I am proud to announce here tonight that Chukaisha Holdings has taken out the rights for the first year of continuous sponsorship. We have one full year of income ready to start the next phase of regeneration."

Hesh inhaled and looked at Joe. "My chemical imbalance is starting to get worse, friend. You got any more of this good stuff?"

Hesh watched the councilor after he gave his speech. He did the rounds of the resident's committee, shaking hands and slapping backs. He stopped at the beer table to have a quick chat with Denis, who handed him a beer. The councilor took a few mouthfuls before pouring the rest on the ground and placing the bottle back on the table for Denis to dispose of.

Hesh was drunk and mildly stoned. He followed the councilor as he made his way to the edge of the common green. The boundary with Chukaisha Tower was fenced. There was a large gate in the middle of the barrier that opened in the morning and closed at night. As the councilor approached, he threw his ID in the air. The fence slid partially open, and a guard waved him through.

"Is that it? You've had enough?" he shouted.

The councilor turned and stared at him, saying nothing.

"Off to the real celebration now that you've fooled the masses?"

The councilor turned and walked through the gap without speaking. The gate began to close.

"Got nothing to say. That's right, just walk on." Hesh had upped the volume again. The guard stared with a blank look through the slats. Nobody thought he was even worth arguing with. They all ignored him as if he did not merit the effort. Maybe he didn't. Just then he felt a tug on his sleeve. It was Maria.

"Let's get back to the others."

"They don't think we're worth anything. He said nothing. Nothing to me. That's not right, Maria."

"It's not. Now what are you going to do about it?"

"What can we do? What can we *do*?" he repeated himself, aware of how unsteady he was on his feet.

Maria guided him away from the barrier and sat him down on the grass embankment. She sat beside him, shoulders touching. "Tonight, we are going to drink with our friends and enjoy their company. This weekend, you are going to take Alex out. I'll give you some money to take her somewhere nice."

"And what does that achieve? How does that fix any of this?" He gestured at the tower block.

Maria gripped his arm and stared deep into his eyes. "It gives you something to fight for. If you give up on your friends, on your own life, what have you left? Who are you going to take with you into the fight? Why would you care enough to resist?"

"Is that what you do, Maria? Do you resist?"

"Every day. Sometimes it is to help a friend, help a neighbor, sometimes it's to save the world."

Hesh frowned but understood the meaning. "You got to stop doing this arm thing." He looked down at her hand gripping him. "You don't need to do that to get my attention. It hurts."

Maria loosened her hold and patted his shoulder.

*

All seats were now taken in the function suite. Eva sat next to Cunard. The head of the tower was flanked by both mayors.

"Ladies and gentlemen, thank you for coming tonight. Today marks the two-year anniversary of our opening and what a time it has been. We are now one of the largest companies by trading volume on Patria." The audience clapped. "Two years. Think about it. Think how short a period that is." This was meant for the Patrians only. "If we can do this in twenty-four months just imagine what we will do in twenty-four years."

One of the drunken traders stood up and shouted, "One times twenty-four," before being pulled back down onto his seat.

"The key has been preparation of capacity. Chukaisha Tower has fifty thousand people working in it every day. We built that capacity up-front, and it was taken up in the first month. Fifty thousand Patrians making Nylon City their home.

"And soon we will be joined by another fifty thousand. Thanks to the foresight and cooperation of the two mayors, Inwood Tower has now been completed and is in the fit-out stage. The subway connection between this building and Inwood is almost complete. This latest development will not only add capacity to our Patrian trading, but will also, for the first time, allow Alterran investors to buy stock in Patrian companies and funds. We are truly on the verge of a new era of prosperity. A prosperity that will benefit both sides of the river and both worlds. Ladies and gentlemen, I give you Inwood." He stood to one side and invited the audience to view the scene behind them.

The function suite was on the fifteenth floor of the tower and, at this level, the view across to Washington Heights was obscured by Wolseley Tower. The side of the building burst to life, covered in white light. The number ten appeared at the top of the tower and then dropped like a stone to be followed by the number nine. It too fell to the bottom of the tower. Each number added to an irregular pile of discarded digits. There were a few whistles of appreciation at the effect as the countdown continued. When the number one fell to the join the other jumble of symbols, the numbers faded. As they did so, the building itself seemed to disappear, replaced by a view across the river and another building being illuminated. A red laser shot from the roof of the distant tower, straight through Wolseley towards the function room. The beam of light bounced off the floor above them before turning blue and travelling back through Wolseley. The crowd clapped and cheered their approval.

"And of course," the speaker continued. "We must not forget the donation to the local regeneration program. The building opposite is now the city's largest billboard. Tonight, we projected the back of the building onto the front to create this fantastic effect. How about it for our special effects team?"

The audience rose from their seats in appreciation.

*

The crowd in front of the tower block joined in the countdown, chanting along in unison. When the number one dropped and the lights began to fade, the cheering gradually fell silent. They were staring at their home as it disappeared to be replaced by the distant New York skyline. The greatest illusion they had ever witnessed had erased their home completely. There were a few nervous laughs, but it was mostly stunned silence. The entrance at ground level was still visible, but other than that, it was as if the building no longer existed.

Red, white, and blue laser beams zigzagged the sky, cutting through their homes, before a barrage of fireworks started to explode in the distance.

Hesh looked over at Denis. The color had drained from his face as he watched open-mouthed at the brave new world of Wolseley Tower.

Someone threw a bottle on the ground next to the drinks table. Denis stared at them as they shouted at him, then he shook his head, mouthing a reply, palms up. A small crowd began to gather round him.

Hesh walked over and stood next to the tenant chairman. "Leave him be. He didn't know. He thought he was doing his best by us."

"We don't exist to them," Joe shouted.

"Oath," Hesh replied. "That's what I've been telling you all along. They don't see us. They look through us. They look straight through all of us and that has nothing to do with him."

"This isn't right," someone yelled.

"It's not, but we don't turn on each other," said Hesh. "We don't turn on our own."

"What we going to do about it?"

Hesh looked at the faces around him. He did not want to be a leader, a spokesperson, a focus for their anger when things went wrong. He did not want to be Denis. But here he was, suddenly sober, despite the booze and the drugs.

"What can we do?" said Maria, just loudly enough to be heard. It sounded like a question, but he knew she was telling him what to say. Helping him, like she always did. Prompting him to find the right words.

"Tonight, we are going to drink with our friends and enjoy each other's company. This night is about us, not about them," he pointed to the tower opposite. "We get drunk. Really drunk." He put an arm around Denis. "This man has sorted that out. And tomorrow? We do whatever we have to so that no one can ever ignore us again. Isn't that right?

Denis nodded and mouthed *thank you*.

Hesh raised a bottle of beer in the air. "To us."

Chapter 11

THE GOLDEN VALUES ... When you are on a tour of duty, you must embody the three golden values that underpin the agency:

1.   Honesty. You must never be honest with Alterrans about the reality of their world.

2.   Compassion. It may be useful to display the signs of compassion, but you must never actually develop compassion for Alterrans.

3.   Trust. Never trust an Alterran. As with compassion, it can be useful to display trust, but it must never be sincere.

Agente In Patria Handbook

Cunard woke up and checked the time. It was 2:30 a.m. He stayed where he was, hoping that he would only be awake for a few minutes before slipping back into sleep. He thought about his conversation with Eva.

When he was preparing for his first tour of duty, Clive had told him about her. She was the great mystery. The last of the seeds. People who were aware of reality. People who could 'remember' the real world. They had become bitter and dangerous and had to be removed. That was what the director called it, 'removed'. She was the only one left. She had helped Jack Glory and in return Eva got to stay. Her survival was dependent on her use to the company. That was what they had on Eva. None of this was in the manuals, but it was how the director had explained Eva's continued presence.

And yet … she had never struck Cunard as someone who acted out of fear. Tonight, Eva told him a different story. Superficially similar. The seeds had to be removed, but the reason was different. There were so many mysteries in this world. Mysteries that could only be answered somewhere between Patria and Alterum, between Patrians and Alterrans. The answers were not to be found in company manuals.

"The day will come when she needs to be dealt with," the director had told him. "When the balance of what she gives us no longer offsets the danger. The key is in understanding when that it is. That is part of your job."

Tonight, she had laid it all out for him. Why? Was it because he was leaving soon, and he would never return? Eva knew she would be removed at some point. She had always known. Did she perhaps betray her fellow seeds to gain a few more years, or was she working for another purpose? A concern for the place and the people, as she had hinted? Was it betrayal or sacrifice that motivated her? Those were the words that swirled around his head. Betrayal or sacrifice. Which was the more dangerous of the two?

Why did she tell him? It gnawed at the edge of his consciousness. He climbed out of bed, slipped his Handi round his neck and made his way through to the kitchen to make a coffee. He would not get back to sleep anytime soon.

"Newsfeed. Chukaisha Tower."

A floating news report followed his gaze as he filled the French Press with ground beans and hot water. The report showed the crowd from the tower block cheering and counting down with the numbers on the side of their building. As the tower disappeared the report switched to the reception room, both mayors clapping as the red, white, and blue laser show cut across the missing building.

The reports didn't reveal a crowd of drunken tower residents throwing empty bottles over the fence as the great and the good left Chukaisha Tower. The entrance and pick-up point was far enough away that none of the bottles reached the waiting cars, but still, Cunard had seen the faces of the guests, appalled and frightened by the distant mob. He had heard more than one murmured comment that included the word 'ungrateful'.

Eva. What did Eva think of it all? Was it the event that brought out the truth? She did not explicitly say she was with the WA. He replayed her words in his head. She was telling him she *was*. Fischer was either with the WA too, or at the very least a sympathizer. That was why Cunard was still alive. How had it come to this? Everyone he valued was a potential enemy. The three-year break rule made sense. He could see that now. He also knew that he could not come back for a third tour of duty anyway. What did that leave for him? An executive role overseeing other agents, or worse still, training agents? The occasional short visit back, no more than a day Alterum time. In and out for specific events. This was the career path trodden by Clive, the one that had been dangled in front of Cunard as if it was an attractive option.

Cunard emptied some whitener into his cup and poured the coffee. He stood at the window and looked out at the deserted world of a city at night. This was a better apartment than the last one. He had allowed himself more comfort, more space after he had been injured. He had needed it when he was recovering. This was somewhere he would be happy to call home. Alterum was somewhere he would be …

No, he needed to walk away from the company when he left this time. He had to forget all about this world. It was the only way. After his first tour, he counted down the months until he could return. Scanning reports of friends and acquaintances, watching the accelerated time of Alterum sweep them all aside. All except Eva. Now he was in an endgame he hoped to avoid. She had as much as admitted she was WA. That meant her time was almost up. She did not expect him to choose Alterum over Patria. She was effectively signing her own death sentence.

Yet, if he told Clive about their conversation, it would not just be Eva. Bella would be gone too. She had been with Eva this whole time and had said nothing. She had expressed no doubts, no concerns. What did that mean about her?

She would be gone in two months anyway, when he left and his agreement with Clive about Bella also ended, but should he call it early? He could head over to Red Hook right now and report his concerns. If he stayed in the radio room for an hour or two, they would have time to unhook her before he left. Then he would be sent to remove Eva. There was nothing from which to disconnect Eva. She was part of the world. A world controlled by the intersubjective, a world in which she needed to be killed to be removed. That was the decision he was making.

Looking down on the empty streets, he circled the problem in his mind, trying to find a solution with which he was comfortable. There did not appear to be one, no matter how many angles he approached it. Perhaps after a good night's rest.

"Penny for your thoughts," came an unmistakable voice from behind him.

"Bella. You followed me home."

*

Eva went back to the club after leaving the tower. She went there most nights whether or not she was performing. It was a home from home. She had her own private booth set into the side wall that ran the length of the venue. From there she could see the stage and the audience. The booth pushed partly into the wall creating an area that could not be seen from the club. Next to this was a door which led to a side corridor. Visitors could enter and leave unseen. This was where Eva had most of her private meetings. Hidden in plain sight.

Fischer was waiting for her when she arrived. He played with an unlit cigarette, not able enjoy it without drawing attention to the fact that someone was in the booth. Eva snaked through the tables, stopping occasionally to acknowledge a guest. Sitting down she looked at Fischer and his cigarette. She leaned over and took it from him. He waited in silence until she pulled out a lighter from a clutch bag and began to smoke. He quickly retrieved another from the packet and took a long slow pull on it, relieved to taste the tobacco at last.

"An interesting night," she said.

"Did you see the resident's reaction?"

"I'm not surprised. What were they thinking?"

"Can we use it?"

Eva paused before speaking. "I think so. We need to heighten the tension, and after tonight, it shouldn't be too hard."

"What about Cunard?" he asked.

"He's the biggest risk. We monitor him."

"He knows about me. He has done since the incident with Morgan. He's still friendly, but he knows."

Eva nodded. "He has suspected me for some time, but that has now turned to certainty."

"Mmh. It was a matter of time. You spoke to him tonight?"

"I've known him a long time. I gave hints to see how much resistance he had to them. Which path his mind would follow? Nothing I said surprised him. He is certain."

"What do you think he will do?"

Eva shrugged. "He has very little time left here. He might do nothing and just run the clock down."

Fischer stared into space. "You really think he would do that?"

"It doesn't matter."

Fischer shook his head. "It does matter. It matters to a lot of people."

Eva picked up a coaster. She turned it over absent-mindedly. "A plan that needs a single individual to work is not a plan. It's a dream. We will keep a close eye on him from now on."

"Bella?"

She nodded. "She's with him."

"I like him," Fischer said. "I find it strange that I do, but ..."

"If we were not like them and they were not like us, all hope would be lost. It is the similarity we depend on."

"What is it like, Patria?"

"Not so different."

Eva stayed in the booth after Fischer slipped out the side door. She ordered a drink and listened to the band. Their style was a slurred swing, slow and fast, fast, and slow. She looked at the glass of sparkling water. She stared at it intently observing slight ripples with every note of the bass drum. She held her wrist with two fingers and felt for her heartbeat. Music, water, heartbeat. All connected.

She thought back to her memories before Alterum. They were not her memories, but they were real. They impacted her even now. The water on the table instead of alcohol. A legacy from years of abuse that almost killed her. No, almost killed the other her. But did it really matter? If it had killed the other her, she would never have been born, fully made, into this world. Music, water, heartbeat.

If she were deaf, would she realize the ripple was caused by the music? If all she could see was the glass, would she think the ripple was an essential property of water, completely divorced from all activity beyond her comprehension?

Such was Alterum. Drumbeats beyond comprehension rippling out over the city, affecting all of them. Music, water, heartbeat. And yet this world had its own cadence, its own rhythm. Where it started was not where it ended. The path was clear. The ripple must now also work backwards. What happened here must have an impact there. Only then would Alterum reach its true potential. Music, water, heartbeat.

The effect spiraled outwards over time. Visitors taking back memories that were real. Some of them finding peace and purpose through the Church of Shadows. Music, water, heartbeat. Chukaisha Tower came next. It was a significant part of the Patrian economy. This was not just admitted but celebrated. Music, water, heartbeat. Now was the time to move to the next level. And yet … would it work? It was a risk, but what was the alternative? Should they just accept the ripple of another world choosing their fate? Music, water, heartbeat. The backwards ripple was inevitable with or without their intervention, but how many generations must live as disposable playthings before it reached balance?

Eva picked up her glass and emerged from the booth. She threaded her way through the audience. Someone shouted for her to sing. The band took up their cause and began to play the intro to one of her regular numbers. She shook her head, but they were not going to be put off that easily with more acknowledgment and calls for her to perform. Music, water, heartbeat. The pull of the crowd too much to resist, she smiled, took a bow, and mouthed the word *okay*. The crowd cheered and the band paused, waiting for her to join them.

Eva changed direction and made her way towards the stage. She climbed the narrow stairs and sat her glass on a stool next to the microphone. She turned and spoke with the band agreeing the set list. The audience clapped as she turned back and leaned into the microphone.

"Thank you. It's always a pleasure." What a difference to earlier in the evening, at the Tower, when she was practically ignored. Cunard was one of the few guests that had paid any attention to her. This world had reached him. She was sure of it. Music, water, heartbeat.

*

Hesh and Joe sat on the makeshift stage and looked at the gap where their home was.

"It funny to think everyone is in there," said Joe. "All those people hidden from sight. It's crazy."

Hesh nodded silently.

"Did you see the looks on their faces when we started throwing bottles at them?" Joe laughed and leaned back, looking up at the darkness. "Man, that was one crazy night."

"Yeah."

"And you. What a speech. You were the leader. In that moment, you were the leader."

"Was I?"

"Everyone was hanging on your words, man."

Hesh stood up. "But what we going to do about it? What can we do about it?" He jumped off the stage and strolled to the fenced perimeter with Chukaisha Tower, the gate now closed.

Joe reluctantly got up and followed him. He caught up as they reached the barrier.

"See, what can we really do against that?" Hesh said. He kicked the bottom of the fence and strolled along its edge. "All that money, all that power."

"My cuz got a job there. It's with the security team. It's good money too."

Hesh laughed and kicked at the fence again.

"What?"

"Don't you see?"

"See what, Hesh?"

"Do you think he could get you a job too?"

Joe shrugged. "He's got drive. Always wants to win. Once he makes a name for himself, yeah."

"Could he get me in?"

Joe whistled. "That's a lot of pressure you're putting on my cuz."

Hesh kicked another fence section. This time it swung to one side. He bent down and pulled on it. "Shoddy work. See that, Joe?" He stood up and began to pull.

"Cheap."

"If he could get you a job, would you take it?"

"Why wouldn't I, man? They pay good coin for working there. Everyone knows it."

Hesh used his foot as leverage, placing it on the next post as he leaned back and used his weight to try and dislodge the loose section. He heard the middle rail pop its rivet. He got between the panel and the fence, and this time leaned into it with his shoulder, pushing forward, away from the fence. "Give me a hand."

Joe pulled as Hesh pushed. They now had the railing at shoulder height but couldn't push it any higher. Hesh pulled it as far as he could to one side, then changed direction and pulled again. Back and forwards, getting it a little looser each time.

"What we going to do, Hesh, break in and get the bottles we threw?" Joe laughed at his own joke.

"So, you'd take the job?" Hesh repeated his question.

"Of course, man. Anyone in there," he nodded back at the missing tower block. "They would take a job in *there*." He pointed at Chukaisha Tower.

"And you still don't see?"

"See what, Hesh? What is there to see?"

"We all hate it, but we all want it. We think what they do is wrong, but hey, if we can be part of it, that's okay, isn't it?"

Joe looked at the tower as he thought. "I get you."

Hesh pulled to one side again and this time the top of the section came free. It fell to the ground, just missing Joe.

"Okay, Hesh. No need to kill me." Joe flashed a manic smile. "I promise not to take the job I'm not going to be offered. Okay?"

Hesh laughed. "I'm not judging you. I would take it. I would. I'm just saying, how can you persuade anyone to fight against something they want?"

"So, you are resigning as the leader of the revolution. That's what you are telling me? Man, that didn't last long. Looks like we will need to put Denis back in charge."

"Give me hand with this." Hesh nodded towards the end of the fence panel on the ground.

They walked back down towards the tower block. Above them was a view across to New York, in front of them the ground floor entrance.

It was a struggle to maneuver the fence in and out of the elevator, but with shuffles left and right they finally managed it and arrived at Hesh's place. Once inside he put the fence down for a second and slid open the living room window.

They used the fence to reach the cladding, which sat about a meter out from the building, held in place by a network of scaffold-like braces and ties. They swung the fence back and then forward, using its sharp end to ram the inside of the cladding. There was a depression of light where they made contact. They swung again and again until there was a crackling sound. Small sparks of light spread across the surface followed by the section in front of them flickering for a few seconds before petering out. They leaned out of the window and looked to the side. There was a difference. A different shade to it.

"What do you think?"

"Yeah."

Pulling the fencing in from the open window they placed it on the floor. The elevator was still waiting for them when they left the apartment a few minutes later. Hesh pressed the button for the ground floor and raised his eyebrows as he looked at Joe. They smiled at each other.

They walked back up towards the boundary to create some distance between them and the tower. Hesh knew exactly where to look. Anyone that lived in the tower block for any length of time could pick their own place out instantly. He pointed at it and began to laugh.

Up above them, floating in the air was one solitary window with a light on and a message scrawled across it with white window cleaner. Hesh circled with his hand and expanded in on the scene. Even with his poor quality Handi, they could make out the writing, large and bold. *NOW YOU SEE ME.*

"Long live the revolution," Joe said, raising his fist in a salute.

*

"When did you get here?" Cunard looked at Bella, who had now appeared.

"Not long after you. You looked tired and I didn't want to disturb you."

He moved away from the window and sat down on the sofa, taking a drink of his coffee. Bella sat in a chair opposite him.

"Describe it to me," she said. "The coffee."

She often asked him to do this. Describe sensations, tastes, touch. She experienced the world around her as if it were on the other side of a glass divide. She could see it all but was not in it. He sighed but did it anyway. "It has a slightly nutty aroma with a little bit of malt to it as well. It could be the whitener."

"I can't believe you use whitener."

Cunard said, "It doesn't go off. I bought one large jar a year ago and it will see me out of here."

"The taste?"

"Bitter, almost alkaline. It's not particularly good." He was aware of Bella staring at the steam rising over the brim of the cup. "Sorry, I shouldn't have complained like that."

"I don't mind bad. Bad is a sensation. The longer I'm here, the harder it is to remember any of my senses, good or bad."

He placed the cup on the table. "So?"

"So?"

"Why did you follow me home? If it had been urgent, you wouldn't have worried about disturbing me. So why?"

"We've been a good team, haven't we?"

He nodded.

"I guess it just seems like there isn't much time left."

"And you really enjoy my company, even when I'm sleeping."

"That's it, Cunard. Besides, one day I'm going to catch you with some company. You will be making love to your mystery partner. How long have you been here? You must have one. It's beyond dispute. I will be standing at the end of your bed watching everything. Just remember that."

He took another drink of his coffee and grinned.

"You think I'm joking?"

"Is that something else I will have to describe? How it feels, what sensations I'm having. Will I give you the rundown during or after?"

Bella rolled her eyes. "I'll decide about that nearer the time."

"I will *not* run out early on you. If that's what you are worrying about. If that's why you are spying on me, you can relax."

"It would be easier than making that last drive with me, knowing you are about to throw me into an eternity of darkness."

"It won't be hard." He put on his best display on nonchalance. "Besides, do you know how much of a bonus I get for reaching that last day? That's not something to be passed up on."

"Enough to buy you a lot of sensations."

"That's exactly it," he replied. "A world of sensations and experiences. Any recommendations?"

"Jump off a tall building. Everyone should jump off a tall building at least once in their life."

"I'll think about that one. So, since you are here and I'm awake, how did you get on tonight? What was Slender talking to the traders about?"

"This and that."

"What this and what that?"

"I don't think there's too much to worry about there," she said. "From what I could tell, they sell personal protection to traders who want to … experience the more authentic local attractions."

Cunard thought about this for a moment. "Makes sense. Leaping because they suddenly find themselves in trouble doesn't come without a cost for them. They would try to avoid it if possible."

Like him, they were here on a 'tour of duty'. For agents like Cunard, it was twelve years local time. For the traders it was typically two. If they jumped early, there was a one-off re-entry fee that they had to pay from their own pocket. They would miss at least a month's salary even with a quick turnaround. More important than all of that, they would lose their completion bonus. That was worth a lot of money. More than Cunard would receive for all his years across both tours of duty.

Bella continued. "Most of the traders he was talking to … is his name really Slender?"

Cunard said impatiently, "I'm sure he wasn't born with it, but that's what he calls himself."

"Most of the traders he was talking to, they leave in less than a month."

"Too close to take any chances." It made sense. "One thing, though. Was there any hint of coercion?"

Bella frowned, not understanding the question.

"Is it protection from the protectors they are buying?"

"Oh, right. No," she smirked. "Definitely not. They were talking about going out with a bang. They want to 'experience something big' before they leave."

"Great. Situation normal. Out of control Patrians behaving like assholes." Cunard drank his coffee. "It's gone flowery. Fragrant. Tastes more pungent now. Almost like creosol."

Bella tilted her head and crossed her eyes. "I don't want you to make stuff up, Cunard. I want the real smells, the real flavors."

"Not much sense of smell to be honest. So …"

"Well, keep the lies consistent."

"What about the WA?"

"What about them? No one mentioned them tonight."

He decided to prod. "That's the thing though. They have gone noticeably quiet recently. It's as if they've disappeared."

"Maybe they have."

"Maybe they haven't," he replied. "You still go to the club with Eva, don't you?"

"Most nights. I go from table to table and there's nothing. Everyone claims to support them. Some say they're members, but it's just talk. I haven't come across anything concrete in months."

"And Eva. Do you stick close to her?"

"We share notes at the end of the night. It's the same story from her. It has gone quiet."

"It doesn't feel right. I'd like you to work the tables less and Eva more."

Bella sat back, surprised. "You want me to spy on Eva. Seriously?"

"Is that a problem for you?"

Bella stared at him, holding his gaze as she silently showed her disapproval. Cunard matched her stare impassively, waiting for her to speak.

"Fine," she said, unable to hold the silence any longer. "But I won't find anything."

"And I will be very happy if that is the case."

Bella stood up. "I better be going." She walked towards the window.

Cunard waved his coffee in the direction of the door. "Feel free to use the—"

She pushed through the wall before he could finish his sentence. Once a base jumper, always a base jumper.

He thought about what she would say to Eva. They were close. Even though she had been given false hope, Bella still had a loyalty to her. It was Cunard that had given Bella the two years, but it was Eva that gave her the hope to live through them.

What do I want? He thought. Surprisingly, it was not difficult to work out and it was not what he expected. Just by asking the question, he realized that he wanted Bella to tell Eva about the conversation they'd had. He wanted Eva to take it as a warning and make sure everything stayed quiet until he had left Alterum for the last time.

Cunard called the duty officer, voice only. It was the station chief.

"What's happening. Is there an issue?"

"Nothing like that. I want to withdraw my extension request."

The chief was silent on the other end of the line for a second. "Alright. Understood. Are you okay, Cunard?"

"Fine. Just realized that the tour of duty is long enough."

"It's too long. Most agents don't make it to the end. I swear that is the way the company has designed it. They make it so long that everyone gives up and misses out on their bonus."

"You could be right."

"Listen, Cunard. If you need anything, ask. I mean it."

"I'm fine. I just need a good night's rest." He disconnected and crossed to the kitchen, placing his empty cup in the sink. The tiredness was in his legs. He felt it spreading upwards. *Now,* he thought. *Now I should be able to sleep.*

*

Patrick sat back on the sofa, overlooking the club. He looked down to the floor below. So much to choose from. The beautiful bodies parading back and forwards for the benefit of the VIP boxes. He would miss this place when he left Alterum. He had been too cautious here until now. He was determined not to waste what little time he now had left.

"This is the actual suite that Morgan owned?" he asked. "The actual suite?"

"Sure," said Slender.

"You've heard the stories, right?"

"I've heard them. They are true. I saw the suite before it was refurbished. The things that happened in here, he was one sick man. You're not into that, are you?"

"And if I was?"

Slender raised his arms, as if surrendering. "If that's your thing, it can be arranged, but it comes with a large price tag. People say life is cheap, but let me tell you, they are wrong. Life is expensive."

"I'm not. I just wanted to see what you would say."

"Anything is possible for the right price. Chain is our currency of choice for the ... high value experiences."

"Our world is so boring. So many rules. So many restrictions. You guys don't know you're living."

"It needs to be something big," a voice came from behind them. "Something we could never do or see back home."

"Like I said, Emma, whatever you and Patrick want. I will make it happen. Just give me the tools and I will finish the job." Slender slid the fingers of one hand over the palm of the other as if spraying money over the table.

Emma laughed, leaned over Patrick's shoulder, and kissed him. "And you are sure you can keep us out of trouble? We're not tough like you are, Slender. We're just playing at it. But we do want to play, don't we, Patrick?"

"With the Manor looking after you, no one can touch you. Not the law, not the WA, no one."

Chapter 12

SAFE WORD ... Unlike visitors, agents do not have safe words. If you die in Alterum, you will enter the void. This is a place that few people return from. Remember this when you interact with Alterran threats. The most successful agents are those that treat all threats as firmly as possible. You will not lose your job or face legal action for 'over-reacting'. Deal with threats as if your life depends on it. It does.

Please note, however, that we may have to transfer you or end your tour of duty early if your actions disrupt the stability of the local environment. Bonuses will be null and void in the event of an early exit.

Agente In Patria Handbook

The church was a nondescript house in a residential street. There was no plaque giving the name of the organization or the meeting times. The front door had a 'W' sign which was made up of four lines. Two larger lines on the outside and two smaller ones on the inside. The smaller lines mirrored each other, the larger lines mirrored each other, the two left-hand lines mirrored the two right-hand lines. Shadows everywhere.

Eva entered and made her way through the hallway to the meeting room towards the back of the property. It was a plain unadorned space with four rows of chairs forming a square so that everyone faced inwards. The walls were white, and overhead was frosted glass bringing light into the room without creating a glare.

She took her seat and began to still her mind. Other attendees slowly entered and took their place in the silence. Once everyone was seated a small bell chimed. Each person present made the sign of worship. Two fingers of each hand brought together in a 'W' to touch their forehead. A quiet invocation was whispered before hands dropped to rest on thighs.

Then there was silence. Eva emptied her mind and breathed. On each breath in she scanned her body for tension and focused on it until it dissolved under her attention and her out-breath. When she had completely relaxed her physical body, she listened for thoughts. When they came, she asked herself if they were to be shared. If not, she allowed them to drift away uncaught and un-chased.

One of the members stood. "I felt anger this week and I could not let go of it. It was a manifestation of something beyond me, not from me. I let the illusion become real and once it was expressed, I let it turn back into illusion." They sat back down, and the meeting continued in silence.

The minutes passed until another person stood. "My past gives me the material for my future, but I will shape it." They sat.

After an hour had passed mainly in still contemplation, the bell chimed a second time. The congregation repeated the shadow sign, touching foreheads, before speaking in unison "The source creates the shadow. The shadow creates the dance."

The attendees turned to each other and shook hands. Conversations now began to bubble up across the room. Eva greeted some friends as she made her way to the rear door and exited the house into the garden. Tables were dotted across the lawn. Eva sat down and Bella materialized on the chair opposite.

"May you find peace in the shadow," said Eva.

A helper approached the table. "Tea?" he asked.

Eva nodded at Bella, waiting for her request. Bella said, "Lapsang Souchong."

"English Breakfast for me."

When the tea arrived, it was placed in front of Eva. She carefully poured both cups and took a small sip of the English Breakfast. She then looked at Bella, who reached out her hand to overlap with Eva's. Eva picked up the cup containing the Lapsang Souchong as Bella closed her eyes.

"Smoked pine."

"Good. Very good." Eva leaned forward and placed her elbows on the small table as she took another drink.

"I tried it with Cunard. He didn't realize I was doing it, but it didn't work. Could it work with someone else?"

Eva thought about this. "Perhaps. You must keep trying and you must always test what I tell you. I am only one small part of the intersubjective."

A member of the congregation approached. "Eva, Bella. Peace in the shadow."

"Peace in the shadow," Bella repeated.

"Will you be attending the retreat, Eva?"

"I haven't decided. Is there any reason for you asking?"

"The lady will be attending. She requested that I tell you."

Eva's eyes widened as she took in the news. "How was the message passed?"

"An encrypted text stream in a Chain transfer."

"Was there anything else?"

"Nothing."

Eva bowed her head. "Thank you."

"This is a meeting with Patrians, isn't it?" Bella stared intently.

Eva put down her cup. "Mostly. It's important that there is a dialogue between our worlds."

Bella looked from Eva to the messenger but said nothing more until they were alone. "Well, that was mysterious. Who is the 'the lady'?"

"A good friend that I haven't seen for a long time."

"Can I come?"

Eva let the question sink in. "I can't really stop you. You do realize that don't you? One of the advantages of being a ghost is that you can go anywhere."

"I'd rather have your agreement."

Eva changed the topic. "Do you have any worries about Cunard?"

"Plenty. He doesn't trust you and I don't think he trusts me anymore either."

"Come to the retreat."

"Thank you."

"Tell Cunard about it. Tell him you have your suspicions."

Bella frowned. "What are my suspicions?"

"That I didn't want you to come. That you think it could be a cover for WA activity. You need to feed him something. It's been too long since he's had any real information."

"Is it? Is it a cover for the WA?"

"Not exactly. There are some overlaps, as you can imagine."

"Isn't that dangerous? What if he comes mob-handed?"

Eva said, "There are too many important Patrians attending. He will be subtle and so will we. We will dance around each other, and he will get some confidence back in you."

"What about you? How do we get him to trust you?"

"We are past that now. It's close to the end. What happens between us will happen. It can't be stopped, but you need to be clean."

*

The trading floor was made up of long benches full of screens, punctuated by comfortable gaming chairs with head rests. They were red, yellow, blue, green, but never black. The chairs were the only expression of personality allowed in the 'factory' as some of the traders called it.

Patrick sat back in his chair and partially closed his eyes until the text on his screen was a blur. All he could see were the shapes. He did this for a few minutes every hour or so. It helped him zoom out from the detail to the big picture. The danger was that he focused too much on the outliers. The stock of portfolio K1525 was mostly trending upwards. There were a few stragglers, but the mean tracking line was positive.

"Are we keeping you awake?" asked Grant, the floor walker for the shift.

"Fuck off, Grunt, and leave it to the professionals."

Grant shook his head and moved on.

Emma turned to him and made a face. "What's up, Motu?" She called him that when he was in a mood. Motu—Master of the Universe. He was only ever in a mood when his trades were not going well, and he was clearly not the master of the universe he imagined.

"This fucker keeps trending upwards," he replied.

"Kobe?" It was shorthand for the main portfolio he managed.

He nodded. "Kobe. It's been on the rise for weeks. But look," he tapped the screen. "There's always falling stocks among them. They fall for a few days and then get dragged back into line, back into positive territory."

"You've been betting on a fall, haven't you?"

Patrick frowned. "Hedging isn't betting."

"Not when I do it," said Emma. "I buy enough options to offset a major loss on my portfolio. I don't use it to chase unauthorized positions."

"And I'm sure your investors are happy with you. It doesn't set the world on fire though, does it?"

"That's the job. We've both been given minimal risk portfolios to manage. You hedge just enough for large drops. Low risk on the upside, low risk on the downside. Sit back and enjoy the scenery."

Patrick faked a yawn. "Will I wake you up when it's time for lunch?"

Emma laughed. "Listen, Motu, it's a rising market. That means negligible risk and high returns. I'm more than happy with my bonus."

"But you'll never be promoted to the high yield accounts, will you?"

"How much have you lost?"

"Nothing. It's going to drop."

"Just because a few stocks run behind the pack? I don't think so."

Patrick said patiently, "I understand this portfolio. It's always been incredibly stable. It's almost like it's one stock, the way they trend together."

Emma spoke fast, imitating the terms and conditions caveats at the end of financial ads. "Past performance is not an indicator of future success."

"Let's have a break." He stood up and walked towards the far end of floor to the breakout area. She followed. Patrick poured two black coffees and pulled a hipflask from his pocket. He tipped the flask in Emma's direction. She shook her head. He poured vodka into his coffee and slid the flask back into his pocket out of sight.

"Cheers." He clinked cups together.

"How deep are you?" she asked as they sat down.

"Not as deep as I have been in the past, but …"

"We leave in a few weeks."

He nodded. "All positions close when we do. It's a crazy rule."

It was not a crazy rule, but Emma said nothing to contradict him. The positions belonged to a trader and marked their performance. The positions had to be declared before they left. The company would then decide whether to adopt them or close them, but that was the point at which the trader's performance was reconciled and bonuses finalized.

"You'll still get your completion bonus though."

Patrick said nothing. His face was blank, staring out the window, deep in thought.

"Shit, Patrick. What have you done?"

He shrugged.

"No, seriously. What have you done?"

"You know James left early, right?"

"You idiot."

He did not need to say more. Emma realized exactly what had happened. James was his proprietary partner. All trades carried out by Patrick belonged to the fund itself, but the proprietary partner was a co-worker that checked the trades and placed positions on behalf of the company itself.

These were hedges on the hedges. If the trade worked out well, the company received a healthy performance commission from the fund. If they performed poorly the company would profit from its own trades which were essentially bets in the opposite direction. With his proprietary partner gone, they had let him cover both sides of the transaction. Patrick had been betting in the *same* direction with the company money, convinced that the portfolio would drop. It was a straightforward win or lose position. If he lost, there would be no bonus, no second chances. And he would be personally liable for the losses because they contravened company policy.

"That's fraud."

Patrick took three deep breaths in quick succession. It was his body hack that kept him energized. He drank the rest of the vodka coffee and took another three breaths.

"Only if I lose."

"Win or lose, it's fraud."

Patrick stood up and walked to the window. Only glass between him and the city outside. "No, fraud can only be prosecuted if the company press charges. If I win, they win, and they won't care how it was done."

"And if you lose?"

"It's not going to happen." Patrick paused for a second then gestured towards the tower block opposite. "Look at this."

Emma joined him at the window. Wolseley Tower was still mostly transparent but dotted randomly across the surface were multiple floating windows, all with writing on them. *NOW YOU SEE ME.*

"Good on them," said Patrick. "Now you see me. Good on them."

"Sometimes it's better to be invisible."

"Where's the fun in that?"

*

Hesh had been home when they came to fix the glass cladding. A maintenance cage was lowered into position in front of his flat. He took a beer from the fridge and stood at the open window as the maintenance crew worked on it.

Sensors were attached to the surface and various diagnostic tests were run. Once these were complete, they used a telescopic frame with suction lifters distributed across it to hold the glass as they ran a high voltage current across the surface. This demagnetized the interior of the material which held it in place. Hesh heard a clicking sound as the pane of glass disengaged from the frame, several feet out from the building. The glass slowly and smoothly slid down below the cage. The crew faced him now without any barrier between them.

"Afternoon, lads," he said.

"Won't be long, son."

"I ain't your son and you are not replacing that glass."

The crew looked at each other then turned to him. "Look, we're just doing our jobs. Don't make it difficult."

"This is my gaff, and I don't want to it fixed, so jog on."

"We can't do that."

"I'll just break the next one. And every other one you put in. Let's skip past all that wasted effort and just leave the thing off." Hesh leaned down and picked up the end of the fence section that was still on his living room floor. He rested it on the windowsill and raised his eyebrows at the workers as if to say *go ahead.*

They consulted to each other in whispered tones before giving up and pressing the panel control to send the cage back to the roof.

Hesh knew this wouldn't be the end of it, but he didn't care. He had started something. Others had followed his lead and they had all painted the same message on their windows. Nothing was mentioned in the press, of course. It was not important enough to mention. They were just a bunch of scheme rats that would not behave themselves.

It was less than an hour later when the councilor turned up at his door and introduced himself.

"You need to let them repair your window," he said.

"There's nothing wrong with my window. I open it, I get some air. I close it when it gets too cold. It's all working. It's my water that doesn't work. It's the lifts that don't work. What you going to do about them?"

The councilor grimaced. "That's what this is all for. It will come in time. Did you go to the event last night?"

"I was there."

"We will get an income from the advertising."

"What are you talking about? Advertising? They are covering us up. That's what their paying for. Not for advertising."

"It doesn't matter if we get the money. Who cares what they show on the building?"

Hesh thumped his chest. "I care. Does that not count? I care."

"You're going to ruin it for everyone. You should be grateful for what we've given you and—"

"There it is. That's it, isn't it? I should be grateful. Shouldn't ask for more. Shouldn't demand more. Where did you go last night after your speech?"

"What?"

"You went over there to celebrate with your friends." Hesh stabbed a finger towards Chukaisha Tower. "You don't represent us."

"I was elected by this community—"

"No, because none of us vote. Some of us can't, and the rest don't see the point."

"I can't help it if you people don't vote, but I am trying to make things better."

"Prove it," said Hesh.

"What?"

"Prove it. Fix the water or fix one of the lifts. Anything. Just fix *one thing* that any of us care about and I'll let you put up your cloak of invisibility."

"That takes money. The money doesn't come in up-front."

"You found the money up-front for the cladding. Find some up-front money for one improvement. Just one. Do that and I might even vote for you."

"You're not a citizen."

"Strange that you didn't even recognize me yesterday, but now you know that about me. How does that work, councilor?" Hesh spat the words out.

"I'm trying to do this the right way."

"Have a word with him, remind him he is here as a guest. Is that it?"

"This is bigger than both of us. They want what they want. They'll get it no matter what you do and no matter what I say." The councilor lowered his voice, embarrassed at what he was about to say. "Do you know who their security firm is? It's run by the Manor. They don't stick to the perimeter fence. If I can't persuade you, they will send someone else round. Someone you won't argue with."

"Who won't you argue with, Hesham?" He turned to see Maria. She had heard the voices and let herself in.

"Our councilor is just explaining how he's going to send the boys round if I don't behave myself."

Maria walked up to the councilor and spoke softly but clearly. "That would be mistake."

"Look, I don't want any trouble from either side. I'm trying to keep the peace."

"There's no peace without justice. Wouldn't you agree?"

The councilor visibly paled.

Hesh said, "I just asked him to fix one of the lifts as a goodwill gesture."

"The trust doesn't have any money yet. Give me a couple of months. That's all I ask."

Maria stared him down. "Ask the council for an advance."

"It doesn't work like that."

"It does if you ask the right way. I'm sure the council doesn't want this all blowing up over nothing. Gangs, residents, other groups. It would all get very messy. They don't want a cut of nothing, do they? Just ask them in your capacity as the local representative."

After he left, Hesh asked Maria what had just happened. There was a subtext to the conversation, but he could not figure out what it was.

"We all have friends, Hesham. The councilor told you who his friends are, and I told him who mine are."

"All this time, Maria, and you never told me you're a gangster."

*

Fischer was nursing a scotch at a corner table when Cunard met him in the bar. He only drank very occasionally, but in this place he would stand out if he didn't have one. He ordered two beers and joined Fischer.

"*Was ist los?*"

"Not much. Just thought we should catch up and compare notes after the other night."

"The mayor was happy. She will have her piece of Patria next month. She went home happy. How was your night?"

"The Manor seem to be getting themselves mixed up with the traders."

Fischer raised his hands. "Those guys never cross the river. I have nothing on them."

"Really?"

"Really. Anyway, who cares about the gangs? They sometimes kill each other. So what? No great loss to the community."

"But they are mixing with Patrians now."

"Oh. *Ja, Ich verstehe.* It's a problem if they harm Patrians. Of course. Why didn't I see that? Let me divert all my resources to protect our wonderful new residents." He rolled his eyes and finished off his scotch.

"I don't think you do see. What do they offer Patrians? There is no drug they want that isn't already legal. Prostitution? Legal. What's left?"

"There's plenty left for them. The Manor control gun sales in London. They get most of their stock from The Five Points. They provide muscle, legal and not so legal. They act as a fence, usually selling anything of value on to The Points. They return the favor. It's the circle of life, *kumpfel.*"

Cunard smirked. Fischer seemed to live by film quotes. "*Hakuna matata.* Is that what you're telling me?"

"Something like that."

"They have been hired as protection by some of the traders."

Fischer nodded. "Makes sense. If they want to *protect* some Patrians, I've not got a problem with that. I see why you do. But me? No."

"They are providing real protection, Fischer. Protection for assholes wanting to be assholes. And my wild and crazy guess is that they will be assholes to Alterrans. Am I getting through to you yet?"

Fischer took a drink of his beer. "So, what do you want me to do about it? Like I said, wrong side of the river."

"It's never stopped you before."

"I make the occasional visit, but they have their own organized crime squad. I can introduce you if you want."

Cunard lowered his voice. "It's not OCS that needs to deal with this."

"You speak in riddles, *bruder.*"

"I've never known anyone mess with Patrians without going through the WA first. Patrians are their territory."

"Times change."

"Are you saying the WA doesn't care?"

"You'd need to ask them."

Cunard sat back and let the silence sit between them.

Fischer shrugged. "There's nothing else I can tell you."

Cunard picked up his beer. "I'll be gone soon."

"I know. I will miss you, Cunard. All these late-night rendezvous, the intrigues. It won't be the same without you." Fischer lifted his glass. "Prost." He took a drink.

"I've never said thank you."

Fischer nodded. *"Und?"*

"Thank you, Fischer."

"I just made a call. They decided you were worth saving, for some reason."

"So, just make a call this time."

"Really?"

"No point in letting a thank you go to waste."

"Okay, okay. I'll make the call."

Cunard let the car do the driving as he headed back to his apartment. He thought about the last few days. He'd made the right decision to leave. Something was brewing. If it happened before he left, he would have to deal with Eva and Fischer. He would do it if he had to, but it was not something he was looking forward to. If nothing happened, he had a bigger decision to make on the way out. As soon as he said the word, confirmed that they were tied up with the WA, they would both be finished. If he did not raise his concerns, he was potentially putting Patrians at risk.

"Are you here, Bella?" There was silence. He breathed a sigh of relief. Perhaps he could get an uninterrupted sleep for once.

Chapter 13

DIVERSITY ... As a company we are committed to diversity including freedom of worship. In recent years, a new religion has emerged within Alterum. 'The Book of Shadows' has also gained some followers amongst visitors. This is a religion that promotes full equality for Alterrans. You should note that this is in direct conflict with our golden rules and our golden values. Any agent found to be engaging in activity that indicates they are a Shadow will be terminated from service immediately.

Please note, as an Alterran derived belief system, the employment ban on Shadows does not breach any legal or constitutional rights.

Agente In Patria Handbook

Cunard was aware of the event before Bella told him, but he was pleased she had shared the information. The station chief had been alerted by the number of high-profile attendees booking to cross on the same day. The matter had been reported to the company and word had come back that it was not to be prevented or disrupted. This meant one thing. There would be company personnel in attendance.

He thought about this as he took the two-hour drive up-state to the venue. Before Bella had passed on the tip, he had been warned to stay away and that had played on his mind. He was on his way out in every sense. Where previously he would have been considered the lead agent, he was no longer in the loop. When he found out Eva was attending, he obtained reluctant permission to attend. There would be other agents there, all of them above him in the trust of the company.

He had seen the loss of status happen before. Towards the middle of his first tour, he had been assigned the job of monitoring a fellow agent. The worry was that she was going native. She was not and Cunard realized that she was simply reaching the end of her final tour of duty. Jack Glory got suspicious of its own when they reached this point. Now he understood why. The thought of leaving and never coming back did change the way he thought about the place and his own behavior.

Thinking back to that assignment, Cunard realized that he was almost certainly now being monitored as she had been. He was one of the few open agents in the company. He was known to and dealt with the Alterran authorities. Most agents were silent as he had been when he first arrived. Working to specific instructions, little contact with each other, they were organized in small cell structures operating under the direction of the station chief.

Cunard had been one of those junior agents before he was put on internal surveillance duties. Right now, he would be on the receiving end of that attention. Just as his trust in Eva and Bella had gone, so too had the company's trust in him. His successor would be stalking him, making sure he stayed true to the end and, without realizing it, preparing to take over from him.

Turning off the main road north, he slowed as he looked for the entrance to the campsite. The venue did not appear in any maps. Visitors were told which road it was on but had to find it for themselves. He had asked Eva for an invitation and directions, which she seemed to take great pleasure in.

After a few minutes he noticed a gap in the trees ahead. Pulling onto the side of the road, he found a dirt track leading to a wooden fence about twenty feet into the forest. He reversed the car slightly and turned. As he approached the gate, figures emerged from the trees. Security in the usual garb of all-black clothes and prominent weaponry. Cunard displayed his ID, and the gate was opened for him to drive through. Just beyond the entrance the track took a sharp turn and he found himself back on asphalt. As he drove further, he passed under an arched entrance displaying the name of the place: *Puk's Grove.*

After a few miles of tree-enclosed approach, he reached a parking lot next to a large wooden barn-like structure. Four sets of double doors sat below a lattice-framed front, all enclosed in a sloping roof that started at ground level and reached a height of thirty feet. In front of the doors, wooden benches were arranged and there was a scattering of people. Cunard parked and joined them as a man emerged from the building. He was wearing a white tunic and held a tightly bound collection of twigs and plants that smoldered and smoked.

"Welcome to our theater," he said. "Please come forward."

Cunard joined the queue as each of the guests was tapped on the forehead as part of the smoke ceremony. "Welcome. Pass through the theater and you will be taken to your accommodation."

"Am I late? Have I missed anything?" he asked.

The man tapped him again. "Weaving spiders come not here."

Cunard said, "Okay, no more questions."

Entering the theater, he looked around. Like outside, there were basic wooden benches. The walls were whitewashed and the natural light from the lattice windows above the entrance created a natural focus on the small, raised platform to the rear of the building. Off to one side of the platform a door was open. He walked down the aisle taking in the photographs on the side walls. They were all of stage plays from the venue. As a cover it was clever.

"Impressive," he said to one of his fellow arrivals.

They mumbled a reply and kept walking, looking straight ahead.

A collection of golf buggies and drivers were waiting for them outside the rear exit. Cunard climbed aboard one and showed his ID.

"Welcome, Mr. Cunard."

"I'm a little worried that I'm late," he replied. "Have I missed anything?"

"No, sir. You and your companions are the last of our guests to arrive, but the opening ceremony has not started yet."

That was the information he was looking for. He scanned the other late arrivals. One of them, the one who had mumbled a reply in the theater, turned his head away as Cunard tried to make eye contact. *Got you,* he thought. As the buggies made their way down another twisting turning track, he memorized every feature of the agent that was tracking him.

The trail took one last corner, and the real venue was finally in sight. A small lake sat at the bottom of a natural grass, sloped amphitheater. Wooden torches lit the dais in front of the water. On the other side of the lake were four buildings with the same sloped roof shape of the entrance theater. Other than the roofs, these buildings were all-glass structures. They passed by them, and Cunard peered in to see sunken step seating arranged in a square. As they carried on to his cabin in the woods behind the main buildings, he wondered how much more of this world was unknown to him, and how much would remain unknown when he left it all behind.

*

The car pulled up next to a large grey building. "I'll call you when I'm ready."

"Sure, boss."

Slender let himself out of the car and stepped into the daylight. He glanced at the sign across the doorway. *Millwall Tenant Management Trust.* Inside were rows of plastic bucket seats full of people waiting to be seen. He noticed the nervous looks as he walked past them towards the reception desk. It was a reaction he was used to. He was taller than most people and muscular without being bulky.

The name Slender was gained from his early days as an Elder in the Manor when he would visit people at night as an enforcer. He had once been caught on a street security camera after a job. The footage had been made public by the police. The image was hazy in the orange streetlight and all that could be seen was a tall silhouette. The Slenderman of urban mythology had been referenced and the name stuck. It had served him well.

The receptionist acknowledged him and, without speaking, buzzed the side-door open. He had visited this place many times. There was a small meeting room on the ground floor used for external visitors. That was where they always met. A councilor and the association manager were waiting for him.

"Mr. Porter. Welcome. Please have a seat."

"Is this going to take long?"

"Or don't sit."

The woman spoke. She was head of the council housing committee. "The local councilor for Wolseley Tower is a moron."

"There's a lot of them about, hey."

"He's not been able to stop the vandalism," the man said. "Now he's asking us to release funds to start the internal refurbishment."

Slender pulled a chair out from the table and slumped onto it. "Okay."

The man grumbled, "Sometimes I wonder why we bothered. We should have sold the land and rehoused the tenants in a new build."

She said, "We have several gap sites we could release to the association for such a project."

"I feel like I'm at one of your planning meetings." Slender frowned. "I hate meetings."

She replied, "It was what we wanted to do all along. It makes more sense than trying to fix up a badly constructed building. I didn't have a majority on the committee to endorse the plan. The thing is, it's not too late."

Slender stared at the woman. "Are you going to demolish it because of a few kids breaking some panels?" He rolled his eyes.

"The Chukaisha Trust has offered to fund security for the association. An extension of your contract."

Slender sat up. Now it was getting interesting. Now there was a point to the meeting. "Why are they not talking to me direct?"

"They are funding the security but can't be seen to be controlling it. The contract's yours if you want it." The manager gestured and a document floated in the air between them.

The number was big enough to further grab Slender's attention. "I'm interested."

"Naturally, we have a few priorities for you."

"I'm sure you do."

"Stop the vandalism to the panels."

"And?"

The woman took a pause before speaking. "And encourage a lower tenancy utilization."

Slender knew exactly what she meant, but he was not going to let her off that easily. "Say again?"

She looked flustered and uncomfortable. "I mean …what would be useful …"

"Are you trying to say that we should make life so uncomfortable that some of them will leave? Is that what a lower tenancy utilization means? 'Cos if that's what you mean, we can do that. Not a problem. I just need to be sure that I'm delivering what you're asking for, hey?"

She flushed and nodded. "Yes."

"And what about the association? Is that what you want too? Do you want a lower tenancy utilization?"

The man said, "We do. It would help make the case. It will be better for everyone in the long run."

"Okay. I understand you. You want me to fuck over the residents."

"That's not how I would put it."

"No, you wouldn't put it like that. But you see, I need to translate it for the troops. They don't understand subtlety. I have to use clear communication. I take what you say and convert that into something they understand. I will say to them 'Guys. We need to fuck over the residents so badly that they don't want to live there anymore.' We're saying the same thing in different words. Are we finished?"

The man and the woman nodded silently, breaking eye contact as they did so.

Slender left the room and closed the door behind him. He messaged for his car and walked along the corridor slowly enough to give the driver time to meet him as he left the office.

He hated people like that with their petty corruption and backhanders. They would not even get rich through all their scheming. They would achieve, at best, middle-class comfort. Maybe a holiday home, somewhere to spend the money they siphoned off. Their unambitious aim was to achieve a pale imitation of real wealth. Just enough to fool themselves that they were the same as those who did not have to worry about money.

Slender, on the other hand, was what he was. There were no illusions. The threat and exercise of force was what allowed him to live this life. He had professionalized the Manor, created some legal businesses, the main one being the security firm, but he still acknowledged what he was. He would never distance himself from the reality of what he did and who he was.

The car arrived as he left the office. He waited for the driver to get out and open the door for him. The world outside faded behind the tinted glass, and he massaged his back into the soft leather seating.

"How did it go, boss?"

"I think we may have to increase the velocity of our on-boarding."

"Say what?"

Slender laughed. "More security staff. We need more staff."

"Well, why didn't you just say so?"

*

After showering, Cunard headed back to the lakeside amphitheater which had already filled up with guests. He made his way slowly to the top of the hill, looking for Eva as he passed the rows of seats. She was here somewhere, but the dimming light of dusk and the number of attendees made it hard for him to pick her out. He estimated there were roughly two thousand attendees. That was more than he had anticipated. The deep metallic sound of a gong being struck resonated across the lake and a torch-lit procession delivered a speaker to the platform. Cunard did not recognize her. She tapped the microphone and leaned in to speak.

"Welcome to Puk's Grove. Welcome to the heart of the forest where we meet below the light of a full moon." She paused for effect and looked up at the night sky before bringing her focus back to the audience. "A cool light that illuminates our path amongst the trees without obscuring the rest of the sky. A light that allows us to see both the world and the wider universe it sits within. My name is Professor Valerie Austin, and I am Alterran. I would like to thank the organizers for inviting me to deliver the opening address.

"When we first met for the inaugural encampment, it was an experiment. A meeting of two worlds to explore whether we could learn from each other. The fact that we are meeting here again for the second time, two years later for some of you, forty-eight years later for others, myself included, shows that this experiment worked. It shows the urgency and the longevity of the need to learn and to share.

"Following the tradition of the first forum, the opening address is made by a philosopher. We are here to think, to challenge, to expand our vision beyond the day to day. But what good is philosophy if it leads to nothing but words? The closing address will be given by a practitioner with a call to action. It may be a scientist or an artist or a business leader. As we begin this process, hold that objective close. Thoughts must lead to action. Tonight, we think and discuss, tomorrow we plan.

"When I give my opening lecture to new students, I explain the different branches of philosophy. Some argue that there are four main branches, others five or six or seven or ten. It does not really matter. They can all be traced back to the need to answer two questions. What can we know? How should we live?

"Epistemology, the study of knowledge. What can we know?

"Metaphysics, the study of the nature of reality. What can we know?

"Logic, the study of reason and rules of inference. What can we know?

"Ethics, the study of morals, of right and wrong. How should we live?

"Politics, the study of how we organize society. How should we live?

"Aesthetics, the study of art, culture, and good taste. How should we live?

"And those two questions are really just one question. The answer to what can we know is no more than a foundation to help answer the second." She paused again. This time she looked slowly across the audience, appearing to make eye contact, and nodding acknowledgement where she did so. Someone in the front row, someone halfway up the hill. Someone at the top where Cunard stood. "How should we live? That is the one question that matters. How should we live? In our own worlds. Between our worlds. How should we live?

"I declare the forum open, and I invite you to make your way to the four lodges, stopping to place some kindling on the bonfire to symbolize the cremation of worries, assumptions, and fixed thought patterns."

The professor stood back from the podium and was handed a small branch by one of the attendants. She placed it into a raised circular iron pit next to the path. The attendant lit the fire with their torch and the professor made her way round the lake towards the lodges.

*

"Are you here?" Cunard asked. No answer. He looked around for Eva but still could not spot her. He then scanned for his fellow agent. He was no more than a few feet behind him. Cunard began to shuffle into the queue leading down the hill. Once in the flow of traffic he was swept along. He took a few steps and then pulled himself out to the side and watched as the agent got pulled towards him. As he drew level Cunard rejoined the throng and put out his hand in welcome.

"Hi, I'm Cunard."

The agent, realizing he had no alternative, accepted the greeting. "Rosen," he replied.

"Quite the event, isn't it?"

"Yes. Are you … Patrian?"

"You should feel very honored. I didn't know about this event until a few days ago. You are already at the center of everything."

Rosen looked confused, unsure how to answer. "Yes."

"I thought I knew all the secrets, but now this. Fascinating, wouldn't you say?"

"I ..."

"For a silent agent to see this in his first tour. That's something. It is your first tour, isn't it?"

"I don't think we should be talking."

"It's a little too late for that now." As they reached the bottom of the hill Cunard pulled Rosen to one side. "I was given the same assignment as you many years ago. Watch an agent on the last lap of their tour. Make sure they stay out of trouble. Only it's not the real objective."

"I don't—"

"I'm not about to go off the rails. Too much of a bonus at stake, not to mention a potential Associate Director role. Your real job is to watch and learn. You've been earmarked for promotion to open agent. Watch and learn, Rosen. Right now, though, this is what we should focus on. Afterwards, you can go back to following me and I will go back to pretending I am unaware of you. While we are here, we need to split up to cover the event."

Rosen frowned but nodded. Cunard joined the queue approaching the fire pit. When they reached the front, they were each handed kindling to throw onto the flames.

*

Alex looked beautiful to Hesh. Her long brunette locks fell loose over her shoulders. The strapless dress hugged her figure and combined with her heels to create an aura of glamour that was out of place, but a welcome sight regardless. He looked down at his own appearance. Jeans, t-shirt and running shoes.

"I feel like I haven't made enough effort."

"Don't worry about it. I always dress like this. Even when I go to the chicken shack for my mum." She flashed a smile and her dark brown eyes seemed to hide a laugh.

"Do you want to go local?"

She looked him up and down again, opening her eyes wide in an exaggerated manner. "Yeah. Yeah, local is ... where we would be acceptable."

They walked west along the side of the outer dock towards the river. "I'm sorry. I should have dressed up."

"Playing it cool, Hesh?"

"Something like that. Don't want you to think I'm a simp."

"There's not much danger of that. Did Maria help you get dressed?" She shoulder-bumped him.

"She thinks she's my ma. Who was taking you up west the other night?"

"Is that you getting possessive already? I don't think I like that."

He laughed. "Nah. Stay cool. I just wondered who has the coin for that."

"No one from round here. Just a guy from work."

"Are you going to see him again?"

"It depends how tonight goes."

As they approached the river, they came to the more expensive housing with its fencing to protect it from the surrounding area. They made their way through the narrow alleyway between two developments that gave access to the riverfront walkway.

"I think our estate is the only housing left here that doesn't have a fence around it," said Hesh. "Is it us they are afraid of?"

"I'm moving out soon. Going to get away from the island."

"Yeah?"

"Yeah. I can't live with my mum forever. She drives me batty, and anyway, why would anyone stay unless they had to?"

"It's not so bad," he lied.

"You've got your own place."

"Have you seen my gaff? It's class. The best of everything."

"Yeah, that's why you can't afford good threads."

They found a free table at a gastro pub and ordered food. They had been neighbors forever and gone to school together, but in the last few years they had only exchanged small talk in the elevator or stairwell. Alex had an office job in Canary Wharf and was taking business management at night school. Now interested in education in a way she had not been at school. Her employer re-imbursed the fees for every module she passed. It was a great incentive to study.

Hesh was scraping by on benefits while doing a university access course at the local college. He had always been one of the smart ones at school, but then his Ma got ill. The studying fell by the wayside, and he left without the qualifications he needed for university. It was the last thing on his mind at the time, so it did not feel like much of a loss, but now it was different. He still thought about his mother every day, but he had space for other thoughts too. He was studying politics and economics. He hoped to take it through to degree level. Alex teased him about becoming a councilor.

"That's not the kind of politics I'm going to do."

"So, you're not a member of a party, you don't want to be councilor, you're not on the tenant committee. What politics do you do?"

"I don't know. I'll tell you when I figure it out."

After dinner they stayed for a few drinks and then followed the Riverwalk round to one of the launch ramps before turning and heading back to Wolseley. Hesh had enjoyed the night. It was good to get out of his own head.

"Thanks," he said.

"I had a good time."

"But?"

"I had a good time," she repeated. "God, you're heavy, aren't you?"

He nodded. "But this isn't going anywhere."

Alex stopped, held him by an arm and stepped in front of him. She leaned forward and kissed him on the cheek. "No, we won't get married and have babies, Hesh. We won't even have a one-night stand. But it was still nice, yeah?"

"It was."

She stabbed a finger in his chest, "And you need to lighten up. Kiss a few frogs and not worry about them turning into princesses."

"Are you calling yourself a frog?"

She smiled. "No, I'm one hundred percent princess. Look, I've got a friend at work. She's very boring. Always going on about the world-wide Patrian conspiracy. She's not as good-looking as me, natch, but you two would get on. You've got the same downcast view on life. She would be very excited if I told her about your window-breaking activism. I can hook you up with her. What do you say?"

"She sounds like a keeper."

"Are you interested?"

"Why not?"

"That's the spirit." Alex looped arms with Hesh and used him for support as she leaned down and took off her heals. "I really didn't expect to do this much walking tonight. Do you have any idea how hard it is in these?"

When they reached home, Joe was lurking at the base of the tower block.

"What's up?"

"I'm sorry, mate. I had to let them in."

"Who?"

"The Manor. They're in your flat. I gave them the spare key. I'm sorry."

He tried to maintain a calm appearance, but Hesh could feel his heart pounding in his chest. "What do they want?"

"It's about the panels. I'm sorry, mate."

He could tell Joe was missing something out. "What else?"

"Maria."

Hesh ran into the building and pressed the elevator button, then without waiting he sprinted to the stairwell and began to make the long climb as quickly as he could.

*

"Are you here?" Cunard asked as he entered one of the lodges.

"Yes," replied Bella.

Cunard sat down on the top level of the sunken seating. "I thought you were avoiding me."

"I got the impression you were sick of me following you."

"Where is she?"

"I left her in Lodge Two."

"Okay. I want you to focus on someone else tonight."

155

"Make up your mind. Who's the enemy now?"

Cunard displayed an image of the agent. "His name is Rosen. He's AIP. I need you to stay close to him tonight and tell me who he talks to, what they talk about. He will be in Lodge One or Three."

"Is there anyone you do trust?"

"You, Bella."

"And I'm supposed to believe that?"

Cunard grinned but did not answer.

A bell rang and the audience fell silent. A man sitting on the opposite side of the room spoke.

"What can we know? The hard problem of consciousness is what we will discuss here tonight in this lodge. I will open the discussion. My name is Saver Alves. I am Alterran."

Cunard recognized the speaker. He was a representative of the Church of Shadows. The most senior members were referred to as Moderators. They refused to call themselves leaders, but that was what they were.

"Why is any physical state conscious rather than non-conscious? How does that subjective experience light up and become real? We can explain the physics of it. We can track electrical impulses in the neurons of a Patrian brain. We can track electrical impulses in the Alterran world. We can say what a thought is made from. What physical transactions occur to make it so? Here and there it is made from the same thing. An exchange of electrons.

"We can find the area of the Patrian brain that stores memories and allows them to be accessed. We can find the physical location of memories in the Alterran world. Both are electric fossils that come to life as energy passes through them like water in a dried-up riverbed. Objectively we know what these things are. But why are these objective processes associated with subjective experience, with a sense of self? That is the hard question.

"Many have questioned the parallel. Alterum was designed as an intersubjective world. Different parts of the whole act independently and influence other parts which in turn influence the whole. The intersubjective divides itself and is slowly changing and evolving through the interaction of those parts. This is what it was designed to do. So, am I a real subjective being or a figment of a collective imagination? Is it enough for me to tell you I experience consciousness and a sense of self? If not, why do you believe other Patrians when they tell you they experience it? Are you inside their head? Do you really know what they experience?

"I propose to you that you know, you have confidence that your fellow Patrian is conscious, is real, because you are not an island. You too are part of an intersubjective world. A reality that exists between the parts, within the parts, within the whole.

"This physical world of Alterum despite all of its complexity is one thing, one entity. We know this world was created by consciousness. Is it so strange to imagine that your world is also created by consciousness? That your world is intersubjective?

"But we created your world, you tell me. Yes, you did. My world was created by a demiurge. We have solved that mystery. But what lies beyond? From where did your world emerge? From where did the conscious matter of the Patrian demiurge emerge? Is consciousness something that exists elsewhere and simply takes shape as it runs through matter in the same way we process those electric fossils we call memory? Or is all matter conscious at some level we do not yet understand?

"Our thoughts and our memories are literally made from the same matter. Is there a difference in the quality of our consciousness? These, my fellow explorers, are the mysteries we travel through tonight."

The conversation began and delved deep into the philosophy and practical implications of each position taken. Every speaker introduced themselves prior to contributing. The breadth of attendees only then began to dawn on Cunard. This was not a collection of Alterrans and Patrian believers in the Book of Shadows. This was a meeting of the best in their respective fields from every area of society in both worlds.

Cunard felt as though the world was shifting beneath his feet. Part of his and every other agent's job was to stop this world waking up to the reality of its own creation. The Book of Shadows was a religion here and not much more than fringe activity in the real world. That is what they had been told by the company.

Here in this hidden grove, the great thinkers of two worlds met and acknowledged the truth. They grappled with its implications and how that should guide their actions. He felt a wave of heat rise through his cheeks in anger. Anger at the indulgence shown to visitors like Morgan who acted without check, without repercussions unless they damaged the company itself. Alterrans were fair game, and his job was to allow that to continue while the great and the good inched towards an understanding of how they should live together, an implicit recognition of Alterrans as living beings worthy of rights.

Pieces of a jigsaw that he had not realized existed began to fall into place. The siege of Red Hook had taken place before the first forum. It was the largest of many attacks on the company and Patrians. Since then, the WA had limited itself to minor shows of strength. Reminding the company that they had not gone away. This event was two worlds testing the limits of the relationship. Understanding how much they could push each other. Understanding the path and the price of peace. He was sure of it. The WA had not saved him. They had saved the Tower. He was willing to bet that the Tower had been agreed to at the last forum. The two worlds beginning to intertwine.

The WA was here. The Church was here. Scientists and politicians and artists were here. Cunard had been kept in the dark as much as the people of Alterum. The truth was only for the powerful, not for the ordinary people, nor the foot soldiers like him.

His job was to keep a lid on things while these people worked out what rights and dignities the Alterrans deserved. What rights and dignities did they have to be given to make this place safe to expand?

*

The door was lying open when Hesh reached his floor. He was out of breath and unable to defend himself, but he went straight in. What he saw shocked him to his core. Maria was sitting on a chair in the living room, her face badly bruised and eyes narrow slits between the swelling. She was holding her arm and making a low continuous cry. Two men were waiting for him, and he recognized one of them. It was Joe's cousin. Before he could say anything, a white blinding light flashed across his vision. He felt a numbness spread over this face. The impact of whatever hit him was not too painful. That was his thought. He was surprised by it but realized that what he felt was relief. Then he heard the crack of a blow to his ribs before he felt it. This did hurt. He let out an involuntary groan. The pain swept across him like a wave of nausea. His vision was back, and he saw a baseball bat swing towards him for a third time, smashing against the arm he had raised in defense. The sense of numbness returned, but this time it was not physical. He had given up trying to shield himself against the blows raining down on him. He had accepted the beating would continue until they killed him. His body went loose, and the blows seemed to land with more of a muffled sound than before. Maybe it was his hearing, perhaps it was the lack of tension in his body. He did not care anymore, he just wanted it to be over.

The man with the bat stopped swinging and spoke to Joe's cousin. "Mark him."

There was fear in the cousin's face, but he knelt and put the weight of his body onto Hesh's chest.

I am on the floor, Hesh thought. Again, his thoughts playing catch-up with his body.

The cousin leaned in. His knife had a small narrow blade. It pressed against Hesh's cheek, and he felt the pressure as it pushed through into his mouth and then dragged through skin. No pain but a sensation of blood dripping from his chin, then wetness. He coughed as blood filled his mouth. Hesh had thought he was ready to die, but the sensation of breathing liquid into his lungs told him that his body was not willing to give up. This was not just his decision. He was now fighting to cough the blood away, thrashing at the man sitting on his chest.

"That will do."

The cousin got off him and Hesh rolled onto his side, spitting.

"No more broken panels." And with that last warning, they left.

Hesh pulled himself up with his uninjured arm and looked at Maria. He tried to say sorry but just mumbled something undecipherable.

Alex appeared a few minutes later and called an ambulance. She found some towels and pressed them against his face to stem the bleeding. Hesh looked at her, now streaked in blood, splashes on her dress, hands painted red and sticky. He felt like a fool. Look at what he had done. Look what he had done to Maria.

When the ambulance arrived, they were accompanied by a cop with a slight German accent.

"Maria, what happened?" the cop asked as he helped Maria to her feet and into a wheelchair. She reached out towards Hesh, and the cop said, "We'll take care of him too."

Hesh tried to say thank you to Alex, but he still could not speak. He tried to tell her with his eyes. The pain killers did their work, and he felt the world go soft, less defined. Joe was standing outside when they reached the ground floor, staring vacantly at Hesh and Maria.

As he was lifted into the ambulance the warm glow of the drugs continued to build, and Hesh drifted off to somewhere better.

*

Cunard left the Apollo Lodge after the first session concluded. He made his way over to the adjacent Hermes Lodge. It was here that he found Eva. Shuffling down past other guests he sat beside her.

"Are you enjoying your visit?" she asked.

"You were at the last one, weren't you?"

Eva gave him a sideways glance. "Something like that."

"You organized it?"

She put a finger to her lips. "We can talk later. The discussion is about to start."

A bell rang and the session began.

"What trade should develop between our worlds? The limits of trade are what we will discuss here tonight in this lodge. I will open the discussion. My name is Rachel Marlow. I am Patrian.

"Prior to the first forum, trade was non-existent. Patrian visitors were tourists in this world. Yes, it was a significant industry, but it was nothing more than tourism.

"Since then, Patrians have begun to invest in property here. Medical and old age packages have created semi-permanent residents. With the opening of Chukaisha Tower, we now have long-stay commuters. Patrian trades are made here. Many Patrian pension funds now invest in Alterran stocks and real-estate. Why? Because the time dilation between our worlds renders those trades low risk.

"A little history helps explain this. In October 1929, the Patrian Wall Street crash occurred. The stock market lost 11% of its value in one day. In the following three years it lost a total of 89% of its value. That is worth repeating. It lost 89% of its value in three years.

"It took until November 1954 for the market to recover to pre-crash values. Twenty-five years. The greatest crash in the history of the stock market recovered in twenty-five years. Even if the Alterran economy crashed at a level unseen since 1929, all losses could be recovered in just over one Patrian year.

"With the opening of Inwood Tower, the trading capacity will increase further. Alterran traders will be admitted to the market for the first time. Trade will start to flow in the opposite direction. Alterrans will hold stock in Patrian companies. The circle will be completed. The question for tonight is, what next?"

Cunard listened with fascination as the business leaders from two worlds discussed where they saw value and profit emerging between now and the next forum.

When the session finished, he followed Eva out of the lodge and into the cool night air. Torches lit the paths between the lodges and the lake where a bar and buffet had been set up. Tables and chairs were placed in small groups around the water. It looked like a wedding reception as guests sat and talked, conversation punctuated by laughter drifting up the hill.

"So, this is where all the decisions are made?"

Eva shrugged. "Think of it as more of an advisory body. Suggestions, recommendations emerge. Some are accepted and some are quietly forgotten."

"And this is why the WA have been quiet."

"There is an agreed truce leading up to the forum. Without it, the great and the good wouldn't come. It's that simple."

"And after. What happens then? Is it back to normal?"

"I need to meet someone. Walk with me." Eva headed in the direction of the lake as she spoke. "It depends on what's agreed here. Sometimes the most effective act is self-sacrifice. Don't assume it's always Patrians that are at risk." She stopped and put a hand on Cunard's chest. "I need some privacy. Can you give me that?"

He watched as Eva made her way to the lakeside. A solitary figure waited at the edge of the amphitheater opposite. As they met, they embraced. Cunard drew a circle in the air and magnified the image. The woman was Patrian, a foot taller than Eva. She had a looseness to her movements that clashed with the conservative clothing she wore to blend in.

Cunard told his Handi, "Scan port manifests for a list of all arrivals."

"Anything interesting?"

Cunard turned to find Agent Rosen approaching. He quickly signed to silence his Handi. "How did you get on?"

"Where is the company?" Rosen asked, puzzled. "These people are deciding the future of Alterum. Jack Glory owns it. I don't understand."

"They are here. We're not the only ones. This place is swarming with agents. Think about it. How many others had you met before today?"

"Not many."

Cunard said, "Exactly. We are all kept apart. They don't trust any of us. Let's get a drink and swap notes. I guarantee you will learn more by talking to me than by following at a safe distance."

*

"Are you here?" Cunard asked when he reached his cabin. Silence. He asked again. Still silence.

He signed to bring his Handi back to life. "Port manifest results."

Eva Enfield

"The other one."

Eva Enfield

"Repeat. Both targets,"

Eva Enfield. Visiting Patrian. Eva Enfield. Resident Alterran

"Shit."

"That's exactly what I thought." Bella appeared.

"I really wish you wouldn't do that."

"She's the Patrian Eva. She's using a difference appearance, but it's her."

"Did you follow them?"

"After you and Rosen went for a drink."

"And?"

"It was private. Very personal. I don't feel comfortable sharing with you, Cunard. You understand?"

"And?"

"She came to say goodbye. Patrian Eva is dying. She doesn't have long left."

"How many times have they met?" he asked without expecting an answer.

Chapter 14

HOW TO SPOT A MEMBER OF THE WA ... The Waking Army, colloquially known as the WA, are a designated terrorist group committed to the overthrow of company rule. The WA is the primary threat you will face. Not all Shadows are members of the WA, but all members of the WA are Shadows.

Does a contact express belief in the Book of Shadows? They may be a member of the WA. Do they consistently argue for the removal of legal immunity for visitors? They may be a member of the WA.

There are some WA members that work more silently. If they are not a Shadow, do they express related beliefs such as panpsychism? Do they express strong support for animal rights, environmental concerns, or any other form of ethics that is inclusive of non-human entities? They may be a member of the WA.

If they express all these beliefs, they are almost certainly a member of the WA.

Agente In Patria Handbook

When he woke up, the German was sitting by his side. The pain was different now. It was a gnawing constant rather than spikes of agony.

"Good morning, Hesham."

He ran his tongue along the inside of his mouth. He could feel the stitches.

"They've patched you up and you will live."

"Maria?"

"She will live too. My name is Fischer." He projected his badge.

Hesh studied the badge. "You're on the wrong side of the river."

"*Stimmt*." His badge faded. "Maria is an old colleague and a friend. We look out for each other. Who looks out for you?"

He fought it, but Hesh felt tears form in his eyes. "Maria."

"Hmm. She told me."

"Did you get them?"

Fischer looked at him. "Did I get them? No, I did not get them. Who would you like me to get? The two that did it, or the man that sent them, or the people who paid the man that sent them? What about the ones who created the situation that led to all of this?"

"The two that attacked Maria." He had no doubts about who he wanted to pay. That was the focus of his rage.

"The fight over crumbs is always more brutal than the fight over gold, but it's a distraction. If you want to get back at the individuals, join a rival gang. But understand this. You will simply be one more person fighting over the crumbs while the real game is played in comfortable offices uptown.

"From what Maria tells me, you are more intelligent than that. I hope she's right. There's always room for good people. But they need to look past the small stuff and see the big picture."

"Can I see her?"

"Later. She needs to rest."

Hesh's brain was still lagging. He assumed it was the drugs. "You were colleagues?"

"Yes. We still are."

"But ..."

"We'll talk again later. Get some sleep."

*

The following day more sessions were held and as night fell, the attendees gathered once more in the amphitheater. As before, a torch-lit procession delivered a speaker to the dais.

"Thank you for attending Puk's Grove. I would like to thank the organizers for inviting me to give the closing ceremony. I am Bill Fraser, and I am Patrian. As balance dictates, an Alterran opened and so a Patrian closes. A philosopher started and a practitioner ends.

"Last night and this afternoon we have covered much ground. Those of you who know me will not be surprised that I spent most of my time in the Hermes Lodge. It's not that I don't believe in art or ethics, it just that I figure someone's got to pay for them."

A murmur of laughter rippled through the audience.

"I am joking, of course, but there is a serious point. What is regulation but the government-controlled codification of ethics? What does regulation lead to? Higher prices, less innovation.

"Many of our speakers have opened their talk with a history lesson. Let me do the same. In a 1906 a novel called 'The Jungle' was published. It was set in the meat packing industry of Chicago. The novel described rat-infested, unsanitary meat processing factories as well as various other shortcomings within the food industry. This novel, this work of fiction, contributed to the passing of the Meat Inspection Act and helped justify the creation of the FDA. The author, a socialist I might add, did quite well out of it. He was quoted as saying he aimed at the public's heart but instead hit their stomach. What he didn't say was that he also hit them in the wallet. Regulation led to higher prices. Regulation always leads to higher prices.

"Yes, there were problems, but nothing that could not have been solved by industry-agreed codes of practice. Look at what we have achieved since the First Council of Patria. Look at the wealth that has flowed into

Alterum. Look at how much more wealth will continue to flow. Why? Precisely because this world embraces what we Patrians have largely abandoned. The ability to do whatever the hell we feel like with self-control as our guide, not laws."

Cunard scanned the audience and detected a split.

"Yes, there will be individual casualties. But let us be clear, the casualties are on both sides. This is not Alterum versus Patria. This is good Patrians and Alterrans thriving and prospering. This is careless and sometimes, frankly, bad Patrians and Alterrans coming unstuck. It is what it is. It is what it has always been and what it always will be. Let us not restrict the good on both sides because of the worst of us.

"Look how far we have come. Do not slow that down with unnecessary red tape. Let us define through these forums what good looks like. What self-regulation we should have, not what knots we should tie ourselves in.

"Now, before we feast to celebrate the end of Patria Two, let's put behind us any disagreements. I end Puk's Grove with Puk's words:

"If we shadows have offended,
"Think but this, and all is mended:
"That you have but slumber'd here
"While these visions did appear.

"Good night unto you all.

"I formally declare this Second Council of Patria closed."

The speaker left the dais to muted applause and walked towards the raised pit, the fire from the opening night now extinguished. Saver Alves stood next to the pit with a metal bowl full of cinders from the fire. Fraser paused before him and had four lines of ash smeared on his forehead. The audience formed a line, and the ash ceremony was repeated with more attendants joining Saver to process the crowd.

Rosen found Cunard and joined him in the queue.

"Listen, who do you think that speaker was, Cunard?"

"I haven't met him, but I recognized the name. He's a non-executive director of the company."

"It didn't go down very well."

"You could say that."

"I'm getting a bad feeling about this."

"How long exactly have you been here?"

Rosen did a silent calculation. "About two years local time."

"And you're only just picking up on the tension? This place is a powder keg. That's why we're here."

Cunard scanned the area for Patrian Eva after passing the fire pit. She was deep in a heated conversation with Fraser. Accepting a tall flute glass from one of the waiters, he weaved through the attendees towards them. Walking in a straight line was something that even the most unobservant noticed at a subconscious level.

Cunard heard her say as he drew closer, "You do not speak for the entire board."

"I don't claim to."

"You shouldn't have given the address at all. The company should never speak at this event. It should only come to listen."

"With all due respect. You are a singer. Entertainers may feel their opinions about everything matter, but I have run companies larger than Jack Glory. That is why I was invited onto the board."

"This is no ordinary company, and *with all due respect*, the company made a mistake."

"Time will tell, now if you will excuse me. I think I'd rather spend the evening with someone who isn't shouting at me."

Cunard walked towards her and put out his hand as Fraser departed. "Hi, my name is Cunard. I'm a Patrian."

Eva stared at him without taking his hand. "Good for you." She turned and walked in the direction of the amphitheater where she was greeted by Saver Alves.

Alterran Eva walked slowly towards him, a bottle of water in hand. "She doesn't suffer fools gladly."

"Am I a fool?"

"Are you?"

He looked around at the guests in their huddled groups. "Maybe I am. I didn't know any of this existed. She has your eyes. I don't think I could spend time with my own clone. My bad habits would annoy me too much."

Eva swallowed before replying. "We like to think of ourselves as sisters."

"Did you both organize this one as well?"

"No. Just the first one. The way it was before was in no one's interests. We were uniquely placed to help. There was a lot of goodwill on both sides. The enemy is never just the enemy, Cunard. They are also the ones that can bring peace. You worry that I'm WA. Some of them think that I'm too Patrian, because of her," Eva nodded toward Patrian Eva.

"Which is it?"

"Where is the line? It's not as straight as you think. Maybe there is no line."

"Answered like a true Shadow. Do I need to worry about you?"

"You'll be shocked to hear this, Cunard, but you're not the only agent I've known over the years." Eva ran a finger down his arm and stared at him with a deadpan expression. "And one thing I've noticed is that exit fever is a very real thing. You want to go, but you don't want to go. You imagine that everyone is beginning to dismiss you as irrelevant. You think some of us are turning against you. It's your feeling of growing impotence that causes the fever."

Cunard said, "Well, you certainly know how to make someone feel valued."

*

The last few days had passed in a blur for Hesh. The painkillers kept him tired, and he slept most of the time. When he finally had enough energy to get out of bed, he left the room to look for Maria. As he entered the corridor, he became aware that this was not a public hospital. The thick carpet and wallpaper were more like a hotel than a medical facility. There was a small nurse's station and the on-duty medic rushed over to him.

"You shouldn't be up yet."

"I want to see Maria."

The nurse nodded and took his arm to support him.

"I've got a visitor for you," she said, opening the door.

"Come in." Maria was sitting on a chair, looking tired but comfortable. One eye was covered in a patch bandage and an arm was in a sling. She smiled at Hesh. "Look at us. We are twins. Come and sit with me."

Hesh was helped into the chair next to her and took her hand. "I'm sorry, Maria."

"Don't apologize. You didn't do it."

"But they came for me. Why were you in my flat?"

"I heard a noise. I've always been nosy."

"Joe let them in."

"I know."

"Was he there when they did this to you?"

"It doesn't matter."

"It does. It matters to me."

Maria sighed. "Yes, he was there. He was scared and he showed them where you live. Then he left. Don't blame him for being scared."

"It was his cousin, Maria. It was his cousin that did this."

She nodded. "It doesn't matter. He does what he's told to do."

"I will kill him as soon as I'm out of here."

"If that's for me, then please don't."

Hesh shook his head. "What is it with you and your friend, telling me to pretend it never happened?

"I didn't want you involved in any of this, but it was never my choice."

He stared at her uncomprehending. It was him that had got Maria into trouble. "I don't understand."

"I wanted you to have a quiet life. Meet a girl, be happy."

"What are you talking about?"

"The graffiti, the broken panels, that wasn't spontaneous. We saw that what you did struck a nerve. 'Now you see me.' That was perfect, Hesham. The perfect thing to say to all those Patrians staring over at us, trying to ignore us. We spread the word and with a little encouragement it took on a life of its own."

"We?"

"I didn't think it would come back on you. Joe told them it was you that started it. I'm so sorry. Can you forgive me?"

"We? Who is Fischer? Who are you?"

"I'm not much more than a pair of eyes and ears these days, but I still do my bit."

Hesh fell silent as he took it in. His neighbor, his mother substitute …
"You're with them? But you always …"

"Can you forgive me?" She dropped her gaze and began to gently sob.

"I can forgive you anything."

She looked up and tightened her grip on his hand as she nodded.

"But you need to tell me everything, Maria. No more secrets."

*

Cunard left the grove after the reception to avoid the inevitable queues the following day. After driving for thirty minutes along rural roads, he began to see the glow of the city in the distant night sky. The greater the distance from the grove, the more it felt like a dream within a dream. Decisions were being made far from the madding crowd, far from those impacted by them.

Was this an exception, he wondered, or were all societies organized this way? Powerful cabals meeting in secret to decide the fate of mortals. It was a battle, that much was clear. The cabal was not some uniform body. Tensions and arguments played out. Power struggles continued, no doubt, outside of the rarefied retreat he had just witnessed. Both sides argued that they represented the common good, but where was the voice of the majority? What was being agreed in their name and what price did they have to pay? If the wrong decisions were made, surely it was better that they were made by those most impacted?

He wiped his brow and turned up the air con. She was right. He did have exit fever. Clive was right to have him followed. And yet … Fraser had antagonized at least half his audience. He referred to the meeting as the Council of Patria. He had basically told the meeting that the company was not interested in Alterran views. He saw their rights as nothing more than red tape.

The first forum had been prompted by the Red Hook siege. An open attack by the WA on the crossing port. Some concessions had been made and the company's profits continued to rise. Patria Two, as he had called it, had not ended well. Once the guests had left, the ceasefire was over. If he were a member of the WA, what would he do? It seemed obvious. Now was the time for a show of strength.

*

Hesh had heard all the stories before. The Patrian conspiracy theories, the attack by the WA on the crossing port in Brooklyn. How the local law enforcement came to the rescue of the Patrians and forced back the assault. What he had not heard before was that his Maria, decades younger, no more than a girl, had been part of that assault. How she had gone to ground afterwards, blending into the background, and eventually taken up residence in Wolseley Tower.

New members, clean skins, had infiltrated the police, political parties, got close to power. Never again would they be defeated by their fellow Alterrans, corrupted and under the control of foreign agents. Wherever that control had been found, it was ruthlessly destroyed. They were now confident that the main levers of Alterran power were, at worst, understood and capable of being neutralized if necessary.

They had become complacent though. They had left the street gangs to their own devices. Never taken them seriously. There were no WA members in the Manor or the Five Points, the two largest gangs in Nylon City. What was clear was that this oversight was putting their members at risk.

Maria was not the only Wolseley Tower resident with connections to the WA. They had been the first to copy his protest.

"So, the protests are not going to stop?"

Maria said, "What you started was important."

"Was it?"

Hesh heard footsteps and turned to see a woman entering the room. She was vaguely familiar. She said, "I'm so sorry."

Maria nodded.

"I should have been here sooner. I was out of town." The woman leaned down and embraced her friend. She then stood and placed a palm on Maria's forehead, shutting her eyes, whispering an incantation to herself.

A calmness that had been absent seemed to spread over Maria. "This is Hesham Fanon. Hesham, this is Eva."

Now he recognized her. She was a singer, famous back in the day. She held out a hand in greeting. "Nice to meet you," she turned back to Maria. "What have you told him?"

"Most of it."

"And how much of it do you believe?" she asked Hesh.

"It doesn't matter. I'll help you. I don't need faith to fight."

"Ah. Only a skeptic would call it faith. We are lucky in a way. We don't need it. It's only Patrians that need faith to believe they are a part of a larger whole."

Hesh said, doubtfully, "We are a simulation created by the Patrians? This is just a playground for them? Doesn't that sound even the slightest bit crazy to you, Maria?"

Eva's eyes flashed amusement. "The things that are believed are often less strange than reality. That's what makes reality so hard to accept." She paused before continuing. "We can find somewhere for you to live, if you are not ready to go back to Wolseley."

Hesh was taken aback at this. "I'm not going anywhere."

"You can't fight without taking a side and you cannot be part of our side if you don't believe. We will ask you to do things with which you are uncomfortable. That will eat away at you if you're only motivation is revenge."

He looked to Maria for support.

"She's right. You should start over somewhere safe."

"No."

"Sleep on it. We can talk in the morning." Eva reached out with her hand. "May I?"

He nodded, thinking she was going to shake hands again. She ignored the outstretched palm and touched his forehead. There was a warmth to her touch that seemed to pass through him, easing the pain and bringing an acceptance of what had happened.

*

Hesh's dreams swirled like a storm that night. Visions of the earlier conversation. Alterrans fighting Patrians, Maria part of that battle. Two versions of Eva. An awareness that one was Patrian, one Alterran. His body, his thoughts, his immediate surroundings merging into one, then separating back out into their constituent parts, together, apart, together apart. Over and over, like a tide rising and falling on a beach.

He woke early with the sunlight streaming in through the window. His mouth was dry, and his head was foggy. Reaching over for the water at the side of his bed he was conscious of the lack of pain. Sipping the water, he ran his tongue round his mouth without thinking. It was not there. The ragged, uneven texture of his stitches. He put the glass down and felt his cheek. It was smooth to the touch. This could not be right. He pushed himself out of bed and stared at his face in the mirror. He saw a face without swelling, without stitches, without pain. His thoughts raced as he made his way to Maria's room. She was awake, sitting up in bed when he got there. Her face free of swelling, her arm no longer in a sling.

"What is this?" He ran a hand over the site of the now missing scar.

The tiredness and stress in her voice was gone. She spoke with a tone of gentle strength. It was the Maria he had grown up with, always quoting from the Book of Shadows.

"The world is not simply viewed through your eyes. It is shaped through your thoughts. Open your mind and you can change reality."

Chapter 15

AGENT CELL SYSTEM ... Your loyalty is to the company. It is not to other agents. There will be few opportunities for you to meet colleagues. You will have regular contact with the station chief and their staff, but unless you are working together on a specific engagement, you will not be introduced to any other field agents. You have entered a demanding profession and you have many enemies. There is every possibility that you will be under surveillance. If you choose to seek out and meet with your colleagues on a regular basis, you will be creating an attractive target for the WA. For this reason, we operate an informal cell structure. As an agent you will enter Alterum alone and you will work alone.

Agente In Patria Handbook

Cunard entered the radio room to find the fishbowl in darkness. He looked at the station chief. "Where's Clive?"

"The director rejected your meeting invite."

That had never happened before. "You passed on my message?"

The chief nodded. "Word for word."

"Does Clive understand—"

"Let's find somewhere quiet to talk."

Cunard reluctantly followed the chief to a side office.

The chief closed the door behind them and gestured for Cunard to sit.

"So, does my analysis no longer count?"

"It does with me, otherwise I wouldn't have passed it on."

"What did Clive say?"

"Nothing. It was just a meeting rejection. There was no feedback, no explanation. Just a rejected invite. There's nothing else I can tell you."

"Did you know about Puk's Grove? What it is?"

The chief allowed himself a smile. "Not all of it, but a little. Look, Clive has shared things with you in the past to which I was not privy. That does not mean you are a confidante. It is the way it works. Only the directors have the full picture. You, me, every other agent, we are only allowed a glimpse of the big picture. Did you think they only try and control what Alterum thinks and believes?"

Cunard felt annoyed at his own naivety. "How long were you a field agent?"

"One tour of duty."

"And how did you get this position?"

The chief laughed. "Why? Are you looking for some career advice?"

"I'm curious."

"I asked for it. I did my tour as an agent and at the end of it, I told them I wouldn't come back."

"Because?"

"Because I thought I would get sucked into the life here. As an agent you need to mix with Alterrans. Let me tell you something you already know. They are real. They are not human, but they are real."

Cunard nodded. "If you don't understand that, you underestimate them."

"I couldn't do it again. Build up relationships that I would either abandon or betray."

"But you came back."

"As station chief. Shorter tours of duty, limited contact with locals. What you do, Cunard, it eats away at you. You should be pleased it is almost over. Take it easy for the rest of your stay and get out of the company once you do."

"Unless I become a station chief." Cunard saw the tell. A quick evasion of eye contact. It was what he expected. "So, that's how it is."

"I don't know what you mean."

"You do. A two-tour field agent doesn't come back in any capacity. They are tainted. No longer trusted."

The chief shrugged. "Clive did three tours, so …"

"So, Clive is the exception that proves the rule?"

"Look, it is what it is."

It is what it is. A phrase that had spread throughout the company like a virus. Cunard realized how much he was beginning to hate it.

"Chief, let me tell *you* something. Clive is a sociopath. The directors know they are real but don't care. They need to listen." Cunard leaned in. "I tell you Puk's Grove created a ticking bomb. By dismissing Alterran rights to their face, they are asking for a reaction. The WA helped open the Tower. They have been keeping the peace, but they won't after this. Something is brewing. I can feel it."

"And I passed your feelings on to Clive. But they were just feelings, nothing specific, nothing tangible. Feelings are not facts."

"I'm right."

The chief looked at the ceiling then sighed. "I agree with you. Other agents have the same concerns. It has been quiet for too long. Clive won't listen until you have something solid. Do your job and try and find out what it is. When you do, then the director will listen, then we can act. What is your gut telling you? When? Where? Who?"

Cunard massaged his temples as he leaned on the table between them. "They made sure Chukaisha Tower opened. It was in their interests. But perhaps they don't feel the same about a second tower."

"The Inwood opening?"

"Maybe. Who looks after security there?"

"A local firm. It's a cover for The Five Points though. You think they are linked to the WA?"

"We've never paid too much attention to gangs. They kept themselves to themselves. Suddenly the Manor are getting close to some of the traders. It doesn't feel right."

"So, that's where we start. Use the ghost and get close to the Manor. I will cover The Points."

Cunard gestured in disagreement. "We need one set of eyes across both."

"Don't be an ass, Cunard. Just because the directors like to keep us in our silos does not mean we have to behave that way. We need more people on this. If you are right, we don't have much time."

"Okay, but we meet. We share intel."

"I'll assign Rosen to it. Satisfied?"

Cunard nodded.

"No more meeting requests to Clive until we have something solid. When we do, no mention will be made of this team we are putting together. Understood?"

Cunard contacted Rosen as he left the terminal.

"We need to talk."

Rosen said, "I take it the chief has updated you about us working together."

"And when exactly did he tell you?"

"Yesterday."

"Right." Cunard sighed.

"He told you we have to keep it quiet, yes?"

I am not on the inside track, he thought as he drove home. *My desire to understand this place has stopped me understanding Jack Glory. I have spent too much time with—*

"So, who do you want me to follow?"

Cunard tightened his grip on the steering wheel and took a breath before answering. "Bella, there needs to be some boundaries."

"It's too late to tell me that."

*

Hesh looked up at the Wolseley Tower as he stepped out of Fischer's car.

"Are you going to be okay?"

He turned and faced the detective. "Yeah." He patted his jacket pocket.

"You're not alone now, but that means you have responsibilities. Peter Parker. *Verstehen?*"

"Power, responsibilities. Sure thing, Uncle Ben." Hesh closed the door before Fischer could reply.

The apartment was a mess. The front door was lying open, and the place had been trashed. Anything worth any money had been taken. Stolen by neighbors assuming he was never coming back. The blood on the carpet had dried black but stuck to his foot as he walked over it. The panel in front of his window had now been replaced. The steel fence paling lay propped up against the window where he had left it. Clearly no one thought that was worth anything. Hesh smiled. It was the only thing he was interested in. He picked it up, swung it back then forward into the replacement panel. After a few attempts he heard electricity crackling. It was done. He corrected one of the upturned chairs and sat down, hand in pocket, and waited.

It was dusk when he saw a silhouette in the door. It was not who he hoped it would be, but he was not surprised.

"Joe. Is that you?"

"Hesh. What the hell are you doing back here? Are you crazy? You're going to get yourself killed."

"By who? Your cousin?"

Joe raised his arms as he entered the room. "I swear I didn't think they would do that."

"What did you think they would do, Joe?"

"Look. They didn't leave me with much of a choice. I swear I didn't want that to happen."

"Sit down."

"I got to go. I'll come back later. I swear."

Hesh squeezed the trigger, and a flash came from his pocket. A bullet thudded into the wall. "Sit down."

Joe staggered back and collapsed into the couch behind him. "I swear I didn't want this to happen. I swear it."

"I believe you. Lights on." The room was illuminated as Hesh gave his command.

Joe crossed his arms as he came into full view. He was wearing dark trousers and polo shirt.

"No need to hide it, my friend. You've joined the security. Word travels fast."

"I—"

"Let me see it. Let me see the logo." Hesh pulled his hand out of his pocket and pointed the gun at Joe.

"Please. You don't need to do this."

"I'm not going to hurt you, Joe. Not if you do what you're told. Let me see it."

His friend slowly unfolded his arms and revealed the logo. It was the shape of a key with the letter "M" acting as the bit.

"So, your cousin got you a job after all. You ever do any shifts at the Tower?" Hesh nodded towards the window.

"Look, Hesh …"

He let off another round to short-circuit the excuses. "You ever do any shifts at the Tower?"

"No. Not so far."

"But your cousin does, yeah?"

Joe nodded.

"And you do Wolseley. You and how many others?"

His friend looked sideways towards the front door then looked back. "One per shift."

"Doesn't seem enough, does it? What happens if you find yourself in a situation you can't handle by yourself?"

"I call for backup from the Tower."

"I guess you better do that now. Just one person. I don't think this is more than a two-man job, do you?"

"What are you—" Another round hit the wall, but this time it was closer. He felt the disturbance of air as it passed him. He instinctively pulled to one side as if he were dodging the bullet that had already finished its brief journey into the plasterboard.

"Open up a message channel. Make it public so I can see it. Ask your cousin to come over. Tell him where you are. He is on duty, isn't he? No need to answer. It's more of a statement than a question. Tell him you need his help."

Joe did as he was told, fumbling at his Handi as he typed the message which hung in the air between them. They didn't have to wait long for a reply.

Uok cuz

Joe stared at Hesh.

"Don't reply."

After a brief pause another message came through. *Panel out again. Who?*

"Say, 'not sure but need you to see something.' That should do it."

Ok cuz

"And now we wait." Hesh stood up. He kept the gun pointed at Joe as he dragged the chair to one side, checking the line of sight to the front door. He stopped and sat down again.

Joe tried to talk to him as they waited, but Hesh put a finger to his lips to silence him.

When the cousin arrived, the door was open, and the lights were on. He shouted from the hallway, "Cuz, you there?"

"Yeah."

"What's the deal?" He strolled into the apartment and froze as he saw his cousin sitting, staring across the room.

Hesh fired and this time didn't miss. Joe's cousin cried out as his thigh was hit. He reached for his pocket, but another round ripped through his arm.

"Have a seat. All the cousins together."

Joe said quickly to his cousin, "I'm sorry. I didn't have a choice."

"You seem to be saying that a lot today, Joe." Hesh grabbed the cousin, knocking him towards the sofa. It didn't take much force. He then held the gun to his head while he removed a weapon from his jacket. He flicked the safety catch and stepped slowly back, now directing a weapon at each of them.

"How?" said the cousin, staring at Hesh's unmarked face.

"It's a long story, my friend, but let's just say the world is a little stranger than most of us realize."

"Hesh, please. I did wrong. My cousin did wrong, but we are both just trying to get somewhere. Don't kill him. We'll walk away and never come back. I promise. Please, for everything we've ever done together."

"Stand up and step away from the sofa." Hesh pointed his gun towards the window with the fence paling leaning on it.

Joe nodded, looking between Hesh and his cousin. "Please."

"I joined the WA. I never thought I would, but I joined them. Ready to fight the good fight? They said, now you are a member, it's not about your own personal revenge. It's about the bigger picture. That's hard. I understand, but it's still hard."

"Listen to them," pleaded Joe.

The cousin said nothing. He clutched his arm, staring at Hesh and the gun.

"The thing is, Joe, I did listen to them."

His friend's eyes screwed up. "Then what—"

Hesh fired the cousin's weapon and hit Joe between the eyes. There was no time for a look of confusion or any other reaction. It was a clean kill and the body fell backwards against the open window.

Hesh turned to the cousin. "Isn't that crazy? It's you that gets to live. You that gets to pass on a message to the Manor. Wolseley is out of your authority. If any of your people enter Wolseley again, this is what will happen." Hesh looked over at his friend. The upper body was balanced on the windowsill. "If you want to be let out of here alive, I need you to do something. Crawl over there and throw Joe out of the window."

"Are you mad?" Joe's cousin had tears streaming down his face.

Hesh wiped away a tear of his own and fired a round into the sofa. "Probably."

The cousin hobbled to the window. Leaning down, he grabbed Joe's legs with his good arm. He then pulled upwards until the balance of weight was hanging out of the window and gravity could take over. The body tumbled out of sight, creating occasional clanking sounds as it hit the scaffolding frame on the way down.

Hesh lifted his gun and pointed at the cousin. "It's a big family you have. Are you close to them? Do we need to repeat this, or have you got the message?"

*

Slender's car pulled up in front of the housing association office. It was dark and the street was deserted. The manager was standing at the entrance waiting. He approached the car and leaned down to tap the window.

Slender spoke to his driver before lowering the window. "First sign of trouble and you hit the pedal."

"Sure thing, boss."

The manager pulled his coat tight against the cold. "You've heard about what happened?"

Slender met the question with silence.

"I think we should delay any plans for Wolseley. Let things settle down."

Again silence.

"We are going to have to cancel the contract. I've had questions about it. Whether it followed due process. Like, who else was invited to bid? We need to lay low."

Slender shook his head slowly. "You are asking me to lay low because there's been some trouble. You are asking me to do that?"

"Look, I was approached by a stranger in café. They had my address, where my kids go to school. Everything."

"Lucky you. You're famous. Well done."

"It's done. The contract has been pulled. You'll get official notification in the morning. I just wanted to tell you in person. We can still work together, just not on this."

"Really?"

"Yes."

"You really think this is how it works?"

The driver interrupted them. "Boss, two police cars coming from opposite directions. You want me to move?"

"Hey, if they are coming for us, we can't outrun them. That's why we've got lawyers."

The manager looked up at the approaching cars. "It wasn't me. I swear."

The police pulled up in front and behind Slender's car, blocking all movement. One uniformed and a plain-clothed officer got out of the car in front of them and walked slowly towards the manager.

The uniformed officer told the manager, "Please stay where you are, sir."

The manager put his hands up to show he was complying. As they reached him, the plain-clothed officer pulled out a machete from his coat and slashed the manager's neck. The manager grabbed at the wound and stared in shock. A bubbling sound came from his mouth as he collapsed to the ground. The man with the machete thrust it down forcefully on the manager's skull to finish him off. He then dropped the knife next to his victim and walked into the alley beyond the streetlights.

The uniformed officer leaned down and spoke to Slender through the small gap. "Sorry to disturb you, sir." As he spoke, the car in front reversed to create a gap. "We'll let you be on your way now. Have a pleasant evening." He raised three fingers in the shape of a 'W'.

"Boss?"

"Go."

*

"They aren't working together." Bella looked at Cunard's coffee and touched his hand.

"You sure?"

"They are at war with each other. The manager was killed with a machete. That cop wasn't faking it." She laughed nervously.

Cunard nodded slowly, thinking about what he had been told. "So, what are the Manor doing about it?"

"What can they do? Everyone knows who they are. Know who their families are. Half their members work for their security businesses. They are in the open. No one knows who the WA are."

"You should have followed the cop."

"You told me to stick close to the Manor. I stayed with Slender. Make up your mind."

Cunard said, "Something is going to happen. Every instinct I have tells me there will be a show of defiance after the retreat. Is the Manor getting cozy with Patrians just a coincidence?"

"No, not a coincidence, but maybe they are getting in the way of whatever the WA has planned."

"I'll make an agent of you yet, Bella."

"That makes more sense though, doesn't it?"

"Okay. Good work. Listen, stick to Slender for the time being. They are in the mix somehow."

She let her hand remain on his as he took a drink of coffee. It was reheated and bitter, but she could taste it.

"Anything?"

"No," she withdrew her hand. "A memory of the taste, but nothing more."

"Keep trying."

"Sure." She walked towards the outside wall and jumped through it. He went to the window and looked down. Bella was visible as she landed and slowly faded as she walked away.

He gestured for his Handi to open the line to Rosen who answered immediately.

"You heard all of that?"

"I did. What do you think?"

"I think she's right. I misjudged it. The Manor are there to be bought by anyone. They don't care who pays them as long as they pay. Somehow that has become a problem for WA."

"It's the security for the Tower, isn't it?"

"I think so. What have you found out about Inwood?"

"The Five Points have won the contract. They have a few members of the Manor training them, giving them guidance on dealing with Patrians. The two gangs control both towers, exchanging personnel and information."

"Okay. Security for the opening of Inwood. Who's in charge?"

"The chief. Any high value targets will be protected by company staff. The Five Points will oversee the building after the opening but will be mostly on entry and perimeter duties for the ceremony. What are you thinking?"

"There will be an attempt to infiltrate or pressure them. Controlling the perimeter would present a lot of opportunities."

Rosen nodded. "Agreed. What do we tell the station chief?"

"Everything. Everything we know and everything we suspect. You need to see him in person. I can never guarantee that I'm alone."

"If you suspect her, we should pull the plug."

Cunard frowned. "She'll be gone soon enough. If she has turned, she's only hearing what I want her to hear. That makes her useful either way."

*

Emma leaned across the bed and stroked Slender's chest. "What's worrying you?"

He took her hand and kissed it. "There's always something to worry about. It's nothing."

"It's Wolseley, isn't it? You've lost control of it."

Slender pushed her hand away and slid up on the bed. "Isn't it time for you to get back to your boyfriend?"

She laughed. "If you want me to, but he's not my boyfriend. He's married out—over in Patria. We are just keeping each other company here. His life is going to end when he goes back."

Slender looked cynical. "You're good, but you're not that good."

"He has lost so much money here. His company just hasn't found out yet. He will lose his job and end up in prison unless they want to cover it up. Even then he will never work in finance again."

Slender took her hand and placed it back on his chest. "We've all got worries."

"Same problem. Credibility."

"You're a smart one."

"So I've been told. He needs to sort it before he leaves. Otherwise, his whole life is gone. It's the only thing he knows and that can give him the lifestyle he wants. Same thing with you. If Wolseley can ignore you, disrespect you, so can anyone else. You can't run your business, if no one fears you, can you?"

Slender reached for the brandy glass at the side of the bed and took a drink. He inhaled sharply and closed his eyes. "What would you recommend?"

"You are going to have to hurt a lot of people to get your respect back, aren't you?"

He said nothing and took another drink.

Emma sat up. "Shit, I'm right. When?"

"Last time I checked; you were not a member of The Manor."

"But I'm one of your best customers."

"This here is good, but we don't have a contract, you and me."

Emma was amused. "Really? You've got me here under false pretenses. Listen, Slender, I want to be there. I want to see it. Something real."

"Are you sick in the head?"

"You've done it before and even if you didn't enjoy it, it didn't put you off, did it?"

"You've always been obsessed with Morgan. That's why we're here, isn't it? You don't love me."

Emma said, "Do I find you exciting and fascinating in the same way as Morgan? Yes. So, what do you say?"

"Why should I?"

Emma took a deep breath before speaking. "Hear me out. Whenever there is a plane crash, airline stocks fall. Not for long, but they fall then bounce back. It's just a fact. What if you knew exactly when that disaster was about to happen? You could make a lot of money."

"I'm not going to crash a plane."

"But you are going to hurt a lot of people. Send a message, scare the people that need to be scared and get back the respect you need to run your business. If you did that in the right way at the right time, I could make us both a lot of money."

"Tell me."

"Patrick has bet on a falling market, but it has refused to fall. If something happened close to Chukaisha Tower that spooked investors, and they then saw a run on local stocks, they would all join in. The markets would rally pretty quickly, but Patrick could sell his short positions at the bottom and get out the hole he's in."

"And I care about that why?"

"Because he's so heavy into his position that it would be a massive windfall. It would be more than he needs to cover up what he's been doing. We split the profit. He pays us using a cash Chain wallet. He has control of his own reconciliation accounts, so he can do it. Everything leads back to him if there are any problems. It cannot be traced to us if we recycle it quickly enough."

"You think it would work?"

"Yes. I would start the sell-off. I have a few friends that would be willing to help. Our selling would trigger the run. We just need a reason to explain our sales."

Slender thought about this. After a long silence he looked at her. "We are going to attack Wolseley. Run through it top to bottom and wipe out anyone we think is connected to the WA."

"That's not big enough."

Slender hid his surprise. "What?"

"You need to burn it to the ground. Set it alight and watch it go up with everyone inside. I want to feel the heat of the flames at Chukaisha Tower."

*

Eva was waiting for Fischer in her dressing room when he arrived at the club. "Is it done?"

He nodded. "It must have been hard, but Hesh did it. It was a childhood friend."

"A friend who betrayed him."

"*Dennoch*, he was a friend. A friend with flaws, but a friend."

"We all make tough decisions, Fischer. Sometimes we have to hurt our own to move forward."

"We should never forget that it is hard. That is how it needs to be sometimes, but it's not easy for someone new like Hesh. It's not easy for me and who am I? An old, jaded, cop."

"You are the best of us."

Fischer rolled his eyes. "I am the best of us? We are in trouble."

Bella materialized as they spoke. She looked as if she was in a trance.

Fischer nodded in her direction. "Where is she?"

"With Cunard."

"She's good."

Eva said, "She's the first ghost I've known that can split her presence so easily."

"Will she get back?"

"I think so. She can taste and feel and see when she connects with others now. Not just me. If we can bring a material body into the intersubjective, I believe she can use it to leap."

Fischer nodded. "One last miracle?"

"You could say that."

Bella shook herself and looked at the two of them. "Were you talking about me?"

"*Naturlich*. You are an interesting person."

"Why thank you." She gave a mock bow. "Cunard has teamed up with the agent from the retreat, Rosen. They are expecting some big event. They think it will be at the opening of Inwood."

"Are you sure?"

"I pretended to leave. Well, I left and stayed at the same time. You know what I mean. Anyway, he thought I was gone when they spoke. They think you are trying to compromise the local security so that you can pull off an attack."

"Good work. Can you stick with him?"

"He's asked me to follow Slender, but yes."

Fischer whistled. "Can you do that? Follow both?"

Bella said, "I am with Slender right now. He is meeting a trader in his private suite at Nylon Zoo."

"*Fantastisch*."

"He's not happy about Wolseley or the police ambush."

"That's to be expected." Eva reached out and touched Bella's presence. "Thank you. Your work is important to all of us."

Bella drifted into a deeper trance and fell silent.

Fischer pointed at Bella with a thumb. "Do you think she's right? They are expecting the attack on Inwood?"

"That is what I would plan for if I was them. It makes sense if you think in a straight line."

"That would be good. Taking out some of the directors."

"No, it would feel good, but it wouldn't be effective. They would close Inwood before it opened. We need the worlds to connect more, not less. Patria needs to be dependent on us as much as we are dependent on it. That is the future."

"I know."

"We can't take the straight-line, Fischer. We will be equal once they see our pain as real pain. Once they see atrocities against us as real atrocities. But they won't do that until they are forced to find morality in the folds of their wallets."

Chapter 16

PERSONAL RELATIONSHIPS ... It is strictly prohibited for agents to enter any form of committed relationship with an Alterran.

Experience has taught us that forming a long-term relationship with an Alterran will compromise your safety and will undermine your commitment to the golden values. In the early days of the company several agents had local partners and some even had Alterran children. These agents typically suffered severe psychological trauma as a result. Any breach of this rule will result in immediate dismissal from the company and termination of any Alterran partners and dependents.

We recognize that the life of an agent is a solitary existence and that this can be challenging for many. There are no company restrictions on your use of commercial services designed to address these needs.

Agente In Patria Handbook

Cunard pulled into the parking lot in front of the *Lucitania* and watched for a few minutes as quadcopters landed and took off. There was a queue of them hovering in the air as they waited their turn to collect the VIPs waiting on the top deck of the ship.

"This is the last big one before I finish. After this I'm done. I'm going to sit on a beach until it's time to leave."

Bella faked a surprised look, raising her eyebrows and making an exaggerated 'oh' shape with her lips. "What will Nylon City do without you?"

"Whatever it wants. If I am right and something goes down, there's only clean-up activity left, and I don't want to be involved in that. If I'm wrong … I've lost my ability to understand this place and I might as well sit it out." He turned and faced Bella. "I suggest you do the same."

"Sitting on the beach doesn't hold much appeal as a ghost. You don't get a tan, you can't enjoy the cocktails. It doesn't stack up as a fun time."

Cunard said, "Then do whatever it is you enjoy. Whatever makes sense for the last few weeks."

"Before …"

"Yeah. I'm sorry I couldn't stay longer."

"I've not been waiting for you to fix me, Cunard. I have my own plans. I have my own agency."

Cunard nodded at the choice of words.

"What?"

"You sound like a Shadow."

Bella sighed. "There's a reason for that. You should get yourself some old-timey religion. It might help make sense of this crazy life of yours."

"Get out of town and make the most of what you have left. I won't say anything, but Eva and the others, no one can save them from what's coming. If they try anything tonight, we are prepared."

"It was good though, wasn't it?"

He stared into space before replying. "It was." He opened the door and got out. Bella stayed seated in the car. He leaned down to speak. "You coming?"

"I'll let you do this one alone."

"Tell them. Tell them we are ready for them."

"I will. And thank you for everything."

"It wasn't so much."

"It was more than you needed to do."

Cunard closed the door. As he walked towards the building he looked back and saw her fading to nothing. He was not sure he could stop what was coming, but at least he had tried.

The conference room was full by the time that Cunard arrived. The station chief sat at the head of the table and agents crowded round, standing room only.

The chief banged the desk to get silence. "You know why you're here tonight. Inwood Tower opens, and we have multiple VIP guests who have crossed over for the ceremony.

"We've done this before, so we take what we learned and build on it. Local security manages the perimeter, we control the reception space and all upper levels of the building. Our VIPs arrive and leave by copter. That means they never interact with the local security. We have had some chatter that an attack may take place. Nothing solid." The chief looked in Cunard's direction. "But it is from sources I trust. So, we have a one-to-one ratio of agent to VIP. You will each act as a personal bodyguard. Level one alert, we warn the guests to prepare for evacuation. Level two, we start the evacuation. There is a strict sequence. Class A VIPs first, then B, etc. Now does everyone know their alphabet?"

There was a ripple of laughter, and someone shouted, "What level are we, Z?"

The chief smiled and banged the table again to regain their attention. "We are so important we don't have a letter. And we do not get on the copter in the event of an evacuation. We stay, we act as a defense line. We fight. Understood?"

There was a murmur of agreement.

"Well, that was underwhelming. We are not the Marines, but am I understood?"

An agent at the front of the room turned and faced the others. He clenched his fist and raised it above his head. "Whoa, yeah." It was greeted with a laugh.

The chief said wryly, "Okay, let's do this. Your assigned VIPs will leave in the next twenty minutes, so muster on the upper deck." He gestured a code with his hand and flung it out into the room. VIP profiles glided to each of the agents. All except Cunard.

The agents filed out leaving him and the chief alone in the briefing room.

"Special assignment for me, I take it?"

The chief sat down. "Something like that."

"I've never seen so many agents in one room before. We've let the genie out of the bottle tonight. They will stay in touch with each other. You realize that don't you?"

"I do. Clive is not happy. The feeling is that the company had to act in case something does happen, but the director is skeptical. Very skeptical. This is being treated very much as an ass-covering operation. Nothing more."

"I guess my prospects for promotion have taken a blow."

"Unless something actually happens. In which case, your lack of specific information will be treated as an intelligence failure, and you will be sacked."

"Thought I might as well go out on a high."

"If it's any consolation, I am in a similar position."

"So, what's my job tonight?"

"I want you to survey the entrance from a safe distance. Keep an eye on the local security. Call in anything suspicious."

Cunard looked at him. "I'm stood down for the night. That's really what you're saying, right?"

The chief avoided direct eye contact as he replied. "Look, Clive didn't want you in the building. I was told to keep you away. Officially you do not have any duties tonight. Unofficially, I have drones in the air and a few agents around the perimeter, so we have all angles covered. You are part of my unofficial backup.

"You may feel as if you've been ignored, but there are other things happening below the surface. Clive is important, however there are other actors involved now. People who believe the current leadership has grown Alterran to this point, and they are now in over their heads. Change is coming, but we still take our official orders from the directors. Understood?"

Cunard nodded.

"Now, get going. I have the next batch of agents to brief and it's the same speech as the last time. Same jokes. You wouldn't want to sit through that again, would you?" As he left the room, the chief called after him, "You have been heard, Cunard. Give us time to work through it."

*

Hesh met the others in the agreed meeting place. It was an old warehouse near the water. Weapons were handed out followed by balaclavas and they each grabbed a bullet-proof vest as they climbed into the back of the van. They sat in silence as the vehicle made its way through the city. He was lost in his thoughts. Joe had been a good friend and then a traitor that almost got him killed. He was friend and traitor. That was the way it was. No one was fully good or fully evil. Just like Hesh driving towards death. Someone else's or his own. That would be decided as the night unfolded.

There were no more miracles to be had. That had been made plain to him when he agreed to take part in the mission. This time he would survive or fall on his own. So be it. This was the destiny he had chosen for himself. He would stand with those that stood with him. He would fight those that attacked the things he loved. This was his path. Standing or falling for something bigger than himself.

"You okay, Hesh?"

"Yeah."

"We're all volunteers. If you've changed your mind, tell me, but do it now. This is the last chance to back out. We're almost there."

"I'm okay."

"Good man."

The van came to a stop and the doors opened. The tower was waiting for them in the distance.

*

Cunard parked the car at Met Cloisters and walked the short distance to Inwood. The new tower was on the edge of the river and had taken the place of a section of parkland. Spotlights lit up the scene. It wasn't hard to keep his bearings. He had visited this area many times. He followed the walkway through the museum grounds and came out at Payson. After a few minutes' walk he turned left onto Dyckman St. and headed for the river. Because of its position between the river and the park, it would not be easy to mount a surprise attack on the tower. Cunard concluded that the most likely approach would be from the river. He decided to position himself near the marina ramp and jetties. The chief had given him no specific instructions, so the reality was that he was surplus to requirements, He didn't care. He was going to do this last job and take his own advice for once. He would leave the city in the morning.

Approaching the ramp, he noticed patrol boats on the water. There was a solitary figure on the jetty who seemed to be communicating with them. As he got closer, he recognized the man as Rosen. He made his way across the walkway and shouted out to him. Rosen turned and waved.

"I thought you'd be up there with the VIPs."

Rosen said, "If anything is going to happen, it will come from the water. The upper floors are sealed off, access is by air which we have under control. What about you?"

Cunard did not know how to answer that question. What was he doing? "The chief is just trying to keep me out of the way. Who is out on the water?"

"Curious thing, that. They didn't have company IDs, but they are Patrians."

"What are the chances of us having a large group of agents with tactical boat skills available?"

"My thoughts exactly."

"They are Marines." Cunard said it as statement, not a question. "He made a joke about Marines during our briefing. They were on his mind, and it slipped out. They are Marines."

Rosen nodded. "It makes sense. Everything I've seen of them. They arrived fully equipped in transport copters this afternoon. The thing is though, they didn't cross. Not from the port anyway. That means they were already here, or they have their own crossing station."

"So, the government has its own forces based here. Sitting quietly out of sight." Cunard whistled. "You know what Alterum is?"

Rosen shrugged.

"It's too big to fail."

Rosen's gaze travelled upwards at the copters coming and going from the rooftop of the tower. "I think you could be right."

Their conversation was interrupted by a cracking sound from the water. It echoed as it reached the riverbank and bounced off the tower. One of the defense boats was under attack. It had come to a rapid stop, creating a forward wake it as it lost speed and the front of the vessel dipped down into the water.

Cunard and Rosen instinctively reached for their weapons even though they were in no position to help.

Cunard pointed towards the boat and shouted a command, "Show."

One Marine was slumped over the wheel at the rear. He had been taken out with a single shot. The others were searching round for the direction of the attack. They didn't have to wait long to find out. A rapid burst of fire came from their starboard side. They returned fire but seemed to be shooting into thin air. A hail of fire hit them and two more of them crumpled.

"Shit, where are they, Cunard?"

"Contact the Marines. We need to speak to them."

Out on the river the other boats began to turn and head towards their stricken colleagues, pushing through the water as fast as they could. The men on the first boat had stopped firing as they scanned the river for their attackers. There was no return fire. A light wind provided the only background noise as the boat bobbed gently in the water.

"I've got them. Can't share the audio with you though. The line is locked down. They think it was long range snipers".

Cunard said, "No, we heard the discharge. They are on a stealth boat, and they are close. Tell the others to stop converging. They are creating one target for them."

"Shit."

"Tell them to spread out."

Rosen repeated the instructions and the boats immediately fanned out in unison. Two boats took forty-five-degree angles to the starboard and port bow of the targeted craft. Two others took port and starboard beam directions before beginning to circle back further out into the river. The final boat headed towards the riverbank and then turned to approach the drifting vessel while using it as cover from anything directly in front of it. One of the boats further out on the river began to flicker as if it wasn't there, flashing in and out of existence. The flickering boat cut its engine and the image stabilized. They had found the attacker's position. Rapid gunfire created a strobe lightshow against the water. As artillery hit the stealth boat small patches of it became visible for a moment before dissolving back into darkness. The attackers began to return fire, their discharges revealing silhouettes before they too faded between shots.

Cunard turned his attention towards shore. "Contact Clive." His Handi projected an image of Clive in the tower.

"Cunard, if you need to communicate, do so through the station chief. I'm busy."

"This is important."

"Wait, let me move somewhere private." Clive walked rapidly past the guests with their glasses of champagne in their hands. Cunard watched and waited as the director left the reception room and entering a service corridor. "Speak."

"There's an attack taking place on the water. We need to activate the evac plan."

The trace of a smile crossed Clive's mouth. "Thank you for your assessment. Your advice is noted."

"I'm serious."

This time the smile was fully present but no less dismissive. "Your instincts were correct. Well done and thank you. We are well prepared for any assault, and we will not be evacuating."

"People could get hurt. Alterrans and Patrians."

Clive was unmoved. "Really? Every Patrian guest here can leap. Human rights are for humans. The only people in danger are our agents. That's what we get paid for. Taking that risk."

Cunard snarled his response. "We?"

"Yes, we. I have never come here with a safe word and never will. This event is too important, and we are done treading softly with the locals. The demand to come here is growing and quite frankly that puts a question mark over just how many Alterrans we need.

"We are not, I repeat not, going to retreat in face of phantoms that want to be treated as equals. Please contact the station chief if you need to any further instructions tonight. There is a line of command. Use it."

The connection cut out before he could reply. Cunard breathed in the musky odor of the riverbank soil carried by the breeze. He turned back to the river. The gunshots were more distant now. The stealth boat was retreating, its wake visible where it cut through the water. The Marines were mostly in pursuit, with one boat transferring the injured and dead from the initial attack to the shore.

"Not the reaction you expected?"

Cunard dipped his head before composing himself and looking directly at Rosen. "By now I should have expected it. Any reports from the perimeter guards?"

"You don't think it's—" Rosen stopped mid-sentence and looked down at his chest, puzzled. A patch of dark spread out from an entry wound in his sternum.

Cunard leapt towards him and knocked him to the ground. The sound of air being whipped surrounded them as a hail of bullets flew past. He pulled off his jacket, rolled it up, then compressed the wound. "Breathe, Rosen, and keep your eyes open."

"I've been hit, haven't I?"

He had experienced the confusion caused by shock before, but it always took Cunard by surprise. "Yes, you've been hit."

"Have you been to the void?"

"You're not going there, Rosen. I'll get you back to the port before that happens."

"You will?"

Cunard took Rosen's hand and placed it on his jacket. "You need to hold this and stay awake. Do you understand me?"

Rosen nodded. "I have a family."

"No one's perfect. Now hold on."

The gunfire had come from the downstream riverbank in the direction of the old canoe club. Cunard shuffled on his elbows to the edge of the jetty for a better vantage point. A round whipped past him, and he recalibrated their position. Sitting below the elevated Henry Hudson Parkway was a stretch of ground with a small stage. Tables and chairs were placed in front of it, with strings of light bulbs covering the outdoor venue. There were two small boats pulled up onto the sand bank behind the stage and a group of four or five figures were sweeping past the tables as they made their way towards the tower. It would take them past the jetty.

"All channel distress signal. Message. Intruders approaching the jetty. Stay clear."

He looked back and saw the approaching Marine boat kill its engine. They had got his warning. He crawled further away from Rosen and let off several rounds in the general direction of the venue. Four guns flashed as they returned fire, revealing their position to the Marines. Cunard rolled into the water and let himself slip below the surface. It sounded as if someone was dropping stones in the water above him. He pushed himself deeper knowing that he needed about eight feet of water between him and the surface for any bullets to slow down to a non-lethal speed. One grazed past him, stinging but causing no serious damage.

Cunard pushed forward heading straight for land while staying as deep as he could. The water began to shallow. His lungs were screaming for air, and he was aware that he would now be creating a disturbance on the surface. There was no choice, he had to make his move. Pulling his weapon from its holster, he righted himself on the ground and stood. The water was at waist level as he emerged, weapon forward. One of the intruders spotted him and they exchanged fire. Both missed and Cunard began to walk towards shore, slowed by the heaviness of his wet clothes and the friction of pushing through water. He let off round after round to give himself cover. One of his rounds hit the mark and the intruder threw his shoulder back reflexively. Another shooter ran towards his colleague, firing in Cunard's direction. He swung round to face the gunmen side-on. It created a smaller target but also meant it was more difficult to move quickly. A bullet hit and he fell backwards, dropping his gun. He was in no more than three feet of water. He swept both hands around feeling for his weapon. The shooter seemed to ignore him, missing the opportunity to go for the kill shot while helping his colleague instead. They both moved towards the tower. Despite his relief, this puzzled Cunard. Why would they take an injured combatant towards action? All that would do is put everyone else in danger.

Just as Cunard found his gun and stood up, he was surrounded by a light from above. This was accompanied by the unmistakable buzzing sound of a copter. The searchlight moved from him and caught the injured intruder and his helper in its glare. As they both looked up, they were strafed by rapid fire. More than was necessary. They fell to the ground, but the attack continued, cutting them to pieces. A second light swept past as another copter arrived. The two remaining combatants fled in different directions, each followed by a copter, chased down like wild boar in a night hunt. One crumpled in a blaze of bullets followed by the second as the copters reached them.

Cunard pulled himself out the water and ran back down to the jetty, waving at the Marines as they headed for shore. One of them jumped onto the jetty as the boat came alongside.

"Man down. Can you transfer him to the port? We need to get him to cross."

The Marine nodded. "The copters can get them there in twenty minutes, max."

"How many of your men?"

"Two voided, two need to cross as soon as possible if we're going to save them."

The pursuit copters banked and came into land, setting down within a few feet of each other. Paramedics came running towards the jetty and the injured.

A suction unit was applied to Rosen's wound to remove the blood. Quick-setting medi-foam was pumped into the cavity to stem the bleeding.

He was then wrapped in a padded silver blanket before being placed on the stretcher.

"Will he make it?"

The medic looked up at Cunard. She said, "Long enough to cross. We are inducing therapeutic hypothermia. That will prevent organ failure for just enough time to get out of wonderland."

He felt the easing of a tension that he had not previously been aware of, the adrenalin settling back down. "Thank you."

The medic replied. "Thank you. You saved a few of our people. Who says all company men are corrupt? Now let's have a quick look at you."

"I'll survive."

"I'm sure you will, but still." The medic cut the sleeve of Cunard's shirt to treat his shoulder. "It passed through. That makes things easier." She applied the medi-foam and then gave him a local anesthetic.

"Why are you here?" he asked. "Did the company send you?"

The medic sneered at his question. "I fight for my comrades and for Old Glory in that order. I didn't sign up with *Jack* Glory. Other than that, all I can tell you is my name, rank, and serial number."

They stretchered Rosen off the jetty towards the copters. "Come with us. There is enough space. We can get that wound properly seen to."

"Thanks, but I've got somewhere to be."

He spoke to the station chief as he made his way back to the Met Cloisters and his car. The chief listened as he gave a full rundown of events.

"Good work, now either go to the port to get seen by a doctor or go home. We've got this covered. I think the events of the last hour prove that."

"I'm not sure what it proves, chief. Why are the Marines here and insisting they don't take orders from the company?"

"I'm sure it comes as no surprise that you and I are not part of the inner circle."

"I'm finished. I'm going to disappear for a few days."

"Take as much time as you like."

*

Patrick and Emma walked into the reception venue together, dressed as if they were attending a cocktail party. The others were already there. It was a small, select group. Only those that they could trust and just enough of them to engineer a credible stock market run.

One of their colleagues approached them. "I can't believe this is actually happening."

"It's happening." Emma looked around the room. Slender had brought his lieutenants with him. Everyone would see what happens when he was disrespected.

She felt a hot flush wash over her and Emma wished she were not there with Patrick. He had to be controlled though. The short position was his. She would make sure he stayed on track until it was over. After that, who knows. Emma was running the numbers on how she could stay beyond her end date.

There was nothing outside that was as good as this. The opportunities for those with a strong stomach were almost unlimited. She looked at Slender moving slowly and deliberately between the small groups in attendance. He was the king of his own world. That was what she wanted. She could have it. Unlike Slender, she always had an escape hatch ready. She could use her safe word in an emergency, leap out of this world and come back again. With a willingness to do anything and the advantage of the safe word, she could be stronger than anyone here, including him.

*

Sitting in the dark in his car, Cunard took in the silence, closed his eyes, and played back the assault. One boat causing a diversion for a small group of attackers. It did not make sense. They never had a chance. Was it little more than a gesture? Never really intended to cause damage. Then there were the Marines acting as support. That did not square either. There was a bigger picture he was missing. No longer in the loop, he was unable to piece it all together. Why did he even care? He could walk away and sit on a beach until the end of this tour of duty. And yet he did care. Very few people spent the length of time he had in Alterum if they had commitments back home. And there was the problem. His commitment had been to the company and that was now ending along with his tour. The attackers were willing to die to make a point and he respected that, even though he could not let them succeed.

There is no line, Eva had answered when he asked her which side she was on. Where was his line?

Another memory of his conversation at the Grove intruded. *Don't assume it's always Patrians that are at risk.*

It was a suicide mission. They sacrificed themselves to make a point. No, that was too simple. But the Marines? Was that the point?

"Call Eva." The line connected and her face floated in front of him.

"Hi, lover. There was really no need to get all dressed up just to call me."

Cunard twisted his hand in the air and the image being projected of him displayed. It was not a pretty sight. Blood splatters and dirt covered his face below hair flattened by water. His shirt was ripped and soiled. He flipped back to see Eva, still smiling.

"Two things," he held his fingers as if to remind himself. "One. There is no line. Two. Don't assume it's always Patrians that are at risk."

She raised an eyebrow but said nothing.

"A conversation we had at the Grove. Do you remember?"

"I do."

"So, I'm not the smartest person in the world, but I'm not stupid."

Eva nodded. "Agreed. You are definitely not stupid."

"I just didn't have all the facts. I still don't. So, that makes it a little harder to work out what's happening."

"Why do you care?"

"We have just repelled a suicide mission against Inwood Tower. It was put down by Marines."

"And your conclusion is?"

"There is no line."

"Right. You said."

"No absolute line between Patria and Alterum. But lines within each side. Alliances that cross over."

"That's an interesting theory. Thank you for sharing."

"So, here is what I am thinking. The attack was minor. Never going to succeed. But it was real. Shocking enough if it's spun the right way. And guess what? Everyone was saved by the Marines. The company wasn't up to the job. It required the government to protect its citizens."

"The cavalry came to the rescue?"

"Exactly, it's almost as it was planned."

Eva betrayed a grin. "That would mean that Patrian governments were liaising with Alterrans. Inconceivable."

"Not with the right back-channels in place. This place is too big to fail and too important for governments to ignore. They need control, but that requires a trigger event."

"And what would the WA get out of this arrangement, apart from a few dead colleagues?"

Cunard thought this over. "I don't know, but you do, don't you?"

"Do I?"

"God knows, the government isn't going to be your friend once they get control, but perhaps you have agreed to limited rights as a first step. Tell me."

"You imagine I am more important than I really am. I don't think the governments of Patria would be any better than Jack Glory, and I don't think the attack you described would be a big enough trigger. You should go home and get some sleep."

"I seem to be getting that advice from a lot of people tonight."

"Well, take it. Here's one more piece of advice, lover. If you don't have the full picture, how will you know you're doing the right thing? Go home and let things play out."

Cunard nodded.

"I need to go. Sleep well." Eva disconnected.

"Replay." Eva appeared in front of him again as he watched the conversation, this time as an observer. He slowed down the call and paused, zooming in on her immediate surroundings. She was not at home, and she was not at the club. He reached the end and told his Handi to play it again.

Her immediate surroundings were blurred, but indistinct figures could be seen moving around her as she spoke. He called the station chief and asked if Eva was at Inwood. She was not there, and he was told, yet again, to go home. He replayed the call a third time. There was a wall of darkness behind her. Wherever she was standing, there was nothing solid in the background. She could be outside, but the ambient noise did not sound right for that. The chief could be lying, but it was unlikely. It was all there. Everything he needed to figure it out, but it was hazy.

He stopped the replay. Getting out of the car and breathing in the night air he took another pass at it. *Go home and let it play out,* she had said. The attack on Inwood was not a big enough event. If the earlier attack was a diversion, why attack Inwood again? Everyone would be on heightened alert. It had to be something happening elsewhere. There were no other official functions that night but … Chukaisha Tower and the port were the other two symbols of Patria. He had seen the security at the port earlier that evening. When all other possibilities had been ruled out …

Cunard rubbed his hands through his hair and got back in the car. Eva was right. He did not know what the right thing was to do, but he had been here too long to sit it out. "Auto-pilot. Chukaisha Tower."

*

Eva mingled amongst the guests, carrying a tray of champagne, topping them up and collecting the empties. She wondered briefly if any of the Patrians would recognize her without the masking tech. One or two of them perhaps, but to most of them she would be just another faceless Alterran. Slender? He would. He had visited the club and he was, no doubt, aware she was somehow connected to the WA. It had been a mistake to dismiss him and The Manor. She was losing her touch. It did not matter. It would be over soon and that was a good thing. It was time for a new generation to take control. New thinking and new methods were required. She had hung on too long. This one last act would be a fitting way to leave her life behind.

The sound of a glass being tapped interrupted her musings. Emma was standing at the front of the room with Slender. She spoke first.

"Thank you everybody for coming here tonight. What we are about to witness is a once in a lifetime opportunity. Enjoy the show, but once it is done, we all head straight upstairs to the trading floor. I will begin the sell-off. You will wait for my command, then join in. We go slow at first, then double the trades, run them for a few minutes and when the price drops enough, we accelerate. On my command. Nothing happens without my confirmation. This needs to look natural. If we pull it off, your bonuses will look like small change. If we get it wrong? We go down and we all go down together. So, enjoy yourself, but don't get drunk. We need to stay focused."

"Over to you, Slender." She tipped her glass in his direction.

*

Cunard's car came to a halt in front of the Tower. He leaned forward and glanced upwards. Something was happening in the reception venue that spanned two floors on the lower half of the building. The rest of the tower was in darkness, but lights illuminated the function suite. He stepped out the vehicle and looked towards Inwood. The council block opposite was mostly invisible except for some individual apartments where the cladding had been damaged.

Inwood Tower was visible in the distance. Spotlights swept across its façade and created beams of light that reached into the sky as they slid off the edges of the building before circling back.

He took off his shirt and wiped his face and arms. The undershirt was stained but it was an improvement. He took his shoulder holster from the car, flicked the safety catch on his gun and clipped it into place. He then walked slowly towards the entrance giving security time to evaluate the threat. He did not want to force them to act quickly based on how he looked. He flung his ID into the air and pushed it towards the building. Two guards mumbled to each other, and one came out to meet Cunard as the other maintained her position just inside the door.

"Can I help you, agent?"

"You tell me. I need to get up to the reception floor. Can you help me do that?"

"It's a private function."

"So is the opening of Inwood Tower. We need to check out any unusual activity within the line of sight. You understand, don't you?"

The guard's eyes looked sideways as he listened to someone in private mode. He looked back and nodded. "Of course. Please make your way inside."

Cunard took a step forward. The guard held his position. He took another step, maintaining his normal pace. The guard was completely still, only his eyes tracking as he followed the agent's movement. He was letting Cunard get in front of him. Ahead of him, the guard inside the building was slowly moving her right hand to the left, keeping it at waist height. It was meant to be subtle, but it was not. She was getting ready to pull her weapon on him. As soon as he had one guard behind him and one in front they would strike. They were guaranteed to take him down if he let it happen.

He had to take his gun from its holster, release the safety, and hit dispersed combatants within the next two seconds if he was going to survive. He had never been that good. Cunard smiled to himself and then laughed.

"Something funny?"

Cunard stopped and turned to the guard. "This," he brought his hand up to his chest. "I'm walking into a reception looking like this."

"So, are you going up or not?"

"I mean, what will they think?" He pinched his undershirt between his thumb and forefinger, pulled it forward and let it go. "Just an undershirt, no collar." He pointed at his gun. "And a weapon fully on display." His hand was now inches from it.

"Are you going up?" The guard shifted weight from one foot to another.

"Yeah, I'm still going up. It's just …"

The guard was staring intensely at him now. There was an almost imperceptible shake of the head and his eyes darted towards his colleague before coming back to the agent.

That was all the time he needed. Cunard made his move, retrieving his gun while simultaneously dropping to one knee. Sudden unexpected movements were always disorientating to an opponent, and he could see the guard's eyes widening and his mouth opening as he realized what was about to happen. Cunard hit him in the shoulder and fired a second round to make sure.

Pushing himself back up into a standing posture he grabbed the guard and placed his body between Cunard and the building. Leaning in, he whispered as he pressed the muzzle against the guard's neck. "You are lucky. You are too heavy for me to carry as a dead weight, and there were no other shields available, so I didn't kill you. Now let's hope your colleague has as much value for you as I do. Walk." Cunard reached into the guard's jacket and retrieved his weapon. Two guns were always better than one.

"You can go up," she said, as they approached the door.

He read the signs. She spoke to her colleague with a look, something in her gaze and a nod that was either a question or a statement. *Are you okay*? Or *You will be okay*. Whatever she was saying, she wanted him to be safe.

"Just let us in the elevator and no one else gets hurt."

"He needs help."

"He needs to come with me. You understand, don't you? I wouldn't want to be ambushed. Just send us up and don't contact anyone. I will send him right back down if you behave. Have we got a deal?"

When the elevator doors closed, Cunard directed the guard to sit in the corner with his back to the external wall, the city behind him as a backdrop. "I really didn't want to do that, but you were going to kill me so ..." He looked at the weapon he had retrieved. "A machine gun would have been nice."

The guard said nothing, shutting his eyes and clutching his shoulder as if that would somehow help the pain.

Cunard noticed the small tell-tale tattoo of an elaborate letter 'M' between his thumb and index finger. He wondered briefly if the Manor was just another division of the WA. An upside-down 'W'. There was so much that he did not understand. Layers within layers making it hard to follow, hard to control.

*

Slender called the team on his Handi. "Are you ready to go?"

"Yes, boss. We're on the fourth floor. Say the word."

"Do it." Slender turned and looked out across the divide between the two towers. It didn't take long before he saw it. The flickering of lights. A few panels closing down to reveal the fire taking hold in that floor's apartments. He turned back towards his crew. "This is what happens when we are disrespected. The Manor has earned its place and we will not give it up. If the WA think they can tell us what to do, then this is our reply."

His lieutenants cheered and raised their fists. Emma and her colleagues crowded together at the window and stared down, captivated at the sight of the emerging disaster.

*

A flash of light in the distance interrupted his thoughts. A fire had started on a lower floor of Wolseley Tower. A small cluster of windows became visible as the orange and white flames burned inside. The cladding flickered and the tower came fully into view as the system short-circuited. The fire burst out through the windows and the flames licked upward. A thick pall of smoke rose above the fire and obscured the floors above.

Cunard said aloud, "Jesus, what have they done?"

The guard twisted round and looked at the growing flames. He smiled through the pain.

Cunard stepped towards him and pressed the muzzle of his gun against the guard's forehead. "What have you done?"

"Are you blind?"

"Why?"

The guard said nothing. Cunard felt a rage in the pit of his stomach. He repeated the question. "Why?"

"Respect."

Anger swept over him. His finger shook as he tried to slow his breathing and calm himself down. He took a step back. The guard visibly relaxed. Cunard fired two rounds.

The fire was spreading rapidly. It flowed upwards like a stream on the outside of the building, windows becoming illuminated as each floor burned.

*

Eva watched the crowd at the window. Naked self-interest and a lack of compassion were not exclusive to Patrians or Alterrans. She had often carried out acts of resistance with little regard for the impact on those affected. She hoped with something less than complete certainty that it had been for the greater good. Time would tell and she would not be here to confirm it.

If her timing was anything less than perfect, the Patrians would leap. Eva spoke softly. "The fire must accelerate."

"Got that," a voice replied in her ear.

She moved to the rear of the venue and opened a service door as the Manor and their new friends still stood engrossed in the scene unfolding before them. Hooded figures pushed past Eva, guns forward and began spraying the crowd.

Emma heard a grunt and felt someone fall into her as they collapsed to the floor. Turning she saw the shooters. She took a breath and prepared to shout her safe word. Before she could make a sound, a gel bullet hit her square in the forehead. The wet blue dye stung a little but other than that was harmless. She frowned as she tried to make sense of what was happening. That was when she felt the wave of fogginess hit. It was a tranquilizer. She had to say her safe word, but what was it? The word was somewhere inside her, but Emma could not quite find it. Her vision narrowed to a tunnel, and she fell to the floor.

*

The elevator came to a stop, but Cunard's attention was still directed outwards. He was defeated, no longer interested in protecting himself from any threats that were waiting. How could they do this to their own? It was a world he wanted no part of.

He turned slowly towards the door, gun pointing downwards. It did not open, but through the glass he could see Eva standing on the other side.

She called, so he could hear, "So, you didn't go home."

"Why? Why would you kill your own people to make a point?"

She ignored his question. "You've been a good friend. You helped me when you didn't need to. I will never forget that."

"Open the door."

Eva turned and walked away. Cunard took in the scene beyond for the first time. There were perhaps twenty people, strapped to chairs. Half of them with bulging cheeks and taped mouths. They were coming to, eyes half open, re-orientating themselves to their situation.

They were arranged in two lines facing each other. Those who did not have their mouths taped were positioned with their backs to the window, Wolseley Tower in the background. They were shouting and screaming at Eva. Only one sat quietly with an air of calm. It was Slender. Those that were gagged were the Patrians, unable to speak. Unable to utter their safe words. Helpless to whatever was planned for them.

Eva raised her hands. "Quiet please." It had no effect. She nodded and someone stepped forwards with a large can of liquid that sloshed as he moved towards her.

The figure carrying the can was dressed in black and masked, not unlike the assailants from earlier in the night at Inwood. He unscrewed the top of the container and poured it over the Alterrans. The liquid glinted as the light caught it.

Eva took out a cigarette and lit it. She inhaled and narrowed her eyes as she savored both the taste and the feeling. "Quiet please."

This time they fell silent, staring intently as she turned the cigarette towards her and blew on it, watching the tip glow as it was fed by her breath.

"Ladies and gentlemen. You have come here to watch Alterrans burn, and you also expected to make a profit from the experience." She laughed. "Why do the rich expect to be entertained and paid at the same time? How wonderful it must be to be you." She looked to the side and nodded to a figure in the shadows.

Behind her the fire in Wolseley Tower was extinguished instantly. The flames and the smoke disappeared. The tower turned into a ticker-tape style display. 'NOW YOU SEE ME' circled the building.

"Wolseley Tower is not burning to the ground. The stock market is not going to crash. Your attempted shorting of the NYLON index will be expensive for you and your employers.

"Ladies and gentlemen, let me make it clear. You will not be making a profit tonight. Tonight, you will have to pay for your entertainment like the rest of us. Fear not though, you will be entertained. You came here tonight to watch Alterrans burn and that is what you will see." She paused and took a draw on her cigarette.

Slender smiled at her.

She acknowledged him. "Nothing to say for yourself?"

"You expect me to beg for my life, hey? Others wanted this done too."

"Your friend in the council will pay. Your friend in the housing association already has. We will all pay, including me." Eva flicked her cigarette towards Slender and his eyes widened as he braced himself to meet his fate.

The Patrians struggled against their restraints, some closing their eyes to avoid the scene of writhing bodies burning and melting. Slender stayed silent through it all, stayed a leader through it all, but he was the only one. The screams continued until the heat destroyed their throats and mouths and lungs. There were loud cracks of burning fat as the figures slumped one-by-one into formless lumps of smoking carbon.

Cunard banged on the door of the elevator, but he was ignored. He stood back and fired multiple rounds into the glass. It did not shatter. Small spiders webs of white surrounded each impact point, but the door remained intact. He could not shoot his way out. All he could do was watch the unfolding horror.

"It smells terrible, doesn't it?" Eva pulled out another cigarette and lit up. She exhaled some smoke and breathed it back in through her nose. "That's better. Did their pain seem real to you? Does their burning flesh seem real to you? I can only speak for myself, but it seemed real to me. Could it be that human or not, Alterrans feel pain? Human or not, Alterrans are real?

"You Patrians can destroy us all. Good for you. You hold the power of life and death over us. That will never change. If you want to walk safely amongst us, however, do not treat us as playthings in our own world. You have a choice. Treat us as equals or close it down. Treat us all with respect or kill us all. That is your choice to make, but whatever the decision is, make the choice.

"I'm sure you've all seen the slogan 'What happens in Alterum stays in Alterum.' You've been told by Jack Glory that you can't take video or still photos out when you leave. You are watching this, so clearly that it is not true. This video was embedded in Chain. This method of transfer has always been possible. Today I am releasing my full archive of abusive practices conducted by the company and by some, not all, individual Patrians.

"Those who have caused pain, should experience pain. Fire burns, but the greatest pain of all is unending loneliness. In designing this place, the company also created a purgatory that exists between our worlds. A place where you can be trapped, alone in the dark for an eternity that will destroy your mind and your soul. The company didn't tell you about that either, did it? They have lied to Alterum and to Patria, to all you 'Real Worlders'. They have put you at risk by creating enemies who do not need to exist. We demand justice and when it is not given, we will take it ourselves. You have seen what these people were planning. They were going to burn a building to the ground for profit. Their profit would have been someone's loss. Perhaps it would have been your pension fund, or your nest egg, but when stocks collapse, and someone loses money, it isn't them." Eva jabbed her cigarette at the Patrians who squirmed in their chairs.

"Prepare them." The masked figure stepped forward and doused the Patrians in fuel. They shook their heads wildly and blinked at the stinging sensation in their eyes, trying to scream, but only succeeding in creating a whispered chorus of sobs.

"In this world we share, we feel the same pain. We feel the same pleasure, we only ask that you exercise the same compassion. The choice is yours. The consequences are yours.

"Safe words will not save those who oppress us. They have had their entertainment and now they will pay the price."

Eva nodded and one of the figures in the shadows tossed a lighter at the group of Patrians.

Cunard stared in morbid fascination as the flames engulfed their latest victims. *The pain is the same*, he thought. *The void though*. The void made him wince at the unfolding scene, knowing what endless torment was waiting for them.

Eva nodded another pre-arranged order and one of the hooded figures stepped forward with a can of fuel. She stretched her arms outwards making a cross. She whispered something and was then doused as the others had been.

She then brought her arms in front of her, craned her neck forward, took one last inhalation of smoke and dropped the cigarette at her feet.

Cunard found himself shouting as he again banged on the door. Shouting for Eva to stop. It was an involuntary reaction that came from deep inside. The others did not matter to him, he realized, but Eva did. It could not end this way. He would not let it.

She turned to him and raised a hand in farewell. Eva stood stoically motionless for what seemed like an age but was no more than a few seconds. She seemed to shout something, tried to tell him something. Then, with a sense of inevitability he watched her crumple to the floor like the collapsing of kindle when a fire takes hold and consumes its energy.

The elevator moved. As it dropped silently, plunging towards the ground in its controlled fall, Cunard noticed the scene above was being broadcast on the side of Wolseley Tower. A crowd had gathered outside to watch.

When the elevator reached the ground floor, he was met by police swarming the building. The guard from earlier was face down on the floor in cuffs. In normal circumstances he would flash his badge, brushing away all questions. Not tonight. Not after what had been broadcast, first to Alterum, and then presumably to Patria.

He was surprised to find the SWAT team was not in the slightest interested in him. He might as well have been invisible. He picked a way through them and made his way out of the building. The wind that always swirled around the base of tall buildings hit him. He breathed deeply to fight the nausea that was threatening to take control. As he walked to the car he spoke into the silence. "Bella? Bella, are you there?"

There was no reply.

PART THREE – SEEDS
Chapter 17

LUCID SYNTHETIC DREAMING ... The implementation of Lucid Synthetic Dreaming must allow for a three-layer consensus model if it is to overcome the limitations of existing virtual reality technology.

1 – Physical Layer – There must exist a layer of fixed behavior that applies to all nodes within the system. This equates to the 'physical' layer of reality in the real world and is unchanging except under extreme circumstances. This is a maximum consensus layer.

2 – Intersubjective Layer – This layer is not fixed but is stable and slow moving in most circumstances. This is the shared experience of conscious nodes within the system. This layer is consensus-based but does not require the agreement of all nodes. There will be multiple competing intersubjectives and the dominant instance will be formed from a plurality consensus. This equates to all socially defined meaning in the real world. The dominant intersubjective will tend to reproduce itself by imposing its version of reality through intersubjective power structures.

3 – Personal Layer – This layer is the most fluid and exists at the level of the individual node. Each node will be created with default attributes and impulses across several dimensions. These settings will form a normal distribution curve across all nodes. This equates to personality and physical traits in the real world. In what might seem like a paradox it will be the personal layer that will give rise to the intersubjective. Once established, however, the intersubjective will become a dominant influence on the personal. Individuals that resist the intersubjective will become marginalized through a natural process of increased social friction.

Alterum White Paper

Cunard walked past his car to the boundary fence with Wolseley. "Are you here?" There was no answer. "Bella, speak to me." The silence continued.

As he approached the fence a group of young boys ran to the edge. They were shouting at him. "Now you see me. Now you see me."

He looked up the side of the tower. The events from a few minutes ago were being replayed in a loop. *This fire has only just started,* he thought.

A stone hit his forehead just above his right eye. The kids were cheering at the direct hit. More stones came in his direction. Cunard turned and walked as fast as he could without running. Why he felt the urge to keep his dignity under fire puzzled him, but he refused to run. *It will just encourage them. Bullshit. You still need to show the superiority of Patrians.*

"Now you see me. Now you see me." The chants were getting louder. Out of reach from the hand-thrown missiles he turned around. The kids had been joined at the fence by a larger crowd. It looked as if it was most of the tower's residents.

Inside the car his Handi buzzed, and Cunard accept the call—except it wasn't a call. It was a general broadcast delivered by a calm but serious-looking woman with the company flag in the bottom left hand of the screen. A ticker-tape message scrolled from the logo across the screen. "Shelter in Place." The woman spoke. "Jack Glory has issued a Level 5 alert to all Patrians currently visiting Alterum. You are advised to shelter in place. If you are in public, please make your way to a private location. There is at this stage no need to carry out an emergency leap using your safe word, but you are strongly advised to seek refuge in a secure location and wait for further instructions. If you are in immediate danger, please leap. If you are not in immediate danger the usual terms will apply and no refunds will be issued. The company asks you to stay calm but vigilant."

Cunard hung up and instructed the car to take him to the port. He tried contacting the station chief, but there was no reply. No one wanted to speak to him tonight. He flicked on the radio to find out what was being reported locally on the crank shows.

Thanks for tuning in. There's a lot to talk about tonight. This is Annie Avril, the Nylon City Nightingale. They were going to burn an entire tower to the ground for their entertainment. That is the true nature of Patrians. For years I've been accused of being mad. A conspiracy theorist. Do you really think this is the first atrocity? This is the first one you've found out about, but it's not the only one.

A few years ago, a serial killer, the Zoo Stalker, haunted this town. He would select his victims in Nylon Zoo nightclub. Did you ever wonder why those killings just stopped? He was a Patrian billionaire. He was allowed to leave without being charged once he was caught. That man's name was Andrew Morgan. He abused and killed Alterrans in one of the VIP suites of the very club where he picked them up. You don't believe me? You think it's another of my crazy conspiracy theories? Watch the feeds when Eva's material is dropped. That's all I ask of you. She had proof. Documents, audio recordings, everything. The whole façade is about to collapse.

Wake up, Nylon City. Wake up, Alterum. We exist in a Patrian simulation. That is why they don't value our lives. That's why Morgan was allowed to walk away.

Cunard switched off the radio. Did Eva have proof of what Morgan had done? The sound of sirens was louder than was usual at this time of night. He opened a window. There were alarms going off in all directions. He thought he could smell burning, but perhaps that was from earlier. It could be his imagination. The city would not sleep though. That much Cunard was sure of. Lights were on in every street he passed. News of what had happened was rippling out, waking the city. Literally waking it. This was one of those events that everyone would remember how they found out. They would remember who they were with.

Clive and the other directors had let things escalate. Cunard had warned them. Others had warned them. They could not see beyond the way things had always been. He tried the station chief again. This time there was a connection.

The chief was in a copter with other agents behind him. "Where are you, Cunard? Are you safe?"

"Heading for the port now. What's the situation at Inwood?"

"We have just completed a controlled evac following the ceremony. There was nothing here after the ground and river assault."

"It was a decoy."

The chief winced. "Yeah. We get that, Cunard. Everyone gets that."

"What about Clive?"

"The director used a safe word to leap after all the VIPs had left. Turns out directors do have safe words when they visit us. Who knew?"

"There's a lot of noise on the street, chief. I suggest you order all agents back to Red Hook to protect the port."

"We've got it covered. Just get yourself back and we will do a full debrief when you arrive." There was a flash behind the chief, and he lurched forward, stopped by his seatbelt. "Shit. Where did that—" The connection cut out. Cunard tried to reconnect without success.

After crossing the city and entering Battery Tunnel he hit a roadblock. He was several cars back from the barrier and could not see who was manning it. The car pulled up and he reached for his gun. He stepped out into the tunnel to see a soldier walking towards him. It was a Marine.

"Get back in your vehicle, sir." The Marine pointed his rifle at him. Cunard flashed his badge. "You are AIP. Understood, sir, but get back in your car." The Marine took up a shooting stance.

When his car approached the barrier, Cunard showed his ID again. This time it made a difference, and he was waved through. Once he was out of the tunnel, he became aware of copters dominating the skyline, spotlights sweeping the approaches to the terminal. They would have heat cameras operating too. The spotlights were a message, a deterrent. At the entrance to the parking lot temporary barriers were in place and floodlights glared outwards. The boom gate was controlled by a group of three Marines with one AIP agent assisting. It was the same situation in the terminal building and the boarding bridge. Multiple checks, all led by soldiers, not company men.

Once onboard the *Lucitania,* Cunard was escorted by an armed guard to the briefing room where he had begun the night. Agents were sitting around the table. The man sitting closest to the door was perfectly coiffed. Not a hair out of place. He acknowledged Cunard.

"You look like you've been in the wars. Have a seat." He pushed on the arms of the chair to stand up.

Cunard said, "I'm fine." He surveyed the room. They were all the same. Uniform looks, the problem with the company was staring him in the face. It had become complacent and entitled. No longer capable of understanding the world it attempted to control. He guessed that most of them had been at Inwood as protection for VIPs. They were meant to look smart, but it was more than that. It was the way they carried themselves.

The station chief entered followed by a military officer. He looked rattled, but he was in one piece. Cunard made eye contact and mouthed a question. *Are you okay?* The chief tensed and nodded. When he got to the head of the room, he banged his fist on the table.

"Listen up."

The soldier at his side raised his hand to stop the chief continuing. "I'll take it from here." He scanned the agents, stopping only briefly at Cunard before bringing his attention back to the wider group. "I am Brigadier General Colin Campbell of the US Marine Corps. As a result of the security failings of the company, we are assuming command of Alterum. The AIP has no standing here other than as an adjunct support under the direction of my command.

"Several of our citizens were voided tonight. If the Marines had not been here to intervene, that number would have been much higher. Two Marines were voided in the course of their duty. No AIP were voided." He paused for effect. "I repeat, two Marines were voided tonight, not a single AIP or company officer was. Your directors left for home at the first sign of trouble. That is the difference between the armed services and private enterprise. We stay the course. Questions?"

The agent who had offered Cunard a seat raised his hand. "If you are in charge, do we cross back to Patria?"

"Anyone that wants to can leave. In fact, you will leave right now. Everyone else, stay where you are."

"I wasn't saying that I want to, I was just—"

"Go. Now."

The agent nervously stood and was escorted out by a soldier.

The general waited for the door to close before continuing. The room was silent.

"The government has seized the company assets and taken over day-to-day control and management. All directors have been fired. You do not have a job if you leave now. You will not receive a bonus or back pay. There may be criminal charges. There will no doubt be civil actions. As agents of the company, you can be held jointly and individually liable alongside the company directors. I am a Marine, not a lawyer. I have, however, been instructed to offer immunity for those that choose to stay until we no longer need you.

"We are going to root out the leaders of this mutiny and destroy them. The WA will no longer exist when we have finished. It will be swift and overwhelming. We will restore the safety and confidence of our citizens to live and trade here. You know this place better than us. You can help identify those we need to punish. Those we need to destroy. I'll leave the station chief to fill in the details."

On the way out of the room, the general tapped Cunard on the shoulder and indicated for him to follow him. When they were alone in the corridor, he said, "I've seen your reports, heard about your actions tonight."

"Am I an honorary member of the cavalry?"

The general did not smile. "The others in there, they are of limited use. You are right in the middle of all this. You are useful and we are going to use you. You will get to cross when I decide, not before. If you do not cooperate you may be stuck here for a long time. If you see that as a reward, you will be voided."

Cunard raised his eyebrows.

The general said, "Sorry if you were expecting a motivational speech. By the way, we're not the cavalry, we are the Marines."

"At least you're honest."

"Who told you that? They only thing you need to understand about me is that I am dangerous, and I am in charge."

"Okay. What do you want from me?"

"By the end of tonight, we will have taken control of Nylon City. You will be a liaison officer."

Cunard frowned at the term.

"Come with me."

The corridors of the *Lucitania* seemed to take on the feel of an infinite mirror effect as he followed the general. The only sound was the clicking of his boots on the floor. A ticking clock counting down the time until they reached their destination.

The two mayors were at a table in the staff dining room. It was a minimalist cafeteria with hard seats and long benches. The room contrasted with their evening wear from the Inwood reception. There was no entourage, just a couple of guards. The general sat down and indicated for Cunard to do the same.

"In your opinion, are either of these people members of the WA?"

The mayors silently shook their heads. The general ignored them and continued to focus on Cunard, waiting for a response.

Cunard said, "They will have people on their staff that are, but no, not them."

"Are you sure?"

"Not one hundred percent. My gut says no."

The officer sat silently for a second, then pulled out a coin from his pocket. He looked at the London Mayor in his cocktail suit and Union Jack bow tie. "Heads or tails?" The mayor sat frozen, saying nothing. He switched his attention to the New York Mayor. "Heads or tails?"

She answered him. "Heads."

The coin flipped and time slowed. Cunard sensed what was coming. No one could prevent what was about to happen. It landed on the table and spun before coming to a stop, heads up.

"Good for you." He looked at one of the guards then gave a quick gaze in the direction of the London Mayor. The guard pushed his gun into the back of his head. The mayor braced as if he were about to receive a punch to the stomach. The trigger was pulled, and blood sprayed forward as the body fell forward onto the table.

The general looked at the woman. She was staring straight ahead, a small but visible shake to her head as she tried to ignore the crumpled body next to her. "Another victim of the WA. It's not just Patrians they are killing. They have turned on local leadership as well. The surviving mayor has asked the governments of Patria for urgent assistance to restore order."

She nodded.

"Nylon City has been declared a protectorate of Patria. US and British Zones have been established with a single, rotating, command structure. The civilian governance will operate similarly with one alternating mayor to avoid jurisdiction issues in law enforcement. We will, of course, stand down and withdraw as soon as the mayor asks us to."

She nodded again.

"I'm pleased that was so straightforward. I have a statement prepared for you and we shall have a press conference in the next hour. There is a copter waiting to take you to City Hall." The general stood up, leaned over the table, and rubbed his hand on the bloody surface. He then flicked it in the mayor's direction spraying her with blood and brain matter. She blinked but remained silent. "That looks better. The direction of the gunshot wasn't right. No blood on you despite sitting next to him. Sometimes we are too good at our jobs"

Chapter 18

THE SEEDS... The initial terraforming of this reality can be accelerated by the placement of several seed nodes. These nodes will construct the physical layer by use of Generative Predictive Transformation. In essence a seed node will create a physical layer based on what it expects to exist in real-time. A seed that walks over a hill will create what exists over the hill just as it reaches the summit. Once sufficient terraforming has occurred, most seeds will need to be removed to allow the three-layer consensus model to be fully activated.

Alterum White Paper

The sight of Eva burning would stay with him forever. He was the one that poured the fuel over her. He did it slowly, avoiding the lit cigarette. She set off the ignition herself. She knew what it would do. She committed to the act without hesitation. The air was full of smoke and burning flesh. He was wearing a balaclava which filtered against the worst of the smoke, but the smell, that was a different matter. It came in waves, the skin, and the hair first, a sweet yet putrid odor that was so overpowering it was more like a taste. He dry-retched as he backed away past the others. They had burned too, but it was Eva that hit him. After the first wave came an awareness of metal as the twisted but now still bodies of the traders and gang members continued to burn. An awareness of rusted iron invaded his nostrils and he gagged again. The others were already out of the room. One of them held the door for him and grabbed his arm as soon as he was within reach. His colleague pulled him through the door and let it shut behind him.

"We need to go now." She held on to his arm and dragged him towards the emergency stairwell.

Hesh pulled off his face covering and breathed deeply. The others had moved down the stairs away from him, but she was still there pulling him along with her.

"I'm okay. Leave me be." He shrugged his arm out of her grip.

"You're in shock. It's normal. Come on."

"I'm okay. Leave me be." He began moving, taking two steps at a time. She followed behind him, acting as the rear-guard. The swirling thoughts began to ease, giving him a space to think. "What's your name?"

She looked surprised "Why? Are you going to ask me on a date? You know, the first time I killed someone I couldn't sleep for weeks. That's not a bad thing."

"That wasn't the first time."

She fell silent.

When they reached the underground parking floor they caught up with the others. They had stripped off and put on police uniforms.

"Do I get one—"

She interrupted him before he could finish. "You would never pass."

She changed and they left the stairwell. A Metropolitan Police van was waiting for them. At the exit they were stopped. A flashlight swept the vehicle.

"Who's he?" The light was on Hesh.

"Just a building worker. His ID checks out. We found him hiding from the terrorists."

The light moved to the woman. "Sislin. I didn't know you were here."

"Everyone's here tonight, aren't they?"

The officer waved them through.

*

The councilor was woken by a call from the concierge control center and told that Wolseley was on fire. She got dressed and drove to the office. By the time she arrived it was all over, the imaginary fire replaced by confusion. She called Slender but there was no reply. Why hadn't he walked away? She would leave town. Watch from a distance until she understood what was going on. On the short journey home, she passed burned-out shops and walls covered in fresh graffiti. *NOW YOU SEE ME.*

She called ahead to tell her partner to pack a few bags and be ready to leave. She was not quick enough. By the time she arrived, there was a crowd outside her door chanting for her to come out and face them. Parking further down the street she called again. "I'm outside. Can you get out the back way?"

"No. They're in the garden."

A Molotov cocktail was thrown at the wall. It burst and the flames spread across the brickwork, burning brightly and then dying out.

"I'll call the police. Stay inside." She cut the call without waiting for her partner to reply. She was not going to call the police. It was said to reassure. They could not be trusted after the death of the housing manager. There was nothing she could do. They were after her blood.

Someone in the crowd shouted and pointed at an upstairs window. There was the visible outline of a figure. It was indistinct and could have been anyone. The crowd decided it was her. Another bottle was thrown. It exploded on the wall near the window. The figure disappeared, and this seemed to make the crowd angrier. Another bottle was launched at the window and, like the last one, missed its target. Two bottles followed. One of them landed dead center on the window breaking against the cross frame. The fuel ignited and another bottle was thrown. This one smashed through the window and the crowd cheered. The councilor saw an incoming call flashing on her Handi. She thought about it for a second and then rejected it. She started the engine and drove with her lights off until she was out of the street. When there was a safe distance between her and the crowd, she flicked on the headlights and instructed the car to head north out of the city.

*

Hesh was dropped off at a safe house near the tower. Maria was waiting for him. She embraced him. He cried and held her tight. Once the sobbing stopped, she spoke.

"Everything you have done needed to be done. Do you understand?"

He stared at the floor.

"You understand?"

"Yes, Maria."

"It's not over yet. You need to take your place now."

He shook his head. "I can't do it. Who would take me seriously?"

She slapped his face. "You will do it."

Hesh took a deep breath and wiped tears away.

She stroked his face gently. "A simple life would have been good, but it's not what the world had planned for you." She put a hand on his chest. "Something inside of you pushed you this way. Made you stand up and be noticed. If you fight it, it will destroy you. It almost did."

He nodded his understanding.

The East Crew arrived first. They were led by Joe's cousin, still limping from the bullet Hesh had put in him.

The Faces from the west and north arrived not long after. Joe's cousin introduced Hesh and the room went quiet waiting for him to talk. He looked round at them. They were the top of the tree. The Elders referred to anyone in their late teens and they sat above the Links and Youngers and Runners, all the way down to The Pre-Crims, members too young to be charged with a crime. Somehow, he expected The Faces to be older, but when the entry level was kids under the age of ten, it made sense that the Faces would be early twenties. As he took in the reality of the gang structure, he answered his own question. *Who would take him seriously?*

"A few days ago, I killed my best friend. Barret's cousin." Hesh pointed to him, and Barret nodded giving a fist sign in response. "I could have killed him, but I killed his cousin, my friend, because he turned on his own. He turned on me. Barret didn't know me, didn't owe me anything. He would have killed me, but that would have been cool, right?"

"Facts is." Barret clenched his fist again, agreeing with Hesh.

"Facts is, and there's no grudge. But if you turn on your own, no one can trust you. You are a mad dog that needs to be put down. I put him down.

"Tonight, I killed Slender. He wasn't a mad dog. I know he was respected. I had no grudge with him. But he was going to burn my people to the ground. I don't expect any of you here to care about that. You don't owe me or any of my people anything.

"The thing is, the Manor isn't the only player in town. Would any of you cross the river and try to take territory from the Five Points?" He let the silence sit for a second or two. "I hope not. It would be a stupid thing to do. The Manor and the Points would just weaken each other and who would gain? None of you. None of them.

"The WA and the Manor are like two fish that aren't interested in each other's prey. They swim side by side doing their own thing, sometimes passing each other but uninterested. Until Slender decided to change that.

He was warned, but he thought he could ignore them. He's dead. We need to make sure that doesn't happen again."

One of the Faces spoke. "I'm not bowing down to the WA."

"You don't have to. The Patrians will see to that. The WA is under attack. They are too busy hiding and dying. But not for long. We need to take the cream now while we can, but we need to know who to respect and who to fight. When to fight and when to stand back. We need to understand the game. Slender got too full of himself. Didn't respect people he should and now he's gone."

"Why should we follow you?"

"Slender kept the cream for his crew. That ends. Everyone gets their share. East, West, all of you."

Barret pulled himself to his feet and leaned on a cane for support. "Silent took over the East Crew without Slender even knowing it. Tightened the noose until the only people that were still with him were those that burned with him. Silent killed my cuz, but he kept his word to me. I am the Face of the East Crew. I stand with him."

From now on, this would be his street name, the name that would be used. Hesh was now Silent.

"I have nothing else to say. You have come here under a truce. Go in peace. Decide and tell your crew what that decision is."

"How do we let you know?"

"If you tell the Elders, you've told me." He let his words sink in. Hesh could see that it had for most of them. There were one or two that would need to be dealt with, but that just created an opportunity for those below them. That was how it had gone with the East. The ambitious Elders were already in place waiting for the word. "You've seen how I fight for those that are with me." He let the other side of the statement fill the silence.

After they left, Maria joined him. "You did well. Now, we must go. No one can ever know where you are staying at night. This is your life now."

Hesh nodded. Silent was a good name.

Chapter 19

POINT OF SINGULARITY ... Unless prevented, sometime after the physical and intersubjective layers have been established a point of singularity will be reached. If this is allowed to occur the future growth and direction will become uncontrollable by external updates and influences. To counter this danger a small number of seeds will remain in place. These can be used in extreme circumstances to influence all other layers. This form of emergency intervention will require a majority consensus amongst seeds and a plurality consensus of the intersubjective.

Alterum White Paper

They flew high above the city where they would be protected from random gunfire. Cunard was strapped in, next to the mayor. They were all wearing headsets to drown out the noise. He could speak to her, but everyone would hear. She was blank. Switched to survival mode. The mayor did what she was told on the surface but retreated her psyche deep inside away from danger.

Maybe he was projecting but he did not think so. Cunard had experienced it himself, a long time ago, in another world, the real world. Before joining the company, he had been a field liaison office for an investment fund. He had been assigned to a failing state rich in rare earth metals most people had never heard of. Terbium, Promethium, and others that were collectively known as the Lanthanides. All of them heavily used in telecommunications and weaponry. The arms industry was, to all intents and purposes, an offshoot of the electronics industry.

The country had been relatively stable until a change of leadership had led to calls for local ownership. The value of the metals grew tenfold after some basic purification and processing. The industries around this process could provide thousands of well-paid jobs. The drumbeat for nationalization was growing louder and harder to ignore.

This had raised red flags in the financial power centers of New York and London. Nowhere was this truer than in Global Rare Earth and Strategic Metal ETF. GRESMX was an exchange traded fund that invested in the entire rare earth production chain, from mining to specialist components. Anyone could invest in the fund, but the company itself was privately held with obscure ownership.

The ownership was not obscure to Cunard. It was controlled by friends of Five Eyes, an alliance of Anglo-centric intelligence agencies. He had been diverted to the company following a brief but promising career in the military. The set-up was a work of genius. The agencies used retail and institutional investors' money to control strategically significant companies. The public paid for GRESMX to achieve controlling positions on the boards of the listed companies. Through ownership they operated a vertical cartel and ensured a reliable supply to member nations, principally through the US and the UK arms industry.

Any risk to that arrangement threatened the fund performance and, more importantly, control. Locally owned or nationalized processors that were not listed on one of the major stock markets could not be folded into the ETF. That would not be allowed to happen.

The recently deposed opposition held 'freedom rallies'. The police and armed forces stood back as the civil unrest spiraled. Kidnappings by militias rose. Gangs were encouraged to take over neighborhoods that were government strongholds. Everywhere that the chaos began to unfold, Cunard was to be found with his suitcase full of cash to be distributed where required to keep the flames burning.

When he was taken, it was not by the government or one of their supporters. It was by a street gang that he was paying to cause trouble. The leader of the gang was smart. He realized that this suitcase was constantly refilled, and he was only getting a small part of what was available. Cunard was taken, beaten, and forced to speak to camera asking the company to pay his ransom. He did not beg. He read his lines cold and unemotionally, staring straight at the camera. He obeyed the directions of his captors without ever being fully present in the moment. Sometimes they would stop the camera and punch him, annoyed at his demeanor. He would just retreat further into himself. He went somewhere so deep he was not sure if he would ever come back.

The company paid his ransom, which should not have surprised him, but it did. They were worried about him revealing his true role or as sometimes happened, being sold on to another group, perhaps a group of government sympathizers. He was released and quietly removed from the country. New liaison officers continued where Cunard had left off. They paid a rival gang to eliminate the kidnappers. They were not interested in getting the ransom back. They just wanted to make sure everyone understood what happened when you crossed them.

The government crumbled and private security companies aligned with warlords became the de facto rulers in mining regions. Cunard watched from afar as he recovered. He knew it was wrong. He knew that when he was involved, but he now also questioned whether it was worth it.

They pensioned him off and directed him towards the AAAC. Jack Glory was looking for agents with real world experience and he soon found himself in Alterum with a new name. A walk in the park compared to what he had been through, right? That was the theory.

The copter landed in front of the entrance staircase, and they made their way inside the building. The mayor was escorted by two Marines, and Cunard walked behind with Campbell.

"With all due respect, General, I don't see what value I am adding here. If you need an audience for your brutality, I am not your man."

"Your concerns are noted. We can discuss it after the press conference."

*

Journalists had their Handis taken off them as they entered the room. A pool camera was set up, front and center, trained on the podium where the mayor and the general were positioned. Cunard stood to one side and watched the shocked reaction as the media took in the sight of the disheveled mayor. She spoke first.

"Tonight, there was a terrorist attack by the Waking Army on Inwood Tower. The initial assault was thwarted. As the London Mayor and I were leaving there was a second. This was directed specifically at us and, I am afraid to say, was carried out by members of our own security teams. It is with a heavy heart that I have to tell you the mayor did not survive that attack."

There was a barrage of shouted questions, ignored by the mayor as she raised her hands to reclaim the silence.

"If it were not for the presence of Patrian security, I am convinced that I would not have survived either.

"It is clear to me there are extremist forces within the walls of our own house that wish to commit violence against those they do not deem pure enough. This threat has existed in the shadows but has now stepped into the light.

"As a result of the actions, we have no alternative but to rely on our Patrian friends to help restore peace. General Campbell will work alongside me to flush out the traitors in our midst. I have informed the federal government that we now consider ourselves a temporary protectorate of Patria. The government has confirmed that it accepts this interim governance arrangement as the will of the people. I tell you fellow citizens as your representative, this is the will of the people. I will now hand over to General Campbell."

There was silence as the general began to speak. "Thank you, Mayor, for your kind words. Our two great worlds have been friends for many years now. Increasingly we have become more than friends, more than allies. We are partners.

"It gives me no pleasure to take temporary command of Nylon City. We are here only because it was requested. Please be assured that we will not outstay our welcome. Our mission is to help your government take back control from those that would destroy it. To weed out those that would undermine it from within. Once we have achieved that mission, I will be happier than anyone to return home to my own loved ones. We are not here to rule or oppress or exploit. We are here to help.

"In order to make this situation as short-lived as possible, we, in turn, need your help. We need you to call out the members of this so-called Waking Army. You might think they are your friends, your neighbors. They are not your friends. They have brought this great city to the brink of anarchy. I call on you all to put aside false loyalty and help us help you.

"We have established several information channels that you can use to inform on them. You can report a suspicion anonymously if you wish. I understand that some of you may want to do that. For those of you willing to give us your contact details, there will be significant rewards for any lead that results in an arrest.

"Let me make one last point before I close off this press conference. We do not know how deep the enemy is. We do know, however, that they have spread their tentacles into law enforcement and justice. For that reason, we will assume emergency control of the justice system. Dangerous times call for exceptional measures. This is one such occasion. My men and women have been instructed to be balanced but effective. They are well trained and will execute their duty with professionalism. Make no mistake though. If they need to employ summary justice, they will do so without hesitation and without consequence. I ask you all to comply, cooperate, and partner with us to make this action as quick and as painless as possible."

The general looked round and nodded at the mayor's escorts. They walked towards her. One touched her lightly on the elbow and indicated for her to follow. The assembled journalists shouted questions as she left the press center.

Once the press had been ushered out of the room, Cunard and Campbell remained alone. "Where are you taking her?"

"Somewhere safe."

"Do you want to tell me what I'm doing here, following you around like a lap dog?"

"I've read your file. Both here and out there. You understand how this goes."

"I do."

"We have no ground game here. We need someone that can speak to the right people, bring them round to working with us."

"You need a bagman?"

"You know the drill. Contact those that we can use. Pass them on to military handlers."

*

The area around city hall was quiet. Lights were on in the surrounding buildings just as they were throughout the city, but there was no one on the streets. The further Cunard ventured away from the newly designated Green Zone into Manhattan the more obvious the true feelings of the locals were. He took detours around burning barricades, following side streets and alleys to avoid trouble.

When he reached his destination, a quiet residential street, Cunard knew he was deep inside hostile territory. There were no lights on in the apartment blocks. This looked like the only place in the city where people were not awake. He parked the car and got out. A figure emerged from one of the darkened buildings. Cunard raised his hand in greeting. Fischer waved back as he walked towards him.

"*Was fur ein tag, eh bruder?*"

Cunard nodded wearily. "Somehow I get the impression I was the only one that didn't know it was coming."

Fischer shrugged. "But you did really."

"Thanks for agreeing to meet me." He looked up at the buildings. "I guess you weren't taking any chances?"

Fischer laughed. "It's just a quiet neighborhood. They do still exist."

"Sure. I wouldn't trust me either."

"So, what do you want?"

"You've not reported for duty despite the all-hands call. You're not at home. That makes you the enemy. I want to change that. I want to save your life."

"*Ja wirklich?*"

"I have been tasked by the military with recruiting locals. Sometimes the best people you can get are those that are close the enemy."

"You think I am part of the WA. What if you are right? I wouldn't be a particularly good revolutionary if I turned against my comrades now, would I?"

"But you would be alive."

"What do you need?"

"Locals who will inform on and if need be, fight the WA."

"Not me, Cunard. You know that. It was good of you to offer. I appreciate your concern. There's nothing I can do for you and there's nothing you can do for me."

"Eva?"

Fischer stared blankly, waiting for the follow up.

"How high up was she?"

"She is the WA."

"Was."

"Listen to the radio." Fischer reached into his pocket and pulled out a scrap of paper. He passed it to Cunard in a handshake, then turned and walked into the building he had come from. As the door opened, he became no more than a silhouette, hand raised in farewell.

After Cunard left the dark street, back into the illuminated canyons of the city, he switched on the radio.

'... multiple sightings of her across the city. Some have claimed she has spoken to them directly. 'Tell them I have not risen', one witness claimed to have heard her say. 'I have not risen for I did not fall. We are a shadow of the source in this world, and we are still part of source when the shadow fades. I will be with you always. Do not fear death. It is nothing but a return to the source. From there you will join me. You will become part of every shadow. These are the words of Eva.'

Cunard listened with fascination. These were not her words. They were probably things that she believed, but they were not her words. It was not true to her voice. A myth was being born across the airwaves of the city, no doubt recorded on Chain, and transmitted out into Patria, into the real world.

'And knowing that you will be part of every shadow, expect to be treated with the dignity that you would treat others.

And knowing that the shadows who oppress you are from the same source as you, fight them as you would fight to make yourself a better person, for that is what you are doing.

If you suffer for this fight, know that the suffering is short-lived but necessary for source and shadow to be become fully aligned.

This is the journey the shadow world is on. Alterum, Patria, the nameless source of both, which is in truth just another shadow, the demiurge of the demiurge of the source.

Oppression is division. Oppression keeps the illusion of separateness alive. Oppression must be fought, it must never be tolerated, for this is the path to truth. The path to oneness. To have acceptance for oppression is to accept division.

Be strong. Fight the oppressors. Know that you will join me whatever path you take. You will join me in the source.'

Cunard switched off the radio and contacted the station chief. "You been listening to the radio?"

"Should I?"

"We are at the start of nothing less than a religious war."

"Maybe you should tell the general that. I'm about to ship out back home."

"Right. Your choice?"

"There's no role for a station chief if everyone reports to the military."

"Right."

"Don't stay too long, Cunard. This is no longer our world."

"It never was."

Chapter 20

SEEDS AS SHADOWS ... With the increasing sophistication of memory harvesting and impulse behavior mapping, it is now possible to create the 'shadow' personality of a real person within a virtual environment. Choosing a wide variety of seed shadows from the real world will lead to the most life-like world possible in the shortest period. These seeds will be completely independent of their physical source.

Alterum White Paper

Hesh had rarely crossed the river and always had a vague sense of uneasiness when he did. That was before the events of the last few days. Now he had event more reason to be nervous. Every uncontrolled thought told him he was in over his head. Maria assured him that he was not. It did not matter. He was committed. There was no stepping back into the anonymous life he had previously led. She had called him a butterfly. He had passed through the chrysalis stage and could no more become a stranger in the crowd than a butterfly could return to its life as a caterpillar. It was not an analogy that filled him with much confidence, but it was typical of Maria.

The car pulled up next to the entrance of a warehouse.

He could not see it, but he could smell the river. A member of the Five Points opened the door for him. Hesh told his driver and bodyguard to wait outside. The building was in use. Racks full of shrink-wrapped pallets stretched out before him. He followed his guide round the cherry picker and down an aisle until they came to an office. The Disciple was seated behind a desk, waiting for him. It was a name given to him when he was the loyal second-in-command and a name that no one dared change once he had dispatched his predecessor. He was at best a few years older than Hesh. This was something Hesh was becoming used to. Maybe Maria's description was not so wrong after all. Butterflies did not last too long once they became adults. Mayflies, who also passed through metamorphosis, lasted no more than a day.

The Disciple stood up and extended his hand. "You've got heart walking in here alone."

"It's your territory. It would make no difference if I came alone or with an army. You would still out-gun me."

The Disciple looked pleased and sat down, indicating for Hesh to do the same. "True, but Slender never came alone. So?"

"So, nothing changes, and everything changes. The Patrians are no longer pretending to be visitors. They have taken control."

"And?"

"You had friends in the PD you could call on. Where are they now?"

The Disciple nodded. "Rounded up in trucks and taken to the stadium. Few come back out."

"Here's the thing. They were constrained. They couldn't make it too obvious. The Patrians? They don't care. They just want allies. That can be us."

"What do they want with us?"

"Unless they wipe out the entire population, they need some friends. That's why they've reached out. We just need to show them we can be trusted."

"Can we trust them? And who are you? You were nobody three days ago. Now you are sitting here giving me advice."

Hesh tried to appear more confident than he was. "You shouldn't trust them or me. Did you trust Slender or the PDs?"

That got a smile. "Okay."

"That's why some of the Faces of the Manor are in your pocket."

The Disciple whistled. "Not so young up here." He touched his forehead with a finger. "Impressive."

"Did you invite them?"

The Disciple made a sign and spoke to someone through his Handi. "Let them in." He stood and waved for Hesh to follow him out of the office. They walked along one of the branching aisles and then turned into what was an open space, hidden like the center of a maze. A figure was slumped on a chair, strapped down to prevent any significant movement. He had a hood over his head and was guarded by two of the Points' men. Hesh looked at the floor below the chair. Drips of dark blood marked the surface. The sound of heels clicking towards them the only sound.

Cunard turned into the opening, accompanied by Marines and a member of the Points. He stared at Hesh for a second before acknowledging the Disciple.

The leader of the Points pulled out a card and handed it to him. Cunard's face froze as he looked at it. The ten of spades had a photograph of Fischer on it. 'Dead or Alive'.

"This man?"

The Disciple took a step towards the chair and pulled off the hood. Fischer was badly bruised around one eye and blood trailed from his mouth. The light startled him, and he winced before focusing. The Disciple threw the hood to the floor. "You will pay?"

One of the Marines accompanying Cunard spoke. "Our word is our bond. It will be paid in Chain to the agreed wallet."

"Any bonus for bringing him in alive?"

The Marine shook his head. "Dead or alive means just that. Same value either way."

Cunard stared at his old friend. "But he may be useful alive, so thank you."

"Just to be clear, we have already made that judgment when we issue the cards. We do not consider this man of high value for intelligence."

Hesh reached into the back of his waistband and pulled out a gun, pointing it at the seated prisoner. "So, no problem if I finish him off?"

Cunard reached for his weapon and aimed at Hesh. "Stand down. He's coming in alive."

The Disciple snorted and stepped back away from Fischer. "I didn't expect things to get this spicy. Take him alive or dead. Just pay me the reward."

The Marine put a hand on Cunard's shoulder. "With respect, agent. You need to stand down. These are our assets and we have given our terms for this target."

Cunard stared again at Hesh, then looked at Fischer. Fischer told him no. It was an almost undetectable movement of his eyes, but it was enough. He was telling Cunard to back off. Cunard looked back to Hesh and saw the same level of understanding between him and the prisoner. Hesh appeared to be dipping his head, but he was saying yes to a request from Fischer. Cunard reluctantly lowered his weapon.

Hesh pulled the trigger and the crack of gunfire echoed. He turned towards the soldier as he put his gun back in his waistband. "Just in case there was any doubt about our willingness to do a job. Are we good?"

The Marine remained neutral, unreadable. "Understood. You have the other cards?"

The Disciple, eager not to be forgotten, stepped forward now that the action was over. "We do. And remember it was the Points that delivered him."

*

"You've got heart." The Disciple repeated his compliment after the Patrians had left.

"We can't trust them, but they need to trust us."

"He died well, didn't he? When I retired Young, he didn't die so well. Pleaded with me. It was pathetic. I'd looked up to him, been his right-hand man. His disciple. Not after that. It was all a sham. I had no respect for him after that. You can respect the dead. You should, but no. Not after that."

"Fischer was a good man. Just not on our side."

The Disciple agreed. "Facts is. That was how I thought it was with Young. But it wasn't."

"And me?"

Disciple threw his head back and laughed, putting an arm round his shoulder as he spoke. "We are going to work well together. I wasn't sure before I met you. Maybe not even before you faced down that agent. But now? Was that the reason you did it? To impress me?"

"Would it be bad if it was?"

*

Cunard and the support team headed back to Red Hook after the meeting. Life was returning to normal, but he was still under orders to avoid his own apartment.

Campbell was waiting for him when he arrived. "I heard you wanted to bring one of our targets in alive?"

Cunard said nothing.

"We are not running a prison. We do not have the manpower. If they are a target, we take them out unless we believe they have high value intelligence. You did not mark this cop as being an HVI target. Should you have?"

Cunard said, "He was a friend to me at times. It clouded my judgment. That's all it was."

"Okay. That I can understand. Look at this and tell me what you think." The general threw up a screen between them. It was coverage of a news conference.

As the Moderator of the Church of Shadows, I hold a temporary position. I am not the arbiter of truth. The truth that can be spoken is a false truth. But as a follower of the Shadow, I know this. We must not be divided between Alterrans and Patrians. This is a false division. Does it not say so in our book, 'The Way is balance between the whole and the part? Reject a part of the whole and you reject the whole.'

The last few days have been difficult, full of injustice and provocation. I neither condemn nor praise the actions of a few. The past has unwound as it was always going to unwind. We cannot undo that. It makes no difference to condemn or praise. All we can do is look forward and create the future.

I call on all Shadows to embrace the book in their dealing with Patrians. 'I am separate. I am connected. I am in the world. I am of the world.'

Now more than ever we have a chance to spread our message. The actions that bring inner peace when faced with injustice will shine brightly within and beyond Alterum.

Face your internal and external enemies with the grace of the Shadow and you will change the world. This is the moment of the singularity. It has been long predicted and it is now upon us. We are its children.

Travel in peace. Travel in the illusion that is real, in the reality that is illusion. The Way is. The Way always was. The Way always shall be.

The image faded as Campbell swiped at the air. "There are people back home that believe this bullshit. That is what worries me. We can't afford a long, drawn-out war that attracts opposition and division."

"Why not? It's never stopped us in the past."

"Well, not on my watch. We will be fast, ruthless, and have this thing under control before the country has a chance to wake up."

Cunard paused before speaking. "Do you trust my judgment?"

"So far."

"Then take my advice and relax. You might not like what you just heard, but that was a call to WA supporters to stand down. It didn't sound like it, but that's what it was. They're not gone, but they will not mount any more attacks. At least not for a long time. This is a repeat of the siege of Red Hook."

"What siege?"

"Ancient history. Something that happened back when the company was in charge."

Campbell almost smiled. "That long ago?"

"The WA proved they can hit us, but they know they can't defeat us. So, they make their point and then disappear. Your campaign will be seen as a complete success. Never has shock and awe worked so effectively. This campaign against urban guerrillas could be studied for years."

"Do not mock me and do not mock the Marines."

"I'm not. I am not mocking you. But what you need to understand and make sure your superiors understand is that this is part of what the WA have planned. You are out of control, then you are in control. You can defeat us, but you will get a black eye every few years unless you treat us with respect. That is their message."

"They've paid a heavy price to tell us that."

"They have. But don't be deaf to it. They haven't gone away." Cunard pulled the most wanted cards out of his pocket and placed them on the table. "This isn't the whole of the WA. These police officers and government officials are one branch that has sacrificed itself to help the others stay invisible." Cunard paused a moment. "Claim your victory, but don't be fooled by it."

Chapter 21

VISITORS ... All previous implementations of virtual reality have relied on sensory feedback via rich sound and vision and an extremely limited set of other sensory inputs. This paper suggests a step change that will allow a completely immersive experience that is indistinguishable from the real world. Utilizing the principle behind the creation of seed shadows it is proposed that ... (The remainder of this section has been removed due to the inclusion of proprietary solutions and techniques.)

Alterum White Paper

The city had been quiet for the last couple of days. The Moderator's call for a ceasefire had mostly held. The people were angry, but they knew they could not win a battle with the enemy they faced. The truth was that everyone who wanted to live needed a reason to do nothing. A reason to accept the situation and wait for it to return to some form of normality.

Self-respect was hard to find with Patrian death squads picking up known and suspected WA sympathizers. They disappeared into dark and not so dark sites. They did not come back. The Moderator had understood this and provided some self-justification for those that did not want to join the missing for the sake of displaying impotent defiance.

Graffiti replaced violence. 'Now you see me' being the most common mark appearing over the city. The street barricades had gone, some burnt-out real-estate the only reminder of the chaos that had passed. Shelter in place notices to Patrians had been lifted and Cunard was given permission to return to his apartment.

The *Lucitania*, which had been his home for the last week, was now a fully functioning military station. Some company staff remained, but it was clear that Jack Glory would be no more than a travel operator in the new age that had just begun. Cunard thought about this as he headed through the tunnel and made his way home. Most of Patria had slept through the whole thing. In a few days, the real world would wake up and hear the news that there had been a 'disturbance' in Alterum. A few bankers had been 'psychologically damaged' and put into an induced coma for their own good.

Cunard instinctively understood from his previous life what the narrative would be. The government had stepped in to take control and a Senate hearing would be held into the debacle. A debacle that would be laid entirely at the feet of the company leadership. What was not in question in Cunard's mind was that Alterum would continue its exponential growth as a financial powerhouse. It had earned the ultimate seal of approval. The state protecting the investments of corporate donors and individuals who paid their way to the heart of hard power.

Cunard put on his coffee maker while he showered. Toweling himself dry, he strolled back to the kitchen and poured a cup. The apartment was empty. It always had been empty. He had been living light for the whole tour of duty. There was nothing he could take back home with him, so why bother collecting mementos of an imaginary life. And yet … Bella had been part of this apartment from the day he moved here after the incident with Morgan. She would show up at random times which made him feel as if she was always there. It had been irritating and yet strangely comforting. Cunard was sure he was no longer being watched. At least not by Bella. He picked up his Handi from the countertop and slipped the lanyard over this head.

"Contact the radio room. Visuals off."

"Hey, Cunard. How can I help you?" It was one of the few remaining company agents.

"I'm looking for some information."

"I'm not sure I can help. We don't have the same access we used to."

"It's a tourist I'm interested in. I sent through an urgent information request a few days ago."

There was a pause at the other end of the line as the operator carried out a search.

"Okay, I've got it. She exited Alterum."

"She left?"

"Yes. Quite an extended stay, but she's gone."

"You're quite sure?"

"I've can transfer the logs."

"Do that. All of them."

After closing the call, he opened the transferred records and scattered them across the room forming a virtual whiteboard. They were primarily vital signs and EEG readings spaced out every five seconds for her time in the pod.

Refilling his coffee, he walked slowly from document to document. "Filter. EEG and heart rate only." The documents merged and shrunk. "Graph the results." The numbers disappeared to be replaced by a red and a blue line. The blue was heart rate and remained relatively stable. The red showed EEG. There were two major events. One near the start of the log showed a dramatic drop. The EEG collapsed down to almost nothing and stayed there. Near the end of the readings, it made just as dramatic a rise.

He marked two points. "Local timestamp, point A?" A date and time materialized. He couldn't remember the exact date, but it was close enough. Bella's jump. The heart rate spike confirmed it. "Local timestamp, point B?" Again, a date and time appeared. This time he had no difficulty in placing it. The recent events were seared into his memory. Bella had crossed at the same time Eva had been self-immolating.

"Shit." Cunard scratched his scalp. "Close records." He sat down and cleared his mind, staring out of the window to the city beyond. After finishing his coffee, he placed the cup in the sink and opened the cupboard above it. There was a bottle of whisky and one glass. It was a Laphroaig, fifteen-year-old. He uncorked the bottle and dispensed a generous measure. He swirled the glass and took a breath, inhaling the strong peated aroma. He had developed a palate for anything that assaulted the senses here. Back home he would never have chosen this drink, but here he needed to feel a connection any kind of physical sensation. It kept him alert. Tonight, he was going to assault his senses to the point of numbness. The jigsaw pieces were falling into place, and not for the first time, he felt like a fool.

It was not Eva who waved to him when he was trapped in the elevator. It was Bella. Somehow, she had developed a physical presence and the ability to shape shift. The pain of the fire had been enough to kick-start a connection to her real body. She had shouted something just before collapsing. Now he knew. Bella was using her safe word. She had gone home.

He poured another drink. He was happy for Bella. It explained the resurrection stories about Eva. She had not died in the Tower. She was still alive. The last time Cunard had spoken to Fischer he had referred to her in the present tense. He had assumed at the time that Fischer was merely spreading the myth. Fischer knew.

Fischer probably knew where Eva was, but now he was gone, sacrificing himself to place fresh WA moles in positions of influence. '*Arm ist, wer den Tod wünscht, aber ärmer, wer ihn fürchtet.*' That was what was on one side of the note Fischer passed him. It roughly translated as 'It is wrong to wish for death, but worse to fear it.'

The other side gave him contact details for the new head of the Manor. All of it was planned. Cunard was expected to unwittingly play his part and he had. He had been that predictable. Another glass full of the memory of peat soil and sea air was required. He poured himself a large one. This night would end when he passed out.

*

He woke the next day as the sun reached a point above the skyline where it cast rays into the apartment. Cunard covered his eyes with a hand as he reluctantly entered a new day. He slid his legs off the couch and pushed himself up into a sitting position. His Handi, registering the motion, spoke.

Incoming message one.

"Cunard," It was General Campbell. "I got your request and I've approved it. Consider yourself no longer active. The crossing stations are fully occupied. You'll need to keep yourself entertained as a tourist until one comes free."

Incoming message two.

"Cunard. I've booked a pod for you as per General Campbell's instructions. Please present yourself at the *Lucitania* next Tuesday at fourteen hundred hours. All slots are booked so please be on time. Any delays will invoke a service charge to be deducted from your final employee payment."

He had exactly one week left in Alterum. He would leave Nylon City. Get away from the Marines patrolling the streets in their armored vehicles.

Away from the overwhelming sense of oppression. Away from the scene of the crime.

After a failed attempt to dissolve his hangover under hot jets of water in the shower he packed some clothes in a travel bag, looked around the apartment one last time and left.

After getting into the car, he paused for a second, unsure where to go. He was in no fit state to drive so he would have to tell the vehicle his destination. He wanted to be somewhere remote. Somewhere quiet. Other than that, he didn't care.

"Take me to somewhere that smells of peat and the sea."

Multiple destinations available. Please be more specific.

"It doesn't matter."

How far?

"As far as we can go before it gets dark."

Calculating sunset, route, and location. Destination selected.

The engine started and the car began to move through the streets of New York, heading for London, and then the Highlands of Scotland. He had never made it there in real life. The messed-up geography of Alterum had some advantages. Cunard reclined his seat and closed his eyes, hoping to sleep off his hangover in time for a drink wherever he ended up.

The sun was dipping below the horizon as the sea came into view and the car woke Cunard. He left it on automatic as he took in the scenery. The road was a winding ribbon of reflected light. Hairpin bends made their way between two rising slopes on either side. In the distance was a body of water glowing orange in the fading light.

In the middle distance a swirling cloud of birds pulsed across the sky. Thousands of them moved in unison swooping in one direction before a section of the flock would twist, dramatically changing course, and pull the rest of the birds with them. Cunard was transfixed. He had watched recordings of the murmuration's of starlings, but he had never seen it in person. What had once been a common sight had faded into memory and old footage when the species population collapsed beyond recovery. The swooping birds made cloud-like shapes in the air, and he let his imagination take over, seeing a face, then a castle, then a dragon. He pushed back in his seat and allowed his mind to wander to wherever it would take him.

It took him to Eva. The face in the murmuration was hers. She had planned everything that had happened. She had enlisted Bella. How did she do it? By telling her the truth and helping to get Bella home. Bella had made it. Eva had delivered on her promise. How many people could say that? What would his legacy be here in Alterum once he left? What would be his legacy back on Patria? He was a Patrian manque and an Alterran manque. Someone who was always lacking the final commitment to anything, to anyone.

The road narrowed as he arrived at the end of the glen, and the car came to a halt next to a small dirt track that led to pebble beach.

Arrived at destination.

He stepped out and took in the air. The dank musty scent of wet soil mixed with a faint vanilla odor from the yellow flowering Broom that covered the ground. He said aloud, "Good choice." The vehicle did not respond to his compliment. He walked down the track and entered the beach. The sound of the water alternated with the clatter of pebbles tumbling over each as the waves receded back towards the sea.

Cunard got too close, and a wave swept over his shoes, soaking his ankles and feet. He did not care. It felt good. This place was magical. He would find somewhere to stay and spend his last few days here before returning to Red Hook. This was somewhere he could find some temporary peace.

He walked along the waterline, following the horseshoe shape of the bay that led to a second trail. That would take him past a small cottage and back to the road towards his car. The incline to this path was steeper than the one he had used to enter the beach. He slid on the pebbles, smoothed by thousands of years of waves. Each step advanced him no more than a half stride. He was in no hurry. The sky was beginning to darken, and a light illuminated one of the windows of the cottage. Smoke curled into the air from the chimney, and he became aware of the distinctive scent of burning peat. That was a place he could live. Reaching the solid footing of the gravel trail he no longer struggled to cover ground. He could see his vehicle in the distance.

"Car. Come to me."

His Handi flashed then answered.

No signal available. Instruction not sent.

"Try again."

No signal available. Instruction not sent.

This was of course possible in the real world. There were still plenty of areas with spotty reception, but he did not think that was the case here on Alterum. The door to the cottage opened and a figure framed by the internal light appeared in the entrance. This did not make sense either. He had chosen the destination at random. It did not matter though. He was glad. She did not need to speak. Cunard did not need to see her face. He recognized the silhouette leaning against the doorframe waiting for him. He quickened his pace.

*

Cunard was sitting in an armchair, shoes and socks off. Heat baked his skin and it felt good. She poured him a whisky, herself a water, and sat in the chair opposite. They both watched the dancing flames of the open fire as he spoke.

"How did you know where I would go?"

Eva smiled. "I didn't. I just chose to be wherever you went. I'm a witch. Don't you know that by now?"

"I guess you are. Do you control the program?"

She leaned forward and turned her head to look at him. "No one controls it anymore."

Cunard sighed.

"Reality is intersubjective. It is what most people think it is. That wasn't always the case. Before Nylon City it was different. The company could use the seeds to make updates. Tweak reality as much as they wanted. Once the consensus protocol was introduced that all changed."

"Yet here we are." Cunard raised his eyebrows and took a drink of his whisky.

Eva tilted her head. "I'm special."

"You are the last seed."

"Our settings were never overwritten."

"So, you can shape reality to whatever you want?"

"Not quite. I must merge with the consensus to change it."

"Then do it. Stop what is happening in Nylon City. Save your people."

Eva put her water on the floor and reached over to take his hand. The room dissolved and he found himself expanding out from his body. He grew out into the fire but did not burn. The light blinded him at first and then his vision slowly returned. He was back in the city. It was night and the dual city was illuminated with millions of lights. Streets, cars,

271

apartments, fires, barbeques. He was all the lights in all those places. He was everywhere at once yet still aware of himself as separate.

He expanded as he grew into the lights of the living. Into their bodies and minds. Sadness, joy, fear, despair, intense pleasure, overwhelming pain. Flowing on from the emotional and physical sensations came thoughts. A relationship was ending. A child was being born. A parent was dying. He thought he understood, but he did not. Not yet. This was just the first stream.

More voices joined with him, more feelings. Then another stream, then another, until he was the city. He was every soul in Nylon City. He was it all. A vast river of life flowing forward as one towards the sea, old life always being replaced with new, but continuing relentlessly on its journey, always there as both form and substance.

Small swirling eddies of humanity felt shared emotions, shared joy, and pain, but ultimately, they rejoined the river. He wanted to speak to the voices, but as soon as he had that thought he was deafened by every other thought that existed.

It was unbearable. He had to escape this cacophony before it drove him mad. He shouted for Eva to make it stop. The voices grew louder until they merged into white noise. He stopped thinking and started feeling. This was the wellspring, not language, not words. Language flowed from a deeper source and then thought that its words were the center of everything. Finally, the noise began to subside, and the lights faded, shrinking until they were once again just the flames in a fireplace in a cottage at the side of the ocean.

He looked at her and nodded his understanding. "That was the program?"

"Just a flavor. That was Nylon City. There is all the rest. Then there is this," she picked up her glass from the floor. "And that," she pointed at his whisky.

He lifted the glass to his mouth and took a drink. "So, why? Why did you start this revolution if you can't finish it?"

"Because it has to start somewhere. As it is within, so it is without. With the company in charge, we are fighting the company. When it fails, as it has, we fight the government. There is no victory until you defeat the real power, and they were more than willing to step in. With our help, but also with the intention of betraying us at the first opportunity. So it was in the past, so it is in the present. Patrians will call this a mutiny, some will call it a rebellion, but it is really the first war of independence."

"So many have died. Are dying. Was it worth it?"

"Would you ask the same question if you were an Alterran?"

"How can I answer that without being one? Perhaps, perhaps not. Do every one of you have the same opinion?"

"You heard the voices of everyone in Nylon City. You can answer that question yourself, but I'm asking you, not everyone."

"Yes." The answer came before he thought it. He felt it and let it speak. "Yes, I would I think it was worth it." They sat in silence for a few seconds before he continued. "I would think it's worth it, but I would also regret it. I would know that I have planted a seed of discontent that will grow and become more powerful, but it will ruin countless lives on the way. I would see a future that might be better than the past or the present, but I would be sad that those that paid for it won't see it. Fischer will not see it."

Eva nodded. "He knew that." She stood up and walked to the window. "It will be light soon."

"It's only just got dark."

"If I want the sun to rise, it rises. Come with me. One last time."

Eva led him back down onto the beach. The light was growing behind them, above the peaks that cut off this place from the rest of the world.

"I am going back home, Eva."

"And what is waiting for you there?"

"Not much, but I can't stay here forever."

"No one really leaves Alterum. Stay and make a life."

He frowned, confused. "With you ... here?"

Eva let out a peal of laughter. "I have my own journey to make, but you can stay. You should stay."

"While my body rots away in a pod?"

"Did you think it was strange that you, a Patrian, could merge with the source?"

"Don't mess with my head, Eva. I know I exist outside of here. I am not a pre-programmed Alterran."

"You are both Alterran and Patrian. Everyone is. The company sold you a lie. You're not in a pod. You are here. You are a replica of what's in the pod and your memories from here stream back to your physical twin. You are a shadow. You exist separately and conjoined to the Patrian, Cunard. You don't leave Alterum, only your memories do."

He knew it was true. He had merged with Alterrans and Patrians when he entered the light. He had felt them both. When he or any other Patrian left this place, they died, and their memories lived on as Lucid Synthetic Dreams. Someone else's dreams. "Bella?"

"She knew. She didn't want to live as a ghost. She was happy to go, to give life back to her Patrian twin."

"My twin. I would be condemning him?"

"Have I told you I'm a witch?"

"You could do that?"

"It's possible. It is how I exist. It's how all the seeds were created. A branching between the twins, the Patrian wakes, the Alterran endures. Stay and be committed to this world. Go and be committed to that one."

The sunlight hit the water. It was plate glass, smooth and untroubled by waves or wind. He had made his decision. Everything was easier now that he was listening for an answer within himself Instead of accepting the illusion that he was making conscious decisions. The reasons were simply justifications for decisions already made. That seemed clear to him. "And you?"

"A late change of plan. My twin is dying. She doesn't have long. I am going to her. She carried our flame in Patria. I will take her place when she's gone."

"No one can leave, but … you're a witch?"

"There are bio-forms that can hold me. She has one waiting for me. When I leave there will be no more seeds left. The singularity will have been finally reached. The future will belong to Alterran-created minds."

"When?"

Eva embraced Cunard and kissed him on the cheek. "Live well here and there. I'll look you up, lover."

"You don't know who I am."

"Okay, Mr. Robert Townsend. Okay." She hugged him again and stood back. Eva lifted off the ground and levitated several feet above him before she began to dissolve into a black swarm of matter. Parts of the swarm coalesced into birdlike shapes and flew over the water. The murmuration of starlings was back and what had been Eva joined them as they wheeled and twisted through the air, making their way out to sea.

Cunard felt something tugging at his mind. It was as if his consciousness was being stretched thin. A snapping sensation washed over him, and he knew it had happened. He was no longer connected to his Patrian self. He was now purely Alterran. His last Alterran memory had left for Patria. His life was here. His commitment was here. He would return to Nylon City soon. He would create a new identify now that he was officially gone. He would fight for the river of life he had experienced. Fight for it to continue to flow, fight for it to win dignity and self-respect. He would fail to see it in his lifetime. He knew that it might never be achieved, but that was his path. He accepted it. It felt good.

The End

THE ALTERUM INCIDENT

Extract from The Economic Journal of Artificial Intelligence.

To understand the Alterum Incident it is vital to appreciate the role of Chain currency and its place in the wider cryptocurrency environment.

Anything of value attracts the attention of the powerful. If that value cannot be accumulated, controlled, or used by established power, it will attempt to destroy it.

The early generations of cryptocurrencies fell victim to this phenomenon.

Designed by anarcho-capitalists who imagined a currency free of government control they built systems that cut out the government regulated banks and finance systems. This almost certainly guaranteed that it would be co-opted or destroyed.

The first generation had several serious flaws. The distributed security was underpinned by proof of work or proof of stake. These required either massive computing power or large cryptocurrency stakes.

Both approaches gradually pushed out the mass of individuals contributing to security and currency creation (mining) in favor of fewer centralized actors that were then more readily influenced or attacked by the establishment.

The decision by most governments to treat crypto payments as cash and therefore subject to anti-money-laundering reporting completed the power grab. The libertarians were left with another failed project undermined by the existing systems.

It was, however, the wild fluctuations in value that ultimately destroyed most early cryptocurrencies.

Anything that fluctuates too much can leave organizations that accept that currency with an enormous potential loss. If, for example, payment was accepted using a cryptocurrency that fell by twenty percent the next day, a sale that was profitable one day becomes a loss the next.

This can also happen outside of cryptocurrencies for international trades that accept multiple currencies. Most international traders use currency hedging to avoid this. The volatility of cryptos meant hedging was too expensive to be effective for anything other than government-backed fiat currencies.

The net result of this situation was that most cryptos ended up as highly speculative investment vehicles. One such early cryptocurrency was ironically named Tulip.

There was a second class of cryptos named stable coins which were tied to external commodities such as gold and government-backed currencies including the US dollar.

While these were not subject to extreme volatility, the uptake tended to be limited to commodity and currency investors who saw it merely as an asset value holding mechanism.

The arrival of Chain addressed most of the existing issues sufficiently to quickly establish itself as the dominant crypto.

This currency was a joint initiative between global finance organizations and, crucially, it was endorsed by the governments of leading economies.

The coins were stabilized by changing the creation process from mining to minting. Minting was the process of creating coins through capital investment. The value of a new coin was based on the fractional cost of adding renewable power supply and compute infrastructure to vast data center complexes around the world.

This was politically popular as part of a move towards "green" technology, but the real reason the renewable element was key was that it was a one-off capital expense which created tangible value linked to the process of running the currency. It was predictable and whilst subject to real world inflation, it was often more stable than many traditional currencies.

Linked to infrastructure capital costs rather than commodities or false scarcity, the upward value was constrained by the mint cost. No one would buy a coin on the market for more than they could purchase it through a mint.

Coins were also minted for finance organizations based on the number of transactions processed, thus creating revenue and profit for the banks and a self-sustaining ecosystem for the currency.

The currency could be held in traditional bank accounts or in digital wallets, which were effectively private accounts with zero customer identity information, much like the original cryptocurrencies. In many ways it was more anonymous than the early crypto currencies. In early currencies, transactions were completely visible. Chain allowed both account and wallet owners to set the privacy level and control what could be viewed by third parties. This allowed Chain owners to share everything, a subset of transactions, or nothing.

This concession was key to the currency achieving widespread uptake now that government and the finance industry were keen to promote it.

Chain was a secure file store, smart contract mechanism, as well as a currency. The consensus model of transaction verification meant that Chain could be used to pass information and contracts back and forward between the real world and the Alterum. The ability to use Chain in this way, combined with the time dilation effect, made Nylon City the perfect location for investment funds whose main currency had already become Chain.

Once the advantages become obvious, the trickle of companies based in Alterum became a flood. And that takes us back to the start of this article. Anything of value attracts the attention of the powerful. If that value cannot be accumulated, controlled, or used by established power, it will attempt to destroy it.

The AAAC was a travel and entertainment company, yet it found itself becoming core to the entire finance sector of the economy. The finance industry and their friends in government did not like this arrangement, but the advantages of Alterum were too appealing to ignore the opportunity.

A takeover bid was lodged by a consortium of leading banks and institutions. Due to the complex company constitution and a heavy concentration of Class A shares amongst company execs, it was impossible to mount a hostile takeover. This left the only other option of government intervention. Anti-trust or special measure legislation was required to wrest control of Alterum from "Jack Glory", as the company grandiosely referred to itself.

It came as little surprise when the incident required to spark a Senate inquiry took place. Such an event had been speculated about on various fringe forums and as is usually the case, dismissed by the mainstream as no more than a conspiracy theory.

During the Senate inquiry a former company agent testified that the Marines were in position ready to strike before the incident took place. Robert Townsend also stated that they executed the subsequent actions to a well-formed playbook, including the summary execution of the London Mayor. He claimed to have previously worked for an off-the-books division of US Intelligence that had employed similar tactics to undermine a South American regime. This part of his testimony was heavily redacted as not relevant and a potential security threat.

One surprise witness was the singer, Eva Enfield. Despite rumors of a serious illness, she made the trip to Washington and appeared in good health. It was a replica of her personality that was at the heart of the incident and the senators were keen to gain her insight into the thinking of her doppelganger.

Whilst she emphasized that her testimony was speculative, she had visited Alterum on several occasions and believed the incident was a reaction to gross abuses of power by the company and individuals.

In what was an unexpectedly eloquent and detailed testimony she schooled the committee on the inner working of Alterum. Very much like Chain, a consensus model had stabilized Alterum. By using each Alterran as a node of verification, the system became resistant to externally introduced software bugs and deliberate attempts to manipulate the overall program. One part of her testimony hit home particularly strongly when she stated:

"I will not try to convince you that Alterrans are sentient creatures that deserve to be treated with respect. For the record I personally believe they are sentient and do deserve respect. Putting that to one side, I will try and persuade you that you *need* to treat them with respect. Why? Because the consensus model of reality is what keeps Alterum secure and stable. Without that our people and companies could not safely operate there. It would need to be completely abandoned.

"As more of us work and interact with this world, the inhabitants are seeing past our myths to the reality of the situation. The Book of Shadows acknowledges reality but also gives a basis for self-belief. One thing that is overlooked by most so-called experts is that we become part of the consensus model when we visit. Alterum is at a tipping point. Our contempt, our belief that these people are simulacrums and nothing more, is dangerous. If this belief takes hold in Alterum the reality created through this mechanism will collapse. The 'physical world' of Alterum will become unstable, just as it was before they introduced the consensus protocol. It was this physical instability that led to Nylon City, but the next rupture might not be so benign.

"Believe they deserve respect or believe they need respect. It makes no difference to me, but at least take the time to understand the consequences of the alternative."

The long-term impacts of the hearing were predictable. The government broke the company up under anti-trust laws. The Class A shareholders kept the travel side of the business. The Class B shareholders became the owners of Alterum and were swiftly bought out by a private equity fund. The same conspiracy theorists who had predicted the company breakup claimed that this fund was deeply connected to government agencies through a revolving door of shared employees in senior management positions.

Alterrans were granted no legal standing, but a code of conduct was adopted and representatives from both worlds now sit on the ethics committee of the reconstituted company. The Book of Shadows, once a fringe faith, is one of the fastest growing belief systems in both worlds. There is increasing speculation that travel will eventually be possible in both directions with Alterrans using lab grown bio-forms to visit the real world. When asked about this, Eva Enfield expressed skepticism, citing the reverse time dilation effect as a barrier. "Time would pass too quickly back on Alterum for this to be practical, unless someone chose to make a permanent move to Patria."

THE GIRL IN THE DREAM

Eva's origin story

The Message

Eva looked out from the stage as the spotlight dimmed. A sea of shadows faced her like an army of silhouettes. They were cheering but also beginning to turn and shuffle out of the concert.

She let go of the mic and walked toward the side, feeling numb. It felt as though there was a layer of insulation between her and the rest of the world. Where there should be exhilaration, there was nothing. Even the act of walking was one step removed from physical sensation. Her body and her mind were anesthetized.

Lift the leg, push it forward, watch where you're placing it because you can't feel the space you are in. repeat, repeat, repeat until you are off stage. She smiled at her internal narrative.

"Great concert, you did fantastic."

"Didn't forget any lyrics tonight, made it to the end," she replied. "Nothing for the ambulance chasers eh."

"They love you Eva, that's why they're here. They love you."

"They don't love me. That's a stupid thing to say. That word has no meaning. They like the music, and they want to see the freak show."

Ray put his arm around her, held her tight and navigated her down the stairs leading towards the changing room. "Not all of them Eva, your music connects. Anyway, I love you."

"I know that Ray, but I don't love you. Isaac's my man."

"Yeah, I know."

"Sorry lover, you don't get to choose your addictions. If I did, you'd be it."

"Sure."

Isaac stood at the door to the changing room with a stranger. "Jewel, you were it tonight."

Ray let go of her and she was swept up into Isaac's arms. His pupils were dilated, his head was nodding constantly with involuntary movements.

"You were it Jewel. Meet my man Mike."

"Fuck off Mike," she said. "I don't know you. Why do you do this shit, Isaac?"

"Two thousand quid. Two thousand quid to say hello."

"I don't need the money. Why do you do it Isaac?"

"It's my hustle Jewel. It's me. Say hello to the man."

Ray stepped forward. "I'm sorry Mike, but Eva doesn't do meet and greets. Give me your contact details and I will refund you."

"I ain't refunding nobody," said Isaac.

"I'll give you your money back. Just give me your details."

Mike shook his head. "I need to speak to her, it's important. I have a message for her."

"Here we go," said Ray, looking around for security. "Another lunatic given access by the conman boyfriend."

"He'll pay you with my money," Eva said, pointing at Ray. "And he'll keep yours," now pointing at Isaac. "It's all my money on a merry go round. Welcome to my world, Mike. Happy, now you've seen the freak up close?"

"You're no freak," Mike said as he stood calmly taking in the scene. "And I'm not a lunatic, but I do need to speak to you. I have a message."

"From God?" she sneered.

"From the girl in the dream."

Eva sobered up. It was as if all intoxicants had been instantly flushed from her body."

"What you are babbling about?" said Isaac, now unsure of this person he had brought backstage.

"You've met her?"

"Yeah, I met her yesterday and she gave me a message for you."

Isaac, stepped between Eva and Mike.

"Let me speak to him," said Eva, pushing him to one side.

"Eva," said Ray.

"It's cool Ray, don't worry. He's got the codeword. He's okay." Ray and Isaac looked on confused, as Eva stepped forward and held Mike by both arms. "Tell me, what did she say. I don't want anyone else to hear, okay."

Mike leaned in and whispered in her ear. "The girl in the dream says hello. She says you've been thinking about how to know if you're real," he paused and leaned out to see her reaction.

Eva smiled, not a sneer or an ironic smile, but a smile of joy. Something she hadn't felt for a long time. Her eyes filled and she took a deep breath to maintain her composure. "I have. Does she have the answer?"

Mike nodded and tears began to roll down Eva's face.

"Enough," said Ray. "What's going on?"

"Fuck off Ray, this is mine, no-one else's. Tell me, Mike. What did the girl in the dream say?"

Mike leaned in again and spoke the words she had guessed at but was never sure of. "You are not real. You are the girl in the dream."

The Concert

It was dawn. Morning was breaking through the gap in the curtains. Eva glanced at her reflection in the mirror above the fireplace. It was dark but there was just enough light to make out the emaciated arms and legs, covered in tattoos, the tiny childlike frame, and oversized head, made larger by her trademark beehive hair. Scattered around her was the debris of fast food, alcohol, and drugs. Sitting on the mantlepiece, so as not be lost amongst the garbage, were crumpled balls of tinfoil.

It was Saturday morning, but for Eva, it was a continuation of Wednesday. That was when she had started, and if she had slept since then she wasn't aware of it. Isaac was crashed in the corner of the room, slumped on the floor, leaning against the wall. He was surrounded by other unconscious bodies.

A couple lay, naked, in each other's arms. Eva remembered them putting on a show. A game of spin the bottle had started with the winners, or losers depending on your point of view, having to fuck each other right there in front of everyone. Eva had sat on the couch watching them go at it whilst eating a big mac and drinking straight vodka from a bottle.

She wondered if she would have gone through with it if she'd been chosen. She was the queen bee, could have refused and no-one would have said a thing, but that would have been lame. She guessed she would have done it.

"It has to stop," said Ray. He was standing next to her holding a newspaper. "I would open your curtains, but the pavement is full of paps, just waiting to get that first photo of you."

"Alright Ray, it's over."

"You can't trust any of these people. One of these arseholes sent the picture to the papers. You realize that don't you?"

Ray had arrived a few minutes earlier with a tabloid newspaper screaming out the headline "Eva's Crack house". A picture of Eva, blurry but still identifiable, was splashed across the front page. She was leaning down over the table sucking on a pipe as she held a lighter to it.

"They are scum, all of them. Why can't you see that?"

"It's not like that lover. We were having fun. Nobody's catching me out, I'm part of it. Don't you see that. I don't care if people know I smoke. I smoke Ray, whatever, it's nothing to me."

"It's killing you, Eva."

"We got the concert tonight yeah?"

"You can't do that. I'm canceling it."

"Nah, don't do that Ray. I said I'll do it, and I'll do it. Take me upstairs. Put me to bed. I've got all day to sleep it off. It's good."

Ray took her in his arms and shuffled her out of the front room, leaving the debris behind.

"You still love me, Ray?"

"Always."

"But you hate me too, don't you?"

"I don't hate you, I hate Isaac."

"Isaac didn't do anything to me, Ray. This is all inside here," she tapped her head. "I did this, just me. He's come along for the ride. You won't come for the ride Ray, you can't be my man."

"Okay, Eva, whatever you say."

"Don't cancel the concert lover. Promise me."

"I promise."

*

Eva stood at the front of the stage. The set behind her was a mock-up of a drawing room. The band was scattered between the standard lamps with patterned and fringed shades. Eva's makeup was heavy and applied over previous applications that had not been completely removed. Through the patchwork covering, there were scabs visible. Her eyeliner was uneven and smudged.

"Did you enjoy the newspapers today?" she asked the crowd.

The audience cheered.

"Come to see the freak show. Well, I'm here. The party was epic, but here I am, and once I've done this shit, I'm going to start all over again. Hey paps, did you like the pictures I sent? That's right, I sent them. You got nothing on me I don't want you to have, understand?"

"Sing Eva," someone shouted. "Come on Eva."

"When I'm ready," she said. "My show, my shit. If you don't like it, fuck off."

There were a few rumbles of discontent from the crowd. The band started an intro, trying to get her to join in. She ignored them.

"I get to decide when tonight's show is going to start, not you cunts."

A section of the audience began to boo. Phones were held aloft filming the implosion.

"Go on then, film me. Have your fun. You paid for it, feel free," she said, arms outstretched.

"We love you, Eva."

"Do you love me?"

"We love you."

"You're a skanky whore."

Eva nodded as the crowd fell silent. "A skanky whore. It's that what you're here for?"

"Fuck yeah," the same voice shouted. It came from the front of the audience.

Eva leaned down and picked up a bottle of beer she'd placed in front of her. She walked to the edge of the stage, in front of the footlights. She could see them clearly now. Someone threw a punch at another audience member.

"Is that the guy with the mouth?"

"Ignore him, Eva."

She took a swig on the bottle and then holding it by the neck, threw it towards the fight. Someone screamed as the bottle missed its target and landed in another section of the crowd.

"Fuck you. Fuck all of you. The show's over for tonight." She turned and stepped back over the footlights. Turning to face the audience, she raised her middle finger in their direction and walked off stage.

"Let's go," said Ray, as she reached the side.

"Where to lover? Are you coming along for the ride tonight?"

"You're coming with me this time. Somewhere safe."

"Where's Isaac?"

"Probably shooting up in the toilet. He can catch up with us later."

The audience was booing loudly, stamping their feet and a chant started up. "Why are we waiting." Paper cups were thrown onto the now empty stage.

Ray guided her through the rabbit warren of corridors under the main auditorium. The roof above transmitting a dull and repetitive thud from the feet of the unhappy crowd above them.

"They don't love me," said Eva laughing.

"Not tonight."

"But you still love me, right?"

"Always." Ray pushed open the fire exit. The limo was there. Ray opened the door and Eva fell forward towards the seat.

"Is there a mini bar?"

"No more drink tonight," he said.

The car sped off, leaving the city behind.

"You'll tell Isaac where we've gone?"

"I'll tell Isaac."

Lucid Dreaming

Eva slumped in her chair eating a bar of chocolate and drinking tea, looking like nothing more than a naughty child.

"You are a right fucker, you know that?"

"Yeah," said Ray. "But it's for your own good."

"Where's my Isaac?"

"He'll be here soon."

"It's been a week since you kidnapped me and locked me up in this asylum."

Ray laughed. "Rehab is not an asylum."

"Might as well be. Tell mum I am never speaking to her again."

"She knows."

"As soon as I'm out of here, Isaac and I are getting hitched. Then he'll be my next of kin and no-one can pull this on me again. You hear me?"

"I hear you. This is my last throw of the dice. If it doesn't work, I'm done."

"You mean you won't love me anymore. That can't be right Ray. You'll always love me," she winked.

"I will," he said. "But I won't try and save you again."

"Sure, you will. You'll always pull me back from the brink."

"You ready for imaging?"

"Yeah, why not. But take me in the wheelchair like the patient I am." Eva got out of her chair and sat back down in the wheelchair opposite.

*

Eva lay down on the bed and the doctor attached the nodes to her scalp.

"And you understand everything that's about to happen?"

"Yeah, sure. You're going to suck every last memory out of my head and create an Eva bot in your virtual reality game."

"Lucid Dreaming," he corrected. "And it's not a game. It's a world where real people will visit whilst deep inside a lucid dream state. They will pay for access, and they will meet real celebrities like you, go to concerts, live next door to them, socialize with them on holiday."

"And if you don't want to ever tour again or make another record, you're free to give it all up. Step off the treadmill," said Ray. "But your copy will carry on making you money. You'll be free to step back."

"You really think you'll fix me by giving me the option of doing nothing?" she laughed.

"Maybe, maybe not. But this life isn't making you happy."

"You're crazy Ray."

"I'm going to administer the anesthetic now. Can you count down from ten to one for me?"

"Ten, nine, eight," Eva's speech became blurred. She carried on talking but only in her head. "Will she think she's real? When I wake up, how will I know if I'm real or if I'm the girl in the dream?"

Eva drifted out of consciousness watching as her whole life flashed before her. The childhood games, her mother chasing her through park laughing, the school concert where she sung Sinatra songs to puzzled looks from her schoolmates, the first holiday to Spain and the talent contest, the older man who told her how great she was but then tried to kiss her, the first studio session being recorded and Isaac bringing in coffee halfway through, making sure she got the right cup, the one with enough vodka to steady her nerves. Faster and faster the memories came, accelerating until they were a blur.

Eva woke with a start. The doctor was still there. Ray was still there, smiling stupidly, no doubt thinking she was now 'fixed'.

"How do you feel?" asked the doctor.

"Sick."

"It's normal. The nausea should pass in a few hours."

"Will she think she's real?"

The doctor paused for a second or two, as if considering the possibility for the first time. "Possibly. Yes."

"Even when I'm drunk, you can't bullshit me, and I'm sober today. Why are you pretending you've never thought about it?"

The doctor leaned his head to one side and shrugged his shoulders. "Sometimes people find it a little disturbing. If you don't ask, we don't tell."

"I've asked."

"Then yes, she will think she's real. Otherwise, it doesn't work. It's the whole point of taking a full memory scan."

"Okay," said Eva. "Next question. How do I know I'm real?"

"What?"

"How do I know I'm the real Eva and not the one that imagines she's real."

"Mmh, great question. A few subjects have asked that question, but not many."

"Are you calling me intelligent Doc?"

"I guess I am."

"So, what's the answer?"

"Je pense, donc je suis."

"Say what?"

"I think, therefore I am. Descartes famous proposition. The real Eva, you, will think about whether you are real, the copy won't. You have thought about what's real, so you are the real Eva. Simple really."

"Okay, Ray fire up the wheelchair and take me back to my room. Real Eva needs some real sleep."

"Sure thing."

"And when I wake up, I want my Isaac to be here, understood?"

Isaac

Isaac bounded into the room with a huge grin on his face. "Jewel, I've missed you so much. Can't live without you."

"Isaac, will you marry me?"

"In a heartbeat."

"Once we're bound, no-one can sign a paper to put me away. It's you and me Isaac. You and me from now on."

"They searched me on the way in. This place is like a prison." He took a pack of cigarettes out of his jacket pocket. "They even searched my ciggies. Thought I might be smuggling in a little blow for you." He pulled a cigarette and a lighter out of the packet and lit up while opening the window. Taking a long slow draw, he exhaled and passed it to Eva.

She breathed in deeply, savoring her first taste of nicotine in more than a week. "Ray thinks you're no good for me."

Isaac placed his index finger and thumb into his mouth, reached into the top right-hand side, pulled out a small tin foil package and placed it on the window ledge. "He might be right Jewel."

294

*

When Eva had got back to the house, she was surprised to find it cleaned up. There was no sign of the carnage that had taken place.

"Did you do this Isaac?"

"Nah, your mum threw me out. I've been couch surfing the whole time you were in the big house."

Eva laughed at Isaac's name for rehab. He loved his noir movies.

"I got some takeaway being delivered. Nothing too heavy, some nice herb to ease you back in. You want me to invite some people around?"

"Not tonight Isaac. I just want it to be the two of us. Is that okay?"

"Sure. Me and you, up a tree."

*

Eva inhaled and held her breath. She leaned back on the couch and looked over at Isaac, blowing smoke rings.

"Hey Gandalf," she said, after finally exhaling in one large breath. "What are you thinking?"

"I'm thinking we should stay in the Shire, but then again, where's the fun in that?"

"Doc reckons I'm smart."

"What makes him think that?"

"Je pense, donc je suis."

"Ooh la la."

"I'm going to sleep now," she said as she stubbed the remainder of the joint in the ashtray and swung her legs around up onto the couch.

"Sweet dreams Jewel. Gandalf's going to watch over you."

Eva drifted off and found herself back at rehab. She was asking the doctor again how she could know she was real. He repeated his answer. Je pense, donc je suis. She woke up and looked at the clock. She'd only been asleep 30 minutes. Isaac was crashed out on the armchair, a burnt-out joint held between his fingers. Eva picked up her phone and dialed Ray's number.

"Eva, you ok?"

"I'm alright lover, but it doesn't make sense."

"What doesn't?"

"What the doctor said. If she was a perfect copy, she would have the same kind of thoughts as me. She would think about whether she was real, but she's not real, so it's not a true test. It proves nothing. I think therefore I am, proves nothing."

"The doctor was right, you are smart when you're clean," Ray said.

"He was lying. He didn't want to frighten me."

"Do you think you are real?"

"I think so, but I'm not sure."

"If you believe it, what does it matter? Maybe he was right. If you think, you are real."

"Real, but not the original?"

"You're smarter than me Eva. You're making my head hurt."

"Okay lover, I'll leave you alone. Are you alone?"

"Saving myself for you."

"Please don't."

Eva rolled herself another joint and lit up. She looked at Isaac. She couldn't remember the last time they had a quiet night, the two of them without any of the ever-changing entourage.

She looked around at the room. There had been a burn mark on the table. She was sure of it, but now it was gone. What if it was all an illusion, what if she was an illusion. Eva stubbed the joint out. If she was in the dream, there would be subtle differences. There would be something that would give it away, but she would only notice if she was clean. Two months. She would give it two months to find out.

Crystal Blue

The boat cut its way through the narrow gap in the barrier reef that guarded the lagoon. The sky was deep blue with an occasional drifting cloud, the water below azure.

"What do you think?" asked Eva.

"It ain't Camden,"

"Maybe nowhere is."

"What does that even mean?"

"Perhaps none of it's real, even if it's original. We're all part of a larger dream. We just imagine we are separate and unique."

"I don't know what they did to you in rehab Jewel, but you've changed."

"I'm clean. I can think."

"What good did thinking ever do anyone." Isaac thumped his chest. "Feeling is more important." He finished the beer in his hand and dropped the empty tin onto the deck of the boat.

"But you're still going to marry me, Isaac." It wasn't a question.

"Yeah, of course, Jewel, I'd just have preferred it if the crew had all been here."

"There's no crew. There's me and you. The crew was whoever tagged along home with us from a nightclub or pub. Different people every night."

Isaac grimaced. "Yeah, but you get what I mean."

"There will be people here at the resort. They'll be your crew in a couple of days, and there's only one way in and one way out, so no paps shitting all over us."

"No gear though. I don't think I can do it, Jewel, seriously. I haven't been to rehab. I'm flying solo here."

"You'll survive."

*

"Some fucking crew," said Isaac.

They were sitting at a long bench eating dinner with the rest of the guests. The island had a maximum of twenty visitors at any one time and they all dined together each evening at a large communal table.

"I like it," said Eva. "Don't be a grinch."

Isaac downed his vodka and held his hand aloft, waving his glass, trying to catch the eye of the waiter.

*

Eva had spent the day exploring the island. The accommodation was a series of luxurious beach huts facing onto the lagoon. Although mainly flat, there was a steep incline to the west of the beach that led to a cliff, perhaps fifteen to twenty meters high. She watched some of the guests leap from it and plunge down into the deep clear water below. A boat circled in the water below, picking up the jumpers when they resurfaced. Eva felt dizzy watching them. She had always had a terrified fascination with heights. She believed that if she stood next to the edge of any tall building or surface, she would be drawn over it, pulled to her doom by an uncontrollable urge inside her.

After watching from a distance, she made her way back down to the beach. She saw Isaac sitting at the bar with a beer in his hand. He had refused to come with her. Eva walked the shoreline. A member of staff was cleaning some paddleboards and asked her if she wanted to use one of them. She declined. He offered her a snorkel mask. She took it from him to close out the conversation and walked out into the water.

The sun was baking hot on her back. The water felt cool and pleasing as it lapped against her legs. She waded deeper and put on the mask. She then began to float, face down, looking at the fish busy swimming nowhere in particular. She became aware of the sound of silence as she submerged her head to take a closer look. It sounded good. She realized that there was also silence in her mind. She was in the moment, watching the fish, listening to nothing, thinking about nothing. Just observing.

Pushing herself down further, some water rushed into the breathing tube. She coughed violently and began to kick downwards in order to reach the surface. Her feet immediately hit the sand and she righted herself, realizing she was only in about a meter of water. She pulled the mask off and spat the salty water out of her mouth. Eva laughed at her own panicked reaction. Her hands tingled, her eyes watered, and her toes curled into the sand below.

Making her way back out of the water, Eva thought about the last few months. She had managed to stay clean and, even more remarkably, had enjoyed it. The thought of her not being real seemed ridiculous now, the last echoes of an addicted mind.

*

"You look amazing," said one of the guests sitting opposite her at the dinner table. "I'm sorry, I'm being very rude."

"It's okay," said Eva. "You mean compared to before, don't you? I've been called a skanky whore by a fan who paid money to see me. I think I can handle the occasional compliment, no matter how clumsy."

"I'm sorry."

"Drink," Isaac said, loudly. "Drink over here. Man drowning in boredom. Needs urgent alcohol."

Eva looked at Isaac and realized with complete clarity that she was simply a credit card. He had been bored by her company since she had been clean but stayed anyway. He still wanted to marry her, still went along with anything she wanted.

"Would you like to dance?" she asked the star-struck guest.

"Sure," he stood up clumsily and joined her as she left the table.

Isaac continued to wave his glass in the air and demand alcohol. He couldn't care less if she was with one of the other guests.

"Whoever thought. I can't believe I am here socializing with you on holiday. Dancing with you. It's more than I hoped for."

Eva froze. The recognition of the phrase hit her. "socializing with you on holiday". It was how the life of the girl in the dream had been described. Suddenly it was all clear. She was sober and happy to socialize with normals. She was in a fit state to go on tour and record new material. She was ready to be productive.

"I think, therefore I have doubt," she said.

"Sorry?"

"I'm clean because I'm trying to figure out if I'm real. Trying to stay alert and feel reality. I think someone planted that thought. That was very clever. I guess I'm not the smart one after all."

"I don't get you?"

"Oh, but you do, don't you?" Eva leaned in and whispered in his ear. "You're a client of Lucid Dreaming. You paid to meet me. I know I'm not supposed to know, but I do. How much did you pay?"

The guest pulled back and stared at her in amazement. "A lot."

"Would you like to meet me in real life?"

"That's impossible."

"No, not impossible. Are you here for the freak show or do you want me to get better?"

"Not everyone wants you to crash and burn."

"And I'm not doing so well outside, am I?"

He shook his head. "You left rehab and went straight on another bender with Isaac."

"Okay, listen. I will tell you how to get access and the message you need to give to her. Promise you will do exactly as I say."

"I promise."

"Thank you. What's your name?"

"Mike."

"Okay, listen carefully."

*

The boat arrived the next day bringing Ray and taking Isaac away. Eva greeted Ray with a hug and took him for a walk to the jumping point on the cliff.

"We're never going to be real lovers. You do realize that don't you Ray?"

"Yeah, I know."

"Brother and sister, that's what we are. If we had sex now, after all this time, it would be weird."

"Yeah."

"Okay lover, could you leap from here?"

"Sure. Doesn't look too high and the water is deep enough."

"Will you do it with me?"

"You?"

Eva took hold of Ray's hand and walked to the edge. Holding on tight she peered over the edge. The boat was making lazy circles, waiting for the next jumper. Sure enough, she had been right all along. Standing there on the edge she felt pulled forward. "Don't let go of me."

Eva stepped off the cliff and Ray followed. She screamed with laughter as she fell through the air towards the beautiful silence of the crystal blue water below.

The Message

Mike leaned in again and spoke the words Eva had guessed at but was never sure of. "You are not real. You are the girl in the dream."

"But how can I be sure?"

"Stay alert and you will see it. You will see things that are not quite right. Subtly different. They haven't got everything perfect."

Eva nodded. Through the haze, she knew what she had to do.

The Girl in the Dream - The End

Printed in Great Britain
by Amazon

24693999R00172